H. E. Bates was born in 1905 at Rushden, Northamptonshire, and was educated at Kettering Grammar School. His first novel, *The Two Sisters*, was published when he was twenty and in the next fifteen years he acquired a distinguished reputation for his stories about English country life, the best of which are collected in *Country Tales* (1938).

During the Second World War he was commissioned to write short stories of RAF life by the Air Ministry. He produced two best-selling collections, *The Greatest People in the World* (1942) and *How Sleep the Brave* (1943), under the pseudonym 'Flying Officer X', and under his own name wrote the enormously successful *Fair Stood the Wind for France* (1944).

In the 1950s he began to write the popular Larkin family novels, starting with *The Darling Buds of May* (1958). He was awarded the C.B.E. in 1973 and died in January 1974. He married in 1931, had four children and lived most of his life in Kent.

H. E. Bates

THE FALLOW LAND

Robinson Publishing
London

Robinson Publishing
11 Shepherd House
5 Shepherd Street
London W1Y 7LD

First published in Great Britain by
Jonathon Cape Ltd in 1932

Published by Robinson Publishing 1988

Copyright © by Evensford Productions 1932

Cover illustration Serving the Hens *by W.P.A. Wells.*
Reproduced courtesy Fine Art Photographic Library Ltd.

ISBN 0 948164 65 4

Printed by Wm. Collins & Sons Ltd., Glasgow

To
Violet & Vernon
Dean

BOOK ONE

Chapter 1

ABRAHAM MORTIMER and his son Jess were setting snares under the old hawthorn hedge that bounded their land on the north. Haws were hanging in heavy crimson clusters among the shrivelling leaves and the pale October sun was dropping behind the line of willows skirting the west of the field. The field was five-sided, a triangular copse of oak and fir cutting across the south-west corner and hiding the farmhouse. Beyond a broken gate beside the copse a cart-track ran down the hedge-side under the willows, which had not been lopped for many years and had thrown up a thick screen of tall smooth branches that looked top-heavy on their squat, misshapen trunks. The field, which was not more than nine or ten acres, even counting the cart-track, was lying fallow and had now lain fallow for three years, although Mortimer had plans for it every autumn. Half-way across the field the land dipped suddenly away, dropping four or five feet. In winter the rains streamed down the slope, washing out the stones and silting the earth across the hollow in a smooth yellowish drift, and in summer the sun baked the drift to a white crust impressed with the iron-hard footprints of horses and men, and the slope dried out into a belt of white stones and pebbles, the soil thin and shallow. It was a difficult field to plough; the horses, going down the slope, could not hold the plough, and they jibbed and stalled returning up the hill, the stones baulking the share and jerking it out of the furrow. For years its harvests had never paid for their seed, and finally, after the worst of failures with wheat and beans, Mortimer had broken it up for one year's fallow. At the back of his mind now was an idea that tares might grow; the field was rank with tough

9

grass and withering docks and the white thistle-heads, and here and there a cluster of wild tares flourished, still purple with blossom. He felt that in the spring he might try tares or lucerne; he would see what the winter brought forth.

The two men half-squatted and half-knelt in the dead grass in the hedge-bottom. Four or five hare-tracks, dry and distinct in the weeds and grass, came down the field and vanished through gaps in the hedge, the gaps clean and freshly printed. Mortimer twisted a noose from a strand of wire and sharpened a hawthorn twig and set the snare. Finally the two men backed out of the hedge and walked along in silence to another gap and Mortimer knelt in the hedge again.

There were signs of a struggle in the second gap; the hawthorn was bitten and splintered, and the dry earth, clawed to dust by a hare in frenzy, was scattered with blood and fur. Mortimer scraped away the fur and dusted over the blood with earth and then proceeded to twist the snare. His son stood by with his hands in his pockets, looking aimlessly about him, a black-haired, decent-looking man of twenty-five or six, with lazy-looking eyes and a half-sardonic, half-humorous mouth that was curiously attractive. His forehead was very narrow between the low fringe of his black hair and his thick heavy brows, which almost met each other. His face had a surly kind of strength and he carried himself with a slight swagger, hardly noticeable, his big shoulders hunched up a little.

He watched his father set the snare without the faintest interest and without offering to help. Mortimer was intent on the snare, twisting a double noose this time and cutting a stronger stake. His white hair shone like snow in the shadow of the big hedge. He was almost an old man; his hands were twisted and skinny and the veins blue and prominent; when he had finished setting the snare he went on to the third gap; he walked with a slight hobble and a heavy stoop of his shoulders, as though all his life he had been carrying loads too heavy for him. The skin of his arms and neck and face was like wrinkled hide, tanned and darkened by sun and earth; the lines of his face were deep and soft, and his eyes, coloured an old pale blue shade turning to grey, were mild with a profound tolerance. There was nothing aggressive about him. He had the same air of patience and servitude as an old horse, too old to canter but still strong enough to work until he dropped. He had worked for over sixty years and had never taken a holiday except on his wedding-day. His old black jacket faded green at the shoulders, his breeches patched at the knees, his short brown leggings plastered with mud, and his old slouch hat, faded and shapeless, were the clothes he had worn for ten years, year in, year out, except that he sometimes changed into an old yellow panama in summer and put on an overcoat in winter.

The sun had dropped deep behind the willows, and a pool of mist, like a casual breath of white smoke, had begun to spread and thicken in the fields lying low beyond Mortimer's. The day had been fine, with heat in the sun, and pink clouds were folded over the sunset. Mortimer and his son worked slowly along the hedge, the old man laying the snares, neither of them speaking. Here and there the old man walked about in the coarse grass, looking for new tracks, and then twisted the snare in the cover of the hedge and set it in the old run again. A flock of starlings flew over and settled somewhere far down in the hollow, chattering wildly with the main flock.

The last gap was broken and yawning, as though something big, like a fox, had trampled through, and it was difficult to lay the wire. The old man cut a stake and fumbled in the hedge, failing once or twice and trying patiently again. His son stuffed his hands in his breeches pockets, spat and watched indifferently the repeated failures until they exasperated him.

'That 'ere run's big enough for a bullock,' he remarked at last.

Mortimer fumbled patiently, twisting a double wire, and did not answer. His son half-turned to walk away, changed his mind, and suddenly began slashing off boughs of haw-thorn with his jack-knife, hung by a nickel chain from his braces.

'You'd be all night a-laying a snare at that rate,' he said.
He sharpened the boughs fiercely, bent down, half-

elbowing Mortimer away, and staked the gap strongly, finishing the job before the old man had time to open his mouth. They backed out of the hedge, the son shutting his knife with a snap, the old man wiping his own meditatively and out of sheer habit across his trousers knee. They gazed at the gap for a second or two; it was make-shift work. The son sidled off.

'All right to catch some old tom-cat in,' he said; 'not much else.'

It was an old jibe. For years Mortimer had laid snares during the winter, but never with much luck. His wire was soft and frequently the hares snapped it or escaped by biting the string and taking the snare itself; someone often pulled his snares, and early prowlers poached the trapped hares before he had time to come down to the field in the morning. During one winter of poor luck, without a hare in six weeks, he had finally trapped a big sandy tom-cat which had torn frenziedly at his arms as he tried to release it, and after breakfast Jess had shot it in the snare with the old shot-gun, blowing it to pieces from two yards' range.

He caught the bitterness in the jibe, but his face remained mild and tolerant. He stood briefly and looked along the hedge, taking a last look of pride at the work he had done.

When he turned and walked away too, his son had already reached the cart-track under the willow trees. Mortimer followed at an ambling, hobbling pace. The willows were turning yellow and the cart-track was thick with yellow leaves and his feet made a light shuffling sound in them. A thin stream ran down the dyke under the trees, and farther up the field, near the paddock-gate, was a bed of watercress. He stopped and squatted by the water, pinching out the young, fresh shoots until he had enough. The water was chilly and he dried his hands on his trousers flanks. It was growing dusk and when he looked up and walked on again Jess had disappeared.

He reached the paddock himself, closed the gate methodically behind him and walked towards the house, a long, sober place of whitish stone standing in a piece of fenced-off paddock thick with ancient apple trees and a few damsons and pears; a tall-doored barn and some cow-sheds and pig-sties of the same white stone, clustered to one side of the house, were divided off by a brick muck-yard where some red and black hens were still feeding. These buildings, the paddock, the fallow field, and two twelve-acre fields lying to the east of the house made up the farm. A narrow road ran along by the paddock, straggled by the house and at the end of Mortimer's land became a track of grass. The copse went with the farm, and the pond swimming with fallen yellow leaves, lying at the edge of it. Mortimer had lived on the farm for thirty years. After twenty years of sweating and thrift and denial he had finally bought the place with all the misgiving and guilty pleasure of buying something he loved and wanted and could not afford.

He crossed the paddock and entered the rickety gate leading to the yard surrounding the kitchen door. There had been a spell of fine weather and the yard was dry and stone-hard, his feet scraping it sharply. He went to the yard pump and worked the handle and swilled his watercress under the spout of water.

The kitchen door was open. He shook the water-drops from the cress as he crossed the threshold and then scraped his chair forward to the table over the bare brick floor. Jess was eating his tea and reading a newspaper, his eyes fixed on the print, and he felt for his food and his cup as though he could not see.

The old man sat down. 'Here's a mossel o' cress,' he remarked.

There was no answer, and Mortimer leaned forward and spooned sugar into the big moustache-cup, like a bowl, from which he always drank. The kitchen was long and low. After a moment Mrs. Mortimer came in through a door at the far end, carrying a basin of milk, a slight, sallow-skinned woman, once fair and now very grey, her face whittled away by work and care and her eyes deepened into a melancholy expressionlessness by suffering and self-denial. She put the milk on the table and emptied the teapot into the old man's cup and then refilled the pot from the kettle and let the tea stew for Jess's second cup. Mortimer never drank a second cup. The woman hovered

about the table until he had taken bread and butter and
salt for his watercress, and then she sat down by the fire,
satisfied. The Mortimers spoke very little, and at tea, because the two men were tired and hungry, they spoke less
than at any other time. They would speak when they
wanted something, and after a silence Jess pushed his cup
across the table and said:

'More tea, mother.'

She jumped up readily and filled his cup, at the same
time pushing towards him slabs of buttered doughcake
and apple tart, showing by her half-eager, half-timid air
that she knew he liked these things and was desperate to
please him. She did not sit down and the restful look did
not come back into her face until he had taken some of the
cake. After that she sat down contentedly enough and
watched him eat it, mouthful by mouthful, watching half-
consciously, her eyes wide and dreamy with the pleasure it
gave her. Finally when he had finished the cake she got up
again and urged him:

'Have some of this apple tart, do. I made it for you,
special.'

But he had finished and had already pushed back his
chair and was wiping his mouth after his last drink. She
knew all his movements and she saw that he was in a hurry
for something and she asked quickly:

'Are you going somewhere?'

'I'm going to get a wash and be off to Staveston. Where's
my Sunday shirt?'

'It's up in the – oh! I'll get it for you. I'll give it a bit
of an airing, while you wash yourself. Sit you still.'

She vanished out of the kitchen and a moment later he
was out at the pump, creaking the handle up and down
rapidly. The mother and son returned simultaneously. He
went through with his bucket to the washhouse and began
splashing and swilling and she came forward to the fire
to hold the shirt low down by the wood embers. Mortimer,
chewing watercress like a cow munching its cud, stared in
silence at this sudden activity and then spoke:

'Where's he off to in such a blamed hurry?'

'He's off down to Staveston, didn't you hear him say so?'

'He's bustling about mighty. What's on at Staveston?'

She turned the shirt, feeling the warmed side with her bony cheek.

'You might well ask. You've been times enough yourself to Staveston Fair.'

'Oh! it's feast, is it?'

He mumbled the words, took a piece of doughcake and reached for the paper Jess had left on the table. He was long-sighted, and without spectacles he could just see the print at arm's length. Holding the paper thus he saw his son hurry from the washhouse and stop to kick off his boots. Mortimer spoke over the top of his paper to him.

'See as them hens are in.'

Jess padded in his stockinged feet towards the stairs, the shirt his mother had warmed flung across his shoulders. He groused 'All right,' as he lifted the latch to the staircase door, drawling the words.

Mortimer fixed his long gaze on the print again. He read very slowly, by great concentration, spelling the words syllable by syllable to himself. He forgot the world about him as he read on, not knowing that his wife had left the kitchen until he heard suddenly the clucking and squawking of hens and her thin, strident voice as she pina-fored and clapped them across the muck-yard into roost.

Chapter 2

JESS MORTIMER took the short cut across the paddock and the path through the spinney, striking the road at the corner of his father's last field. The path ran close by the dyke under the low hedge. White rows of wheat stubble, sharp in the twilight, came to the very edge of the path itself. Mortimer ploughed his headlands to the limit, not wasting a row, and the stubble was scythed short and neat, hardly an inch of wheat-stalk standing. The dry ground between the stubble rows was also clear of straw; Mrs. Mortimer had gleaned the field ear by ear, carrying the big gleaning bundle home on her head.

He climbed the stile and paused to see if the stubble had scratched his light-brown boots, which he only wore when he had finished the Sunday evening milking and on Saturdays and on his very rare holidays. He was a big, muscular man and the dark-brown jacket fitting him tightly across his shoulders and his fawn breeches across his thighs made him look bigger still. He wore his jacket unbuttoned for comfort and his trilby hat cocked slightly back from his forehead; in his hat-band was a little jay's feather and across his waistcoat the broad double-loop of a thick silver watch-chain, which his mother had given him for a keepsake. He walked down the road with long loose strides, easy in his bearing, except that he was conscious at times of his best clothes and did not know quite where to put his hands. The sky was not yet dark, and lower down the road, catching the faint sweetness of some honeysuckle, he stopped and straddled the dyke and gathered the spray, just able to distinguish the pale flowers in the twilight. He threaded the stalk through his buttonhole. With the flower in his coat he looked flashy, a bit of a dandy, a little louder and more attractive.

He met no one coming up the road. The track ended

at the farm and no one but the Mortimers came up after darkness. The land on either side of the road sloped away and there were no trees in the fields except a few ashes spared by hedge-cutters and in the distance a triangular copse or two like the one by the pond at the farm. In the clear half-darkness, unobscured by trees, he could see a long way and he walked along with his eyes hovering on the light in the sky ahead of him. On a windy night, with the wind blowing that way, he would have heard the music of the fair.

In the hollow the farm-track joined the main road, leading one way to Staveston and the other to St. Neots, both market towns. It was four miles to Staveston, but presently, by taking a field path, he could cut a mile. He found the stile and walked across the meadows, knowing every turn of the path and every tree and hedgerow in the darkness. He walked quickly but carefully, trying to keep the dew from his boots, and finally when he left the fields and reached the first lights of the town he stopped and gave the boots a secret polish, rubbing the toe-caps lightly on his breeches.

The clocks were striking eight as he reached the market square. The streets were thick and noisy with people, with noisier knots of men and women by the open doorways under the pub-signs. He smelt the beer as he walked past, and after mingling with the crowd for a minute or two he ambled across the square and under the big whitewashed arch of *The White Hart*. The walk had made him thirsty. He looked in at the door of the bar and searched the faces among the mist of tobacco-smoke for a sign of someone he knew. There was scarcely room to stand and two women pushed their way through the drinkers and drank their beer on the doorstep, fanning their flushed faces. As he stood craning his neck for the sight of a familiar face the women watched him, becoming facetious at last. He moved off. They called after him:

'Look at his bouquet!'

He turned his head and grinned sardonically. They called again, but he did not stop or speak.

The night air was very mild and long trestle-tables had

been set out in the pub-yard. He sat down and ordered a beer and drank it quickly and ordered another.

'It's a big fair,' the barman said. He wiped the beer-ring off the table neatly with a dirty cloth and set down the second beer.

'Ah,' said Jess.

'They tell me there's a boxing show.'

'Boxing?'

His voice became slightly eager without losing its laconic tone. The Mortimers were uneasy with strangers, their minds suspicious of familiarity, and he simply sat and drank his beer, only nodding, while the barman told him about the boxing show. There were exhibition bouts by the professionals and challenge fights for anyone out of the crowd who cared to stand up. There were money prizes for the winners and a chance of a better bout if you looked handy.

Someone called the barman away and Jess finished his beer quickly and walked away up the pub-yard in the thickening crowd towards the fair.

He pushed his way through the throng at the gates, by the winkle-stalls and the women selling brandy-snaps and gingerbread. The bright paraffin-lights of the stalls and roundabouts blazed full in his face and he took a strong breath of vinegar and winkles and paraffin-flames and warm dust and trampled grass. The roundabouts were playing gay melodies, there were sounds of rifle-shots from the shooting-ranges and everywhere the rising and falling murmur and laughter of the big crowd.

The boxing show was at the far end of the fair and the proprietor was shouting hoarsely from a platform at the crowd he had gathered; he was a short, dark unshaven man with quick hard eyes like peas, and eloquent, dirty hands; his eyes were cunning at the business of weighing up the crowd, and he talked to them like an orator, waving his hands and twisting his voice swiftly from indignation to flattery, cajoling and arresting and humouring them unceasingly. His four boxers stood behind him in dressing-gowns, lined up before the green-and-scarlet curtains at the entrance; they stood impassive, staring formidably, arms folded, arching their chests and knotting their fists

18

under their arm-muscles impressively. Over the entrance a big lamp burned with a white light and under the light hung a big brass bell and a punchball.

Jess pushed his way into the crowd.

The proprietor was just shouting:

'And last of all Flip Thomas, a young Australian, middle-weight. Thomas is going to be a champion and the man who beats him will be a champion! Six rounds and a purse of fifteen shillings, any weight up to twelve stone. Thank you? Thank you? Young feller with a buttonhole there. Thank you. Just throw the gloves to the young feller with the buttonhole.'

He leapt back across the platform and began to clang the brass bell. Someone flung back the entrance curtains and the crowd pushed forward to the pay-boxes.

Jess elbowed through to the booth with the gloves in his hands, and a little man with a towel flung over his shoulders pointed the way to the dressing-room, a little canvas tent behind the main booth, and he went in, feeling awkward in his best clothes and brown boots and the honeysuckle in his buttonhole. Three other men came in and all four stripped themselves. Mortimer stripped to his waist, not saying much, wondering if he should take off his boots and if his Sunday jacket and shirt would be safe in the tent. Two of the boxers changed into drawers and rubber shoes and did a little shadow-boxing, loosening their limbs. Finally the little man with a towel thrust in his head and asked: 'Chappie who's having 'em on with the Australian?' Jess slipped his coat over his shoulders and the trainer said:

'Are you 'im?'

'Ah,' said Jess.

They went into the booth together. The crowd was thick on all sides of the ring and the ring itself was flooded with light. Two boxers were prancing about the ring, feinting and tapping each other with light humour, finishing an exhibition bout. They ducked and struck at each other and missed simultaneously and the bout ended as Jess walked up to the ring, the crowd laughing and applauding.

Jess took off his boots and gave his coat to the trainer and hoisted himself into the ring and sat down. He looked slow and heavy-fleshed and his face was half-solemn and half-surly. The Australian climbed into the ring and worked his muscles lightly on the ropes, Jess, watching him, holding out his hands at the same time for the trainer to push on his gloves.

The gloves were tight on his hands and the trainer whistled.

'Got some big fists, young feller.'

'Ah,' he said.

The proprietor came into the ring and the gong sounded for silence and he introduced the boxers, clap-trapping about fair play and the honesty of the show again until the crowd were restless and ripe for the bout to begin. Finally he called the two men together, whispered a rigmarole about low-punching and clinches, and sent them back to their corners again, the gong ringing a moment later.

Jess moved slowly into the centre of the ring, squaring up, surly and gloomy in appearance, his guard low. He was bigger than the Australian and his arms and neck and face were burnt to a bright brownish-red where the sun had caught them. The Australian, lighter and quicker, tapped his cheek smartly and neatly before he had time to move; he led back with his right and missed, the swing looking cruder because it did not connect. The Australian taunted him, knocking his head aside with the flat of his hand; he felt a fool; the crowd laughed and he clinched, aiming powerful body-blows, the Australian taking them all on his gloves and slipping away along the ropes unpunished. The round ended tamely. In the second round the Australian enticed him about the ring, thrusting his head forward invitingly, unguarded, for Jess to hit, and then feinting beautifully at the leads and flat-handing him before he had time to recover. The crowd, half-bored and half-amused, began to cat-call, urging the men to fight. Jess aimed a powerful swing with his left and half lost his balance, catching his man with the heel of the glove. The Australian danced back, worked in quickly and jabbed twice, powerfully and rapidly, under the heart, staggering him momentarily into a kind of numb sickness. The blows were like a revolution. He had ambled to and fro like a man in a stupid dream, but suddenly he rushed forward tempestuously, forcing the Australian to the ropes with big slogging punches. His face was suddenly livid with temper. He worked his arms with a kind of vicious inspiration. His punches were dynamic and furious. The Australian covered up with his elbows, finally turning his back and pitching forward against the ropes. The crowd roared and the Australian went down on his face, rolling over as the referee counted to ten and held up Jess's right arm, shouting hoarsely:

'The local man! Local man the winner of the bout!'

Jess dragged loose his hand, climbed out of the ring and cloaked his jacket about his bare shoulders. The proprietor climbed down behind him. In a quick voice Jess asked for his money, his face dark and hot with temper. The proprietor leered back sarcastically:

'Hot-tempered and hard-up, eh?'

'Ah, give us the money.'

The proprietor counted out the silver and held it out and Jess snatched it.

'All right, hothead, don't snatch. Ain't looking for trouble, are you?'

Jess glowered; his hands were trembling with anger.

'Want a bit of advice from an old hand?' said the proprietor. 'Well, look after your temper afore it masters you. That's all, me old cock. That's all. Now clear out.'

Jess, ambling off through the crowd, heard the trainer throw a soft taunt after him: 'Fists like legs o' mutton.' But he did not halt or look back. His anger had surged up into his eyes in a dark mist and he felt half-drunk with it. The faces in the crowd were vague masks and the darkness outside the tent was throbbing and quarrelling with a chaos of painful stars.

He put on his clothes and walked slowly out into the light of the fair again. His anger was lessening little by little, but it surged back in hot waves whenever he thought of the punches over his heart or whenever the pain twinged him again. His temper had stupefied his mind and he could think of nothing but two things, the pain and the money he had won, and he wanted to do nothing but forget the pain and spend the money.

His mind began to clear a little as he stopped at a shooting gallery and took a rifle. His hands were still unsteady and the little rainbow-coloured balls dancing on fountains of water were like mad things. He blazed at them and missed. He swore at their dancing mockery as he wasted his shilling. He paid again and began firing madly at the bottles hung in rows behind the fountains; they were easy targets after the quivering balls and he fired until the gun was warm in his hands, making a wild noise with his gunshots and the rapid crashing of glass. The stall-woman began to mutter remonstrations. He turned his back on her sharply and walked away without a word, swaggering a little in his independence.

He spent a little money on the dart-boards and a game or two of chance, but they bored him after his wild shooting and he walked from one stall to another quickly, searching for a game where he could waste his money with glory. The money had made him like a child; he would be filled with restlessness and joy and misery until the last penny had gone. He kept jingling the silver in his pocket, remembering that it was perhaps only once a year that he ever had so much. The farm was too small and poor to make a profit; the Mortimers scratched up a bare living, and in a good year his father tied up perhaps ten pounds in a little cotton meal-bag and put it aside to meet disasters like the death of a horse or illness or an attack of swine-fever. There was nothing to spare for wages; he was expected to work for his board and lodgings and he worked for them, knowing that the farm would some day be his. His father gave him a shilling or two for his pocket and his mother bought his clothes and gave him half a sovereign once or twice a year, begging him to say nothing to his father. He always spent it before the thought of saying anything had occurred to him. She never questioned what he had done with it. His mother was quiet and sound about money. His father was a fool. He hated to spend and he was afraid to charge. A certain shilling was worth a doubtful pound. Very often he would sell a pig for half its price because he needed the money and was afraid of asking more and not selling it at all.

Jess stopped to look at a hoop-la. There were watches and clocks and painted vases and bracelets on the board;

the prizes were set wide apart and the rings were large. He paid for a dozen rings and began to throw. He was long-armed and without leaning far over the rail he could drop rings plumb on the board. The thought of his money was still burning in his head, but his mind was clearer and his hand steadier. He threw slowly and deliberately, watching his rings carefully, aiming for a watch. The stall-man flashed by and flicked up unlucky rings with a cane. 'Better luck next time, better luck next time!' he yelled. 'Gentleman here wins a pearl necklace, a real pearl necklace.' Under the bright lamps hanging from awnings the nickel watches and pearls and painted ornaments were jewelled with light and from the centre-pole hung a notice printed like a text in letters of blood: 'God helps those who helps themselves; but God help those who help themselves here.'

A ring fell over a watch and Jess held up his hand. 'Gentleman wins a solid silver watch!' He took the watch and paid for a dozen hoops. The watch was ticking. He dropped it into his pocket among his money and threw again.

He suddenly began winning with frenzied luck, paying for more hoops while he pocketed his necklaces and trinkets. He felt excited and reckless again and he flung his rings at a gilded vase until he won it. Turning, he gave the vase to someone in the crowd which had knotted itself about him. He began to swagger a little, throwing aimlessly, not knowing what he wanted to ring.

He wasted a dozen rings and then his luck returned and suddenly a voice said:

'Have a go for me? – for a necklace?'

He turned his head. A girl was standing at his elbow, holding his gilded vase. He stared at her.

'You seem to have all the luck,' she said.

She wanted to give him sixpence. He stared, refusing dumbly.

'A green necklace. Go on,' she said. 'Have a go for me.'

He did not know what to say to her and he was glad to turn his back and try for the green necklace with the rings he had still in his hand. His luck had left him again and he wasted the rings. When he pulled out his money to buy another dozen the girl entreated him to take her sixpence and not try again.

'Ah, I'll be shot if I ain't man enough to do a little thing like that,' he told her.

He turned and threw his hoops and at his fifth throw the hoop dropped over the necklace. He threw the rest of the hoops carelessly, as though tired of it all, and then pushed his way out of the crowd.

Clear of the crowd he stopped. The girl was at his side and he looked at her with some kind of understanding for the first time. She was a small, compact, bright-eyed creature; her face was pointed and sallow, slightly resembling his mother's, and she had the slight, sharp prettiness of a sparrow. Her body was so small and narrow that he could have picked her up with one hand.

Chapter 3

THE brassy mechanical organ of the big roundabout, a switchback of gilded peacocks and white swans, came to the end of its tune, and the air seemed strangely silent when the cars had rumbled to rest. Jess shifted his feet awkwardly and played with the necklace. The girl's bright perky eyes, very dark and vivacious in the full flood of the fair-lights, were unaccountably arresting. He felt that he could not escape them. He dropped the beads abruptly into her outstretched hand. The beads were a soft pale green, like young wood-nuts. She smiled in a sharp quick way. He had an impression from her smile that there was no nonsense about her.

'I've been wanting a green necklace a long time,' she said. 'I'm sure I don't know how to thank you.'

'If I couldn't win a bit of a thing like that with all that luck I wouldn't be a mucher.'

'But you made my heart stop beating, throwing like you did.'

'Ah?'

'I could see you wasting every penny just for the sake of wasting it.'

He did not know what to say.

'The things you must have won and then you kept on throwing!' she said. 'My heart turned over.'

'Ah! them rings ain't much.'

'Oh! I know, but one of these fine days you'll be glad of all that money.'

'Money ain't everything.'

'You can't do a sight without it,' she said. 'I can't abear to see folks throwing money down the gutter. I take care of what bit I've got.'

'You're like my old dad,' he said. 'He wraps his up in some old bag and hides it.'

25

'He'd have a fit at you throwing money away like you do, wouldn't he then?'

'He'd have a fit at anything I did, I reckon. He don't give me much. I won all this a-boxing.'

He told her about his fight and she was disgusted and impressed because he had won fifteen shillings by merely knocking a man half-senseless, and finally he said:

'We're standing here talking and we might be having a glass o' beer or else a ride on them peacocks.'

'It's just money thrown away on peacocks, I think,' she said.

'I could do with a glass o' beer anyhow,' he said. 'I don't know about you.'

'I could do with a bit of a sit-down,' she said, 'but I don't want more than half a glass.'

They walked out of the fair together and down through the crowded yard of the inn; they found a vacant seat among the benches where he himself had sat under the whitewashed archway.

He ordered the beer and while the barman had gone she fastened the beads about her neck. They looked pretty and neat on her, the milky greenness blending softly with her sallow skin.

'Do they look all right?' she asked.

'They do fine,' he said awkwardly.

She pressed her chin into the hollow of her neck and glanced down at the beads. There was instantly something prim and neat and old-fashioned about her, something almost puritanical in her pale face, her sane, candid eyes, the white collar of her dark dress.

The barman came with the beer and Jess took a long drink and wiped his lips. She watched him, not touching her own glass.

'I look well, I warrant, sitting here with a stranger, don't I?' she said.

'You're all right,' he said. 'Your mother won't say nothing.'

She was watching the creamy bubbles of beer twinkling and breaking in her glass.

'It'd puzzle my mother to say much,' she said, 'and my father too. They've been buried long enough.'

26

Again there was nothing he could find to say. He drank again and stared at the people sitting at other tables and at the crowd streaming past under the archway. Sometimes he looked at the girl slowly beginning to sip her beer. She attracted and disconcerted him. He felt embarrassed whenever he met her bright perky eyes and he was glad when she had finished sipping her beer and was ready to go again.

They threaded their way into the crowd and back into the fair again. In the crush at the gate they were separated and he lost her. He wandered about until finally he found her again under the lights of a gingerbread stall.

'It's a wonder I ever found you again,' he said. 'You're like some little dillin pig, you are.'

'What's a dillin pig?' she asked.

'In a litter o' pigs there's allus a little mite. That's what a dillin is.'

She laughed and he went on:

'We allus feed the dillin up a bit if the sow don't lay on it. I reckon that's what we'd better do with you, too. While we stand here a-talking we might be eating a mite o' brandy-snap.'

'Oh! I couldn't eat a crumb.'

'Ah? What about a plate of mussels? They'd slither down like new peas and you wouldn't know you'd had 'em.'

She shook her head.

'Let's have a bout or two on the peacocks and then eat summat,' he urged.

'You won't rest till you've dragged me on those peacocks I know,' she said. 'You're a Tartar, you are. Oh! I don't know – it's throwing your money in the street, but I'll come just once.'

They walked through the crowd and waited on the steps of the roundabout until the cars slowed to rest. He shouted in her ear above the blare of music and the thunder of wheels:

'Which'd you rather – a peacock or a swan?'

'Oh! a swan – somehow I never could trust the look of a peacock. It's all show and nothing else.'

The cars halted and he climbed after her into an empty swan and said:

'Did you ever see a string o' swans a-flying over?'

27

'No.'

'When we were ploughing the day afore yesterday a string went squawking over. They're pretty to look at a-flying.'

'Are you a farmer then?'

'Ah, we got a bit o' land,' he said, 'such as it is.'

The cars began to move and bore them with a gathering of speed up and down the switchback. Voices screamed with shrill shrieks of pleasure over the blast of music as the cars went faster and the world below became giddy and rolling, swirling with coloured lights, a chaos of silver and rainbow. 'D'ye like that tiddlin' business?' he shouted and she nodded silently, half-sick with the thrill of pleasure repeated and repeated as the cars plunged down and up again.

The cars slowed down and stopped and she wanted to alight, but he would not hear of it.

'What's a fiddlin' bit of a ride like that?' he argued. 'You don't know as you've had it.'

'You know what it's like when you've had one as well as when you've had a dozen. It's a measly bit of a ride for tuppence, too.'

The swan began to move.

'Ah! The second ride's the best,' he said. 'And what's tuppence?'

The roundabout soared and dropped and surged into an ecstasy of noisy speed. The girl lay back in the neck of the swan, holding herself stiff for the sickening thrill of the downward rush and the upward switch. Gradually she came to like the thrill of the laughing waves of pleasure rippling up through her body. Jess sat in the tail of the swan and pitched comically like a drunken man whenever the cars lurched with speed. For long intervals they sat and smiled at each other and when the cars came to rest again he squeezed himself into the neck of the swan with her and they talked above the pandemonium of wheels and music and the crash of cymbals and the shrieking of voices. Finally when the noise was deafening and the speed was at its height he asked her suddenly:

'What's your name?'

She said something in reply, but he could not hear, and at last she pulled down his head and shouted in his ear:

'Deborah.'

She pushed his head upright again with a playful gesture, knocking his hat askew. He turned to her with the drollest smile and she flung her head backward to laugh at him until her face was flushed. They went on into the fourth ride and she did not protest. She began to laugh at the little gilded Italian figure with big moustaches stiffly conducting the organ with doll-like beats among the forest of golden organ-pipes. She laughed in spite of herself, her laughter sharp and quick but happy. Jess watched her and pondered on her name and finally shouted again:

'Deborah what?'

The cars were coming to rest and there was no need for her to shout in reply.

'Deborah Loveday,' she said.

He told her his own name as the cars were rattling into speed again. They had never heard of each other. She lost herself for another moment or two in the riot of organ-blasts and noise and laughter and then she remembered herself.

'I don't know what you think, Jess Mortimer, but you've about thrown enough money away on this thing,' she said. 'Off we get, quick.'

They alighted and wandered off through the crowd again. She made mental calculations: he had thrown away half a crown; and she was horrified.

'It wouldn't take long at that rate to spend a week's wages,' she said to him.

His hat was still cocked askew. He looked rakish and care-less and he derided her softly:

'All depends what you call a week's wages.'

She told him in reply, in her quickest voice, serious at once:

'I get five shillings and all found.'

'What doing?'

'I'm in service,' she said.

He caught her arm quickly. 'Wages or no wages, I'm off in that there show to see the Wild Man from Borneo. And you're a-coming too.'

She hung back a little.

'Ah, come an' have a look outside, anyway,' he urged. 'They won't bite you.'

She allowed herself to be taken into the crowd gathering about the entrance of a side-show painted like a jungle; there were emerald palm-trees crowded with monkeys, and prowling among the palm-trunks were tigers with scarlet mouths and leopards sulkily feeding on bloody prey; on smaller trees sat cockatoos, and snakes were coiled up or poised ready to strike in the shadows under the tropical trees. In the centre of it all, over the crimson entrance curtains, a tattooed south-sea islander with red nostrils was snarling, spear in hand, at the animals painted on all sides of him. Over the entrance were letters of blazing light: 'Purchase's Living Wonders.' A young girl in a dirty green dress fluttered through the curtains and danced, and presently another, dressed in pink, came out and joined her; they danced a lifeless duo, their painted faces bored and unsmiling; when they bowed themselves away the proprietor, in a frock-coat too tight for his fat paunch and a top-hat stuck far back on his bald head, appeared in their places; red in the face, he bowed and rubbed his hands and spouted:

'The young ladies you have just had the pleasure of seeing will play with a pair of snakes. Live snakes! They will kiss them like babies. Have you ever seen a young lady wind a snake round her body? Have you ever seen a wild man dance on red-hot irons and swallow fire and not hurt himself? Have you ever seen him drive needles through his naked flesh and not draw blood?'

It was too much and the girl allowed herself to be taken through the crimson curtains. The sixpence admission was a silly, wild, delicious extravagance, but she smiled in spite of herself, and finally when they came out of the show again she was cold with a delicious horror. The black man had eaten fire and had wounded himself with spears and the girls had kissed the snakes and hugged them to their breasts.

She was shaken out of herself by horror and joy. Jess swung her away into impossible gaieties. He dragged her to the top of the helter-skelter and pushed her down, half losing his hat as he followed her; he paid for giddy turns on the cake-walk; he hurled himself at coco-nut-shies and they drank the milk of the coco-nuts when the laughter and warmth and dust had parched their throats; he lifted her into a yellow gondola and pulled the ropes with all his strength until the boat swung in a mighty arc which numbed her whole being with the deadness of terror, so that she could only cling to the ropes and shut her eyes against the sickening swing that hurled her up against the stars in the blackness of the sky and then plunged her headlong down to the lights and the crowd again. He rolled coins in a game of skill where his luck ran wonderfully. After he had won back double the money he spent she, trembling, tried her luck too, with a single penny; she lost and tried again and still lost; her lips became thin with disappointment. He took threepence and won back the money she had lost, but she was adamant and would not take it. 'If I'm fool enough to do it I'll be the one to suffer for it,' she said. And when his luck finally seemed to be turning she begged him to give up. He obeyed at last and with the money he had won he paid for joy-rides on flying-horses, he bumped the saddle ludicrously and fetched his horse resounding smacks on the buttocks as they flew round, and gradually her joy returned.

He guided her into the crowd again, looking for shows they had not tried. The thought of spending burned in him like a fever. She tried to calm him, constantly horrified by waste and recklessness.

'Let me spend something,' she begged. 'I've got a shilling or two.'

'I want to try my strength on that bell,' he said. 'You can spend what the pipe you like after that.'

'Oh! that's a daft thing, just trying to ring that bell up there and nothing for it.'

But he had notions of exhibiting his strength. He wanted to impress her. He took her away and paid his money and flourished the great wooden hammer and spat on his hands before she could protest again. He braced himself to swing and then rested on the hammer, eager to bet with her:

'Bet a shilling I don't ring the bell six times out of six?'

She looked up at the great scarlet and yellow pillar, marked like a huge thermometer, with the brass bell gleaming against the black sky.

'I shouldn't wonder what you could do,' she said.

'Ah! you daren't bet,' he gibed softly.

'Oh! I dare, but I'm not such a fool,' she said.

'Ah! just for once?'

She tightened her lips, smiling shrewdly, and shook her head.

He swung the hammer and crashed it down mightily; the iron finger soared up the pillar like hot mercury, hovered for one second short of the bell and fell swiftly again.

He turned to her with grinning triumph:

'See? First time an' I don't hit it. You could have minted money.'

'You did that on purpose,' she accused him. 'I know you.'

He pretended innocence, protested, and finally spat on his hands again and made exaggerated flourishes.

He struck, the finger shot upward like a rocket and the bell gonged deep over the noise of the fair.

'I knew you could do it. I can see through you like water,' she laughed.

He grinned and swaggered, glad to have exhibited his strength. And she gibed softly:

'But you couldn't do it again if you tried all night.'

'What?'

He swung swiftly, crashed the hammer and gonged the bell in a moment, and when the finger had fallen he swung and struck and rang the bell again. Having caught the knack of it, he made the finger fly up and down without rest, the gong ringing out with regular beats like a parson's bell.

Finally the sweat poured down his face. Tired of it all he flung down the hammer and took the girl away.

'What d'ye think of that?' he said.

'Oh! all very well,' she said, coolly and wickedly. 'You'll be a strong man when you grow up.'

He pretended anger and tried in revenge to rush her away into some fresh gaiety, but she was tired and hung back. He thought of eating again.

'Come an' have a mite o' brandy-snap or something,' he urged.

She shook her head; he cajoled and humoured her.

'A mossel o' gingerbread? I'm that hungry I could eat a loaf myself. Come on, a bag o' butter-balls?'

She kept shaking her head, until finally he was inspired:

32

'Hot taters!' he exclaimed. 'You could tuck a couple away and not know as you'd had 'em. Come on.'

She relented and they went off to where he remembered having seen the potato-oven, standing among the fortune-tellers' tents and the skittle-boards, an old, twisted white-bearded man sitting on a box in charge of it, warming his hands at the red cracks of fire in the black oven and munching potatoes, peeling off the roasted skin with faltering hands and dropping crumbs of potato among his beard; the air was warm with the heat of the fire and the fragrance of roasting potatoes. The old man doddered to his feet and Jess shouted:

'What are the taters, dad?'

'Two a penny.'

'Give us a dozen.'

The old man trembled into activity, opened the oven and began pinching the potatoes.

'Ah, give us one for a going on,' said Jess. 'I like 'em blinding hot, I do.'

They took a potato each, warming their hands with it, and then they broke the skins and blew on the steaming flesh, white and soft as flour. Jess ate with big, noisy bites and swallowed his first potato before the girl had begun to nibble hers. He broke his second potato, and with his mouth full said to her:

'You chimble away like some little old mouse. Ain't it good?'

'It's grand,' she said.

'Did you ever have 'em baked in a twitch-fire? That's about the only blessed thing about our land, plenty o' twitch, so's when we like we can have a bit of a fire and roast a tater or two. That's about all it's good for.'

'What's wrong with it?' she said. 'You grumbled once before about your land.'

'Ah, an' I expect I may grouse about it. It won't alter nothing. It's like a bit o' bread gone sour. You can't do nothing with it. It tears your insides out. I hate the thoughts of it.'

She looked at his face, strong and warm and red in the light glancing up from the potato-oven, and she said quietly:

'You don't look amiss on it.'

33

'Giveus another tater and don't let's talk about land. I'm only waiting for some old body to die and leave me summat. The land's no good to me. I'd get shut of it to-morrow if I could.'

'If you're waiting for a fortune I expect you'll wait a fine old many years, like me,' she said.

'You're about right.'

He turned to the old man and said:

'Give us another one, dad, a big 'un this time.'

The old man opened the oven. Simultaneously the girl paused in the act of peeling her potato. Somewhere a clock was striking and she could hear the notes dimly over the pandemonium of the fair. It was eleven o'clock.

'Oh! I'm done for now,' she burst out.

'What's a matter?' Jess said.

'I can't stop to tell you. I shall have to run, that's all.'

She began to walk away immediately. He snatched another potato and paid the old man and ran after her.

'I'm a-coming too,' he said.

'I ought to have been in not a minute after ten, and here I am,' she groaned.

They hurried out of the fair under the archway of the inn and into the streets. The tables were deserted and the inn was closed. The crowd was going homeward. They hurried in silence out of the town. The night was calm and black and freckled with stars and light mists were settling and drifting across the fields, drowning the hedges and the trunks of trees. She stopped at last before the white gates of a house faintly visible at the end of an avenue of poplars.

'You better take these trinkets I been hawking round,' he said.

He gave her a handful of the prizes he had won, a clock and a vase and a bangle of blue beads. He took the spray of honeysuckle from his button-hole and gave her that, too.

'You come up to the farm Sunday afternoon and we could have a bit of a look round for some mushrooms,' he said to her. 'How'd you like to come?'

'You'd have to fetch me,' she said.

'I'll fetch you.'

'About three o'clock?' she said.

34

They stood for a moment and looked at each other in the darkness, not knowing what to say or how to part from each other. She lifted the honeysuckle to her nostrils and he heard her breathe its fragrance.

Suddenly she said good night and turned away and half-ran along up the avenue of poplars. He turned away after a moment also and began to walk slowly homewards, eating the still warm potato and thinking about her. The jingle of the fair floated suddenly across in the clear darkness. He put his hand in his pocket, fingered his money, and turned his steps suddenly back towards the fair.

Chapter 4

DEBORAH LOVEDAY woke as a clock was striking six. Her mind, faltering between sleep and wakefulness, counted the strokes, and the first sensation of the day leapt through her body. As though the clock had frightened her, her body gave a great start into consciousness. She stared for one second at the light of the breaking sun and then sat up and reached for her clothes and leapt out of bed.

Her bedroom was like a box. By its little square window stood a painted washstand, with a white ewer and basin, and against one wall a chest-of-drawers in varnished deal and against another a single black iron bedstead with a frilled bottom canopy and a black shawl spread over the blankets. The wallpaper was trellised in parallel lines of faded pink and emerald poppies; here and there the paper had begun to peel away, showing the plaster damp and green with mould beneath; there were a few pictures in frames of bird's-eye maplewood and a single one in a large black wooden frame, a coloured oleograph showing Ruth in the cornfield. It was the only thing in the room that the girl possessed besides the black shawl on the bed. On the shawl the date of her birth, May 20th, 1862, was worked in neat grey figures in one corner.

She dressed and combed back her hair in great haste. She had not time to wash herself. Her hair she parted rigidly in the centre and then swept it back and knotted it tightly, holding the comb in her teeth. Her movements were quick and sharp and deliberate. She acted as though she had no time to think.

When she was ready at last she carried her shoes in her hand and went to the door and opened it. Before her stretched a long, broad landing, with many closed doors; she walked along it soundlessly and at one door she stopped and listened and then went on as soundlessly again. At the end of the landing she ran quickly down the flight of carpeted stairs and at the foot of them she sat and put on her shoes. All about her, on every wall, hung cases of stuffed birds and fish and animals, and there was a silence and odour about the house like the silence and odour of a museum. It was like death. The doors were varnished and the varnish had blistered and gave off a strong acrid smell; every door was closed, and the passage leading from the foot of the stairs was filled with a musty twilight.

The girl did not notice these things. She laced up her shoes and hurried along the passage and down a flight of four steps. She opened a door and was in the kitchen.

The kitchen was even gloomier than the passage. The walls and the stone floor were utterly bare and there were odours, very stale and damp, of things that would not mingle, grease, cooking, linseed oil, soot, whisky. There was a dresser of varnished deal filled with wineglasses and a dinner-service with immense white meat-dishes and plates and tureens, and opposite the dresser was an immense iron cooking-range which covered half the wall.

She knelt down before the range and began to rake out the embers. By the clock on the high mantelpiece it was ten past six. She hurried; there was a sort of implacable mechanism about her movements. She fetched sticks and paper and lighted the fire and the flames licked upward. After watching them for one moment she moved away to fill a kettle with water at the sink. Suddenly a gush of smoke blew back down the chimney. She rushed to the range and bent down and blew back the smoke, coaxing a flame. As soon as her back was turned again the flame died and the smoke puthered out again. She went on like this, blowing and coaxing, until she was out of breath.

The kettle did not boil until a few minutes to seven. She had meanwhile set out on a painted iron tray a cup and saucer and a teapot. The house was utterly silent beyond the movements she herself made. She moved with extreme care. When the kettle boiled at last she made the tea and waited. Bright daylight was coming in at the window, and some sparrows began quarrelling in the ivy-leaves that covered the house. Suddenly she looked at the clock again and her body

37

gave a sudden start as though she had for one second fallen asleep and was waking again.

She poured out the tea. She behaved as though performing a ritual: she measured the sugar and poured the tea slowly to within an inch of the cup's edge; she added a thimbleful of milk and waited a moment and then added a spoonful of whisky.

After waiting another moment she took the tea away upstairs. The clock was ready to strike seven. She walked with grave deliberation upstairs and along the landing. Finally she stopped and tapped at the door at which she had listened when coming down. Nobody answered and she went in.

She looked at once at the thing that always struck her first as she entered the room: the bed itself. She always shot one rapid glance at it, a glance of apprehension and wonder. She was struck with wonder because the bed itself, a great mahogany four-poster hung with deep red velvet curtains and pale pink silken cords, was as large as her own room, and she was faintly afraid because of the person who slept in it.

After setting the tea on a little walnut table at the bedside she pulled back the curtains across the windows. The windows were tightly shut and the room had about it the same odour of lifelessness and damp darkness as the stairs and the passages. She felt that she could not breathe.

As soon as she had pulled the curtains she approached the bed again. Very timidly she put her hand on the coverlet and whispered:

'Mrs. Arbuthnot.'

The old woman in a pink flannel nightdress who lay asleep on the pillows did not stir. She was incredibly ugly; she was like a spiteful caricature of a woman fashioned in clay that had begun to shrink and crack, her skin having about it a curious yellow pallor that looked unclean and hideous, her head so nearly bald that the remaining threads of hair looked as though hastily glued on as part of some clumsy and impossible make-up. The hair had the same faint yellow colour as the face, and the lids of the eyes were stained yellow too; her lips were invisible; the upper jaw had dropped, sucking in the lips and the wasted flesh of the cheeks. She breathed with strange lightness and there was something inhuman about her immobility, and so forbidding was that motionlessness that

38

the girl could not touch her. It gave her a sensation of numb horror merely to lay her hand on the coverlet and call her name.

The old woman did not answer. The girl turned away to pick up the tea-cup. Instantly, like clockwork, the old woman opened her right eye and watched her. With that tiny action she sprang to life; her face had been a mere mask of hideousness, as lifeless as a model; it became suddenly vivid with diabolical suspicions, watching with fixed acuteness, the light of the eyes sharp, penetrative and sinister.

The girl turned with the tea-cup in her hand after a second or two. The eye closed at once; the face snapped back into its immobility before the girl could speak.

'I've brought your tea, Mrs. Arbuthnot.'

Then the eyes opened slowly. The lids were heavy, the light in the pupils was misted and drowsy. There was a groan, as though it were all an intense pain; the eyeballs rolled and dropped and trembled; the life seemed to ebb away; and then the body itself made a movement. The old woman tried to struggle upwards; she sank back, struggled and sank back again. And then her voice came to life:

'Help me up, can't you?' she croaked fiercely. 'Don't stand there like a dummy, you fool. Help me up. I can't drink lying on my back, can I? Help me up, help me up!'

Very timidly the girl put one hand under the shoulders and helped to raise her. The old woman began to cough as soon as she sat upright, retching and breaking into great sighs and muttering grouses against the girl. There was a devilish strength in the voice:

'I might die while you stand there! I might die, I tell you! Why don't you use your wits?' she half screamed. 'You'd just like me to choke, wouldn't you? I know!'

The girl stood nauseated and horrified, but unafraid. She had conquered the fear that the voice and the words had once had for her. They were a mere rigmarole that the old woman hurled at her every morning; they were a mere ritual which she looked upon as meaningless.

'Drink your tea,' she said.

The pretence of coughing and pain went on, lessening a little; finally it died away, and the old woman took the tea-cup.

She groaned and sighed for another moment or two and then she raised the spoon and tasted it. The spoon dropped with a clatter.

'You've poisoned it!' she shrieked.

'Oh! Mrs. Arbuthnot, what a story! Oh! what a wicked thing to say.'

'You've poisoned it!'

'Oh! Mrs. Arbuthnot, you know I wouldn't do anything of the kind.'

'You've poisoned it! What have you put in it? Tell me what you've put in it!'

Deborah was silent.

'Why don't you answer me?'

'It's just a nice cup of tea, that's all. I didn't put nothing in it except the whisky. Why, I'd drink it myself. Come, you just taste it again. It's your fancy.'

'Fancy!' muttered the old woman.

Her voice was weaker and querulous and wretched.

'Come, you drink it,' said the girl. 'You'll never be able to start your poems this morning at this rate. Now drink it while it's still hot.'

Slowly and cautiously the old woman drank again; the girl humoured her with soft, encouraging words; at every sip there was a long, suspicious pause and after every pause the old woman muttered something.

'I don't like it. It's queer. It's queer.'

Gradually she took deeper drinks and there were shorter pauses and she muttered less and less.

'Bring my shawl and put it round my shoulders,' she said at last.

The shawl hung in a great mahogany wardrobe standing at the farthest end of the room, and behind the tall, dark-polished doors, in which the room was reflected in bright lights and sombre red shadows, hung all the dresses and coats and skirts and capes that the old woman had worn for the past forty years. As Deborah swung back the doors she breathed the stale scent of the garments and the curious fragrance of camphor and lavender and the odour of the old mahogany itself. The mingling of soft odours was in some way lovely and comforting; she lingered over it as she reached for the shawl, and she stood for a second or two taking in a long leisurely breath of it before closing the doors.

Instantly there was a croak of frightened suspicion from the bed.

'What are you doing there? Come away at once, come away, come away, I tell you!'

The girl shut the doors and took the shawl to the bed.

'I know! You're after something there! You want to steal something. First you want to poison me and now you want to rob me!'

In silence the girl wrapped the shawl round the old woman's shoulders, taking no notice of the words. They broke out again immediately:

'Why don't you say something? If you're not trying to steal, why don't you say so?'

The girl turned away and walked to the door and opened it. Before she could leave the room the voice had changed its tone abruptly:

'Oh! don't go. Don't leave me for a moment. Come here a moment. Come here. That's it, stand there. You didn't hear anything in the night, did you? Something walking about and sighing? You didn't hear anything, did you? I keep thinking I heard something. Did you hear it? I heard it! I know I heard it, a man's voice, and someone moving up and down. Didn't you hear anything?'

Deborah shook her head; the old woman was cold and quaking with excitement.

'Oh! I know I heard something!' she went on. 'I woke up. It wasn't a dream. I woke up and I felt he was in the house. My son, Leopold, the son I lost. He was in the house. He was walking up and down –'

'Oh! Mrs. Arbuthnot, you were dreaming, you were having a dream, that's all.'

'Oh, no! oh, no! I heard him. I know his voice, I know his voice.'

'Hadn't you better lie back on the pillows and rest while I make your breakfast? You were only dreaming. You'll work yourself up into such a state again and you won't be able to write your poetry.'

'But he will come back, he will, he will.'

41

'Lie back, you lie back and think of your poetry.'

'His clothes are ready for him when he comes back. You know where they are, don't you?'

'Never you mind about that. You lie back and think of your poetry. What are you going to write about to-day?'

The old woman relapsed gently back against the pillows, dazed and exhausted by her talking and her delusions.

'Aren't you going to write a poem to-day?'

'Yes, oh, yes! About the leaves, about the autumn. "October with her sweet and faded face, Majestic in her form of moulded grace." I shall begin like that. I thought of it in the night when I woke up. Oh! are you sure you didn't hear anything?'

'You lie quiet. You won't be worth a hatful o' crabs if you don't. There!'

The old woman sighed and Deborah went out of the door and closed it behind her. She hurried downstairs and into the kitchen. The fire was smoking badly and it was half-past seven. Kneeling by the stove she blew the fire until the smoke lessened and flames crackled upward and she herself was out of breath again. After that she hurried hither and thither, in and out of the kitchen and the pantry, preparing the old woman's breakfast of arrowroot. While the milk-and-water for the arrowroot was boiling she cut slices of bread and butter for herself and searched the pantry for something to eat with her bread and butter. She was famished and to her joy she discovered a piece of cold black pudding which she ought to have eaten for her supper on the previous evening and which in her haste in coming home she had forgotten. She decided to warm it; she might frizzle it gently before the fire on the toasting-fork. She wasted precious minutes finding the toasting-fork and it was nearly eight o'clock when she finally began toasting the pudding. Her every action was part of a fight against time.

Suddenly from upstairs she heard a long shriek. She made a motion of impatience with the toasting-fork. She knew the words that followed the shriek without even listening to them: 'Oh! Deborah, I feel so ill. Deborah! I'm dying, I'm dying. Oh! Deborah!' Intent upon the pudding she let the shrieks continue and finally die away. Like the accusation of poisoning and all the rigmarole of the voice sighing and groaning in the night they were meaningless to her. Every morning for two years the old woman had accused her of putting poison in her tea, and night after night she had suffered the delusion about he son. From the first moment of waking life became foi Deborah a complexity of suspicions and accusations, of running up and down stairs, of scrubbing and dusting, of cooking and shrieks about illness and death. Precisely at seven o'clock she took up Mrs. Arbuthnot's tea, and a little after seven, morning after morning, she was accused of having poisoned her; at eight o'clock she took up Mrs. Arbuthnot's basin of thin arrowroot, and shortly after eight she was accused of having poisoned her again. After breakfast she washed the old woman with luke-warm water; it was like washing some petulant, ailing child; the old woman fretted, cringed, groaned and half-wept. Deborah, phlegmatic and inexorable, washed her without mercy. 'Even if you never do get up,' she said to herself, 'I'll see you're clean, that I will, and clean you shall be.' Before she had finished washing her and had dressed her in her pale mauve dressing-jacket it was ten o'clock, and the old woman, pretending exhaustion and faintness, took a little whisky. It was only the whisky, she said, that kept the life in her at all. Without the whisky she could never have written her poetry. She began tow rite her poetry about eleven. Half-lying back against the pillows she pencilled verses in a large, black-covered book with a gilt clasp and a tasselled silver-and-purple book-mark, writing steadily and with a curious expression of dreamy fervour until the poem was finished or the spirit had forsaken her. She wrote a poem and sometimes two poems every morning and having finished a poem she would call up Deborah to hear it read. The girl had to leave her work and go upstairs and stand at the bedside, aproned and black-handed, and assume the proper expression for listening; generally she clasped her hands before her and stared at the mahogany wardrobe and wondered what price it would fetch if ever the old lady died and the things were sold up. She listened to the poems vaguely; they were easy to understand and she knew also what to expect in them. If it were April the poem would be about showers and daffodils or larks and sunshine; if it were October about the frosts and falling leaves, a sad poem; if the old woman woke up and it was snowing the poem would be all about the white mantle of purest snow and a robin red-breast on the window-sill. Without her whisky Mrs. Arbuthnot could not have written her poems and apart from her poems there was no other reason left for her to live.

Deborah always listened to the poems patiently. In her unexcitable, phlegmatic way she thought them wonderful, and when at last Mrs. Arbuthnot had finished reading and asked her opinion she always said 'All right' or 'Very nice indeed.' Even when a poem about death or grief had sometimes made her feel that her own heart was weeping and half-breaking she could say nothing else. When she suffered it was as though her body hardened itself deliberately against both her suffering and the thought of showing that suffering, caging and binding in her emotions until they tore themselves into an agony in trying to escape. Her will was so strong that she would let it break her sooner than her suffering should show in her face. She had suffered a good deal in her first months with Mrs. Arbuthnot. It was a week before she realized that she was to be alone in the house with her and a month before she realized that no one ever called. She found she was expected to work from six in the morning till ten or eleven at night, with Sunday afternoons or evenings and one week-night free, but often on those days Mrs. Arbuthnot complained that she was dying and Deborah never had the holiday. She slaved and never complained of her hours, or her food, or of Mrs. Arbuthnot's accusations of lying and poisoning and stealing and dishonesty. 'I'm in a rare shop, and no mistake,' she said, and that was all. Inexorably she forced herself to tolerate it and actually to argue that it was most providential and lucky that a girl of twenty-five, without parents, should have a roof over her head and a bed to sleep in. There were times when the long day sickened and wearied her and when the last hours grated with pain over the sharp edge of her nerves and patience. She schooled herself not to flag or

44

surrender. There was a streak of fatalism in her and a sort of dry philosophy: 'I got here myself and I'll be the one to suffer for it. That's all.'

The days were not so trying now. She had learned to accept Mrs. Arbuthnot's accusations and cries of distress as though nothing had happened. Thus she sat and toasted the piece of black pudding with a kind of wilful pleasure until the cries died away. 'She's no more dying than I am,' she thought. Once she had believed in these cries, until one afternoon, discovering Mrs. Arbuthnot sprawling across the bed in a state of coma which she thought was death, she had fetched a doctor. 'I'm afraid she's dead this time, sir,' she said. 'Dead?' he repeated. 'She's drunk, that's all.' Since that day more than half the fears and trials of her life had vanished.

She finished toasting her pudding; it smelt delicious as she put it on a plate in order to keep warm while she stirred the arrowroot. Like the tea, the arrowroot had to be measured and made with extreme exactitude and served at a precise moment. Deborah stirred it and tasted it. It was soft and excellent. As the kitchen clock began to rattle before striking eight, she seized the tray and hurried upstairs with it.

The old woman was dozing. Deborah roused her and put the tray on the bed and told her not to spill the arrowroot. Before Mrs. Arbuthnot had time to taste the arrowroot she was out of the room again. A shriek followed her along the passage and down the steps to the kitchen:

'You've done something to it! It's poisoned! Deborah!'

Not heeding, the girl hastily shut the kitchen door and poured herself a cup of tea and put her frizzled pudding on the table. She took a long drink of tea and relaxed. The day behind her seemed long and old already and this was her first moment of bliss and quietness. The kitchen was her absolute province; it was her home; she could do whatever she liked there. The old woman never came downstairs and perhaps never would come downstairs again. She took another drink of tea and listened. The cries had subsided. Breaking her bread she dipped a piece of it in the fat that had dripped from the pudding over the plate. She began to eat hungrily and went on eating for some moments without wondering why she was so hungry.

Quite suddenly she remembered. She had eaten no supper. For the first time since waking she gathered her thoughts; in a second she remembered everything, the fair, the hoop-la, the roundabout, the wild-beast show, the hot potatoes, the way she had crept upstairs listening at every step for Mrs. Arbuthnot's terrified voice. She ate her pudding and drank her tea a little absently, thinking about Jess Mortimer and trying to disentangle him from a confusion of fresh impressions. She did so at last steadily and unexcitedly; she went back over the bright events of the fair, half-remembering the tone of his voice, things he had said, the way he had looked at her. Farmers, she thought. She knew nothing about farmers, since she was town-bred; she knew only that farmers kept sheep and cows and grew corn and she supposed the Mortimers did these things too. She lingered over her breakfast longer than usual; she tried to arrest and fix the impression of Jess Mortimer in her mind and contemplate it, but it was elusive, like a tune she had heard only once and could not catch complete again. For a moment or two she became lost and dreamy and then her conscious self awoke again. 'Here, I should think you're going to sit day-dreaming over a chap you very like won't set eyes on again,' she told herself. She cleared her plate quickly with a crust of bread until it shone bald and white and then drained her cup. 'I should think so!' A second later she remembered something else. Her heart gave a curious leap in spite of herself. She sat as though petrified at the remembrance of her promise to meet him on Sunday.

'You've done it now,' she thought. 'You've done it now, Deborah Loveday.'

She had promised, and to her a promise was something irrevocable and inescapable. She pushed back her chair. She had promised! She emptied the luke-warm water from the kettle into an enamel basin and went slowly upstairs to wash Mrs. Arbuthnot.

'You've done it now,' she kept thinking.

46

Chapter 5

IT was Sunday afternoon. Jess Mortimer and Deborah were walking across the paddock towards the farm; they had walked beyond the Mortimers' land, over neighbouring pastures, looking for mushrooms. Jess was carrying the mushrooms in his handkerchief, knotted up. Deborah had an armful of spindle-leaves, the berries and leaves a lovely dying pink. She had no success with mushrooms. Jess had told her how to walk about the field and how she would know a mushroom when she found it. 'A mushroom's real white or else a bit brown. You'll see 'em shining a long way off. And underneath they're pink or pinky-black if they're gettin' old. I'll show you one and then you'll know better.' She watched him roam about the field, how he turned sharply and knelt down, as though he scented the mushrooms. She wandered off, saw something white in the grass, gathered it and went back to him. 'Ah, that's only an old puff,' he said. 'I tromple on 'em, I do. They're no good.' He showed her the mushrooms he had gathered, the flat white mushrooms with beautiful pink under-gills that he called fryers, the tiny half-grown buttons like globes of satin, and the big, thick-stalked kind that were best for stews and ketchup. She marvelled because he knew so much. He told her how they grew best in warm wet weather and under the moon. They separated again and she came back to him with her hands full of toadstools. 'You can throw *them* away,' he said. 'Some folks eat 'em, but I reckon they're poison. I don't think I s'll start.' She was disgusted with herself because she knew nothing. 'I'm a fine mushroomer and no mistake, I am,' she said. 'Why *can't* I find them?' And finally coming across the paddock she had been so sure of success until he had told her she was gathering blue-legs.

'Well, blue-legs or whatever they are, I will say I gathered something some good,' she said.

47

She gathered a dozen blue-legs and cupped them in her hands while he held the spindle-leaves.

'Th' old dad'll eat 'em. He'll be glad on 'em,' said Jess. 'I'll take you in now and you can give 'em to him while I milk.'

She hung back suddenly.

'Oh! am I going to meet a lot of folks?'

'Only th' old dad and mum.'

'Haven't you any brothers and sisters or anybody?'

'No.'

'What does your mother say about me coming?'

'Nothing. She would say nothing to what I done.'

They walked slowly towards the house and Jess opened the paddock-gate and locked it again when they had entered the farm-yard. A black rough-haired pony came across the paddock and looked over the gate. Deborah walked away.

'Nag, back, nag, back!' said Jess. 'Git back! Nothing for you. Git back there. You ain't frightened of him, are you?'

'What's his name?'

'Tom. Tom, back there! He won't hurt you. He's getting old. Tom, back!'

She inwardly derided herself because for a moment she had been afraid of the horse. Her will asserted itself and she went back to the gate.

'Tom, Tom, here, Tom,' she said. 'I want to stroke him. Make him come.'

The horse came back and she ran her fingers lightly down his nose. He tossed his head and a spasm of fear shot through her, but she persisted and the horse quietened.

'Good Tom, good Tom.' He hung his head submissively and she felt warm towards him, stroking his head softly. 'Good Tom, good Tom.'

'I've got to milk,' said Jess at last. 'Bring him a mite o' bread after tea.'

She gave the horse a final caress and then followed Jess across the farm-yard. The sun was dropping quickly, the tops of the barns and stacks catching the yellow light and throwing longer and larger shadows across the yard.

Above the pond the tall, black poplars caught brighter sunlight, their pale leaves burning and flickering, and in the spinney the yellowing elms were vivid against the dark green firs. Beyond the spinney a mist was whitening thinly across the lower fields in spreading pools, the bright colours of trees and hedges, the colours of leaves and hips and haws and spindle-berries fading in the falling light. It reminded Deborah of a piece of description in one of Mrs. Arbuthnot's poems. She stopped suddenly and looked back over the fields, admiring the colours.

'It's just like a bit of poetry,' she said.

Jess laughed and they went into the kitchen.

The kitchen was empty. The Mortimers were in the parlour, in the front of the house. Deborah followed Jess, looking about the big kitchen and sniffing the old sour milk and wood-smoke smell; she caught sight of hams and sides of bacon hanging under the rafters, the salt on them glistening like a hoar-frost; she had never seen such bacon; but the floor was dirty with dry boot-scrapings, and hen-droppings and feathers, and the idea of dirt jarred on her. She followed Jess into the parlour with two impressions sharp in her mind. 'They don't live bad, with bacon like that,' she thought. 'But I bet I'd let hens come and muck all over the kitchen floor. I can see myself!'

In the parlour Mrs. Mortimer was setting tea on a heavy round mahogany pedestal table. She had not heard their footsteps against the clatter of her own crockery and she was saying to Mortimer, who was sitting on a shiny American-leather chair, fidgeting with the fire: 'If you're going to put some wood on, put some wood on. Man, you urge me, puttin' such skinny-flint bits on. What heat is there in bits like that?'

Jess and Deborah entered before Mortimer could speak.

'This is my mother and this is Deborah Loveday,' said Jess.

'Oh! Good afternoon, miss.'

'And this is my dad. We bin a mushroomin'. She's brought a tidy handful o' blue-legs, Dad.'

'Blue-legs?' said Mortimer. 'Ah!' He rose quickly.

Mrs. Mortimer brought a plate for the mushrooms and

blue-legs and Jess went out to begin milking. His mother followed him into the kitchen and called after him into the yard.

'Tea's pretty near ready. Don't go off, Jess.'

'Tea'll have to wait, that's all. Cows got to be milked. It'll be dark else.'

'We'll wait for you,' she said.

In the parlour the old man was saying:

'Loveday? You ain't no kin of Jaby Loveday? Big man, a carrier, used to talk down his nose? They used to twit him a lot about talking down his nose.'

'I got no relations much,' said the girl. 'Not as I trouble about.'

'I used to work with a man name o' Loveday, Ike Loveday –'

Mrs. Mortimer came back, carrying a seed-cake and a basin of stewed pears.

'Ah! you start,' she said sharply to Mortimer. 'Start an' fill the gal's head with your old tales afore she's here in the house five minutes, I would. I wonder how many more times! I wonder!'

'Shet up!'

'Folks'll think you got nothing else to do but sit and tell fool's tales like that. Take an' fetch some wood in. That'd be more sense like.'

The old man fell silent, staring at the fire. The girl felt awkward, pitying him a little, drawn to his curious soft meditative voice, the mellow flavour of the tale that had been told and told again. He fidgeted aimlessly with the fire again and she could not look at him. Her eyes wandered over the parlour, over the wallpaper with faded blue roses and the faded blue skirting-board and the walls covered with faded family portraits in red plush frames. On the mantelpiece were vases and ornaments set so close that they touched each other, cheap things of yellow and blue glass, tinsel-painted ornaments filled with wild grasses, and the gilded vase that Jess had won at the fair. The curtains at the window were of patterned lace and dyed to a cream colour and looped with blue lace sashes; there were many chairs and a couch of slippery American leather

50

to match; in one corner was a family chest of rough-carved oak with a large clasped Bible standing on it and a pale maidenhair fern in a brass pot standing on the Bible; along the window-ledge stood more ferns and ivy-leaved geraniums, still in bloom, white and pink and purple, the room aromatic with their queer fragrance; under the window-ledge stood a lace pillow, the bobbins spread out like a gaily painted fan on the old print. The room had a stale, fusty, shut-up smell, but Deborah felt that beside the big dead rooms of Mrs. Arbuthnot's house it was fresh and beautiful.

The silence became awkward, and searching for something to say she thought of the blue-legs.

'Jess says you eat the blue mushrooms,' she said to Mortimer.

'Ah, he'd eat any old truck,' said Mrs. Mortimer. 'Stinking old herbs and I don't know what he'll bring home some days and stew 'em.'

'Shet up.'

'That old hound's tongue you bring home, that's fit to choke a pole-cat.'

'Mash the tea, woman. I want to get locked up afore dark.'

'I'll mash the tea when Jess comes in and not until.'

He poked the fire gloomily.

'And leave off with that fire.'

Mortimer sat and listened with patience and great forbearance. He protested gently, never raising his voice. It was as though he wanted to be eternally left alone. The girl was struck by the soft lines of his face, his white hair, his speech, his mind working back to old tales and reflecting on the past.

Mrs. Mortimer cut bread and butter. In the kitchen the kettle sang to a boil and she went out and brought it back with her and set it on the parlour hearth. In a minute or two everything was ready. Mrs. Mortimer sat down.

'Jess'll be here in a minute,' she said, addressing the girl. 'It's been a grand day.'

Everything must wait for Jess.

She leapt up when at last his footsteps scraped the kitchen

step. She made the tea half-guiltily as though afraid it would not be ready for him. He came into the parlour at last.

'Come on, Jess. Sit you down.'

She took no notice at all of Mortimer. The old man shuffled to the table and sat down and took a slice of bread and butter and folded it on his plate.

'And you, miss, you sit here aside o' Jess.'

She spooned out the pears, sorting out the cloves on Jess's plate and putting them back into the basin, knowing he disliked them. Mortimer stretched out for the pears, but he could not reach them and Deborah passed the dish to him.

'Shall I help you?' she said.

'Ah, do.'

She filled his plate with pears.

'Plenty of syrup,' he said.

She spooned until the pears swam in the pale red juice.

'Whoa!' he said. 'Lovely.'

She smiled and they were intimate.

Mrs. Mortimer talked rapidly. It was a great and unusual thing to have a visitor and she must be warm and talkative towards the girl that Jess had brought home. She asked a great many questions, often putting the questions through Jess, making her inquisitiveness polite.

'And what is it this young lady does, Jess?'

'I'm in service,' said Deborah.

'Oh! in service.'

It was something more than a common thing to be in service.

'I wanted Jess to be a gentleman's servant,' she said.

'Tah!' said Mortimer.

'Ah! you can tah! It's a better job than farming. Look at Arabella's boy. He'll be a gentleman himself afore he's done, and so might Jess have been.'

Mortimer was silent. Everything revolved to Jess.

The girl was glad when tea was over. After tea she remembered the horse.

'She wants to take a mite o' bread out to old Tom,' said Jess. And then to Deborah herself: 'You better go along o' dad while I feed up.'

52

'Ah, come along o' me,' said Mortimer. 'I'll show you round a bit.'

'Keep her out o' that muck,' said Mrs. Mortimer.

'Shet up.'

They crossed the yard and looked at the cows still standing in the barns, waiting to be turned out. Somewhere behind the big barns the pigs were squealing and Jess walked across the yard with the swill buckets on the sway-tree. The twilight was deepening and Mortimer took off his hat and clacked and herded the hens to roost in the old hen-house against the cart-shed. An old white hen ran perversely round and round the muck-heap, clucking and cackling in defiance. Mortimer flung his hat in vain and the hen struggled into gawky flight and floundered on the muck-heap, red and panicky and shedding feathers. 'You go one way and me the other,' he said to Deborah. They separated, penning the hen in the corner of the stables, half-catching her and losing her again. They hunted in dead seriousness again, putting the hen into flights of terror. They could not chase the hen at last for laughing and loss of breath. In the roost all the other hens were clucking in panic. The old white hen flew for refuge among the wagons. Mortimer and the girl stalked her quietly. The hen drooped her feathers and crouched like a partridge behind an old trap, where they pounced on her at last, Mortimer swinging her up by her legs, rousing her into cackling terror again. The girl's eyes streamed with tears.

'It's been a fine old many years since I laughed like this,' she said.

Mortimer flung the hen into the roost and dropped the trapdoor and found his hat. He unbolted the doors of the big barn and they went through the barn into the stack-yard. In the darkness of the barn there was a dry smell of grain and chaff and potatoes and in the stack-yard the air was sweet with the scent of straw. Beyond the stack-yard stood an old thorn-hovel, leaning drunkenly on its posts, housing an old landau that had once been painted golden and black. The paint had blistered away and the shafts were cracked and it stood like a symbol of a vanished prosperity, a scrap of broken elegance.

'Missus wanted a conveyance to drive out a-Sundays and I picked it up at a sale cheap. But I don't know when we rid in it last now. I dare say it's ten year, perhaps, and above that.'

They went on to the paddock and the old horse ambled across to the gate. Mortimer took the bread from his pocket and showed the girl how to hold the bread in the flat of her hand so that the horse could take it and not hurt her. There was a long story about the horse and he told it in catches and fragments as they walked back across the yard to the house, beginning the tale at the end, losing the thread, breaking off for long silences and standing still without warning to make a gesture or to look back at the horse.

'If you look at him you'll see how he holds his head up. Straight as a reed. That shows his breeding. A man told me, a man as knows, Sep Sturman, a man as knows about horses if any man ever did, he's dead now, he said he believed he was trained to be a race-horse but something must have gone wrong somehow. Look at him. Won't go away from that gate until we've gone. And see his head? Straight as a reed! He ain't much good now, but I wouldn't part with him for a sight.'

Back in the house they sat and talked together in the half-darkness, the old man searching his mind for stories that had lain there untold since the last new listener, every tale mellow and wise with the print of his meditative, tolerant mind and of his spirit half-living in the past. She heard odd tales, sometimes without an end, of his boyhood and youth, of old fairs, of gypsies and prize-fighters, of crinolines and murders, of harvest-suppers and plough-Mondays, of remoter, vanished country things. He sometimes half-sang a song to her, his voice broken. He found something warm and responsive in her and she, never having heard of such things, was spell-bound and happy. She felt that she had known him all her life and that they understood each other, even though to him the past was the past, and like some vanished heaven would never return, and nothing could ever be the same or as sweet again.

When Mrs. Mortimer came in at last and Jess followed

54

her the tales ended, and the talk fell to ordinary, common things. Mortimer got up and lighted the oil lamp and set it on the table. Uninspired, he sat for a long time silent, leaving Jess and his mother to talk.

He fidgeted and poked the fire for a short time and finally he rose and went out into the kitchen. They heard him moving about there, setting up mysterious sounds. He came back at last with a plate of bacon, thickly sliced, a dozen mushrooms and a few blue-stalks. They were for Deborah.

'I'll tell you how to do the blue-legs,' he began.

'I should think the gal's going to be bothered with your old blue-legs!' broke in Mrs. Mortimer. 'I should think so!'

'Shet up.'

'It's you that should shet up.'

'You put 'em on a toastin'-fork and frizzle 'em gently and then pepper and salt 'em.'

'And like cucumbers,' said Jess, 'throw 'em down the drain when you're done. They're about as good for you.'

Mortimer persisted gently.

'You try 'em, my gal, and when you come again tell me if you like 'em.'

He shuffled from the room and returned with apples for her, a few walnuts and some green pears to lay aside for Christmas. He packed them all into a string bag for her, and Jess carried the bag for her when they left the farm and she went home.

'How do you like our old farm?' said Jess.

'Oh! I like it! And your dad.'

'Come up again next Sunday.'

She made her promise. He took her arm and as they were standing outside the gates of the house, awkwardly wondering what to say in parting, he suddenly seized her and drew her against him and gave her a strong, clumsy kiss. She gave a warm, happy laugh, not knowing what to say, and he kissed her again. She was warm in response and she pressed his hand with hers when they parted.

In the kitchen, quiet after she had settled Mrs. Arbuthnot for the night, she sat and mused over the kiss and the new emotions it brought her, going back from the kiss to all that had happened at the farm. She fried some bacon and frizzled a blue-stalk and cooked some mushrooms. She had never eaten such a supper.

'Well, if I don't live and do like a lady,' she thought.

She ate her supper in a state of bliss. The taste of mushroom was soft and delicate and the bacon had a faint, smoky, half-sweet, half-bitter taste like the smell of the kitchen at the farm. She soaked her bread in the sweet black gravy of the mushrooms, feeling that life had never been so wonderful.

Chapter 6

EXCEPT in the worst weather and when Mrs. Arbuthnot was not too ill or perverse to be left alone Deborah went up to the farm every Sunday through the autumn to Christmas. The farm became a separate life to her, attractive and warm with its smell of smoke and milk and of earth itself. The days between Sunday and Sunday went heavily. I'll go off my head if Sunday don't soon roll round, she sometimes thought. Yet Jess was slow in coming to life for her. He was bound up with his mother, and she, having sacrificed herself utterly to him, idolized him. He was her absolute possession; he was wonderful. Deborah, instinctively calm and unimpressed, stood firm on her independence. 'He's only a man,' she thought. 'And I can see myself going off my head for a man.' She scorned the blindness and stupidity of Mrs. Mortimer's sacrifice, her mind going sharply to the root of things: 'The more you do for men the more you may, and the less they think of you.' Her emotions about him remained simple, explicable, bearable; she walked arm in arm with him coming home from the farm in the darkness and they kissed each other in the barns and at Mrs. Arbuthnot's gate and sometimes the remembrance of a kiss brought about a queer sensation of bodily pleasure, the same sensation as she had experienced riding on the roundabout when the cars had plunged downward. It came quickly and passed quickly, a momentary flicker of unusual joy. She never paused to explain it.

She began to understand the relation of things at the farm very early. She realized that there was and had always been a struggle. She became aware of the existence of the land. The land was something more than the earth; the earth was something vague, primitive, poetic; the land was a composite force of actual, living, everyday things, fields and beasts, seed-time and harvest, ploughing and harrowing, wind and weather; bitterness and struggle; the land was an opponent, a master. The earth was sweet in spring and autumn, natural, eternal, yielding flowers and loveliness. The land was eternal also, but a man worked on the land, sweating, breaking his back, his work never done. Unlike the earth the land never rested or relented. The land ate into the body of a man and the land and the man became at last part of each other, bonded together and lost without each other, like two old enemies drawn to each other at last by a kind of bitter love.

At the farm there were eternal arguments about the land. By the fire in the evenings, when Jess had finished the paper, and Mortimer was dumb for tales, the land came up. Deborah had no part in it; she knew nothing of the land except that in some way the land and the farm were all part of each other. She realized quickly also that Jess and his mother hated the land.

Mrs. Mortimer's hatred was absolute and her theories were simple.

'Say what you like, the land don't pay. It ain't worth the candle. You slave your whole blame life long and then you're where you were when you started.'

Mortimer had theories also, long and elaborate, difficult to put into such brief simple words as her own. These theories he had worked out by long processes little by little, in the solitude of the fields and by laborious readings on winter nights. His schemes were obsessions; he theorized about collective farming, communal marketing of produce, a great, absurd, visionary system in which the land belonged to the people. He had read somewhere of the versatility and industry and cleverness of the French peasant; the French cultivated every inch of their land and pooled their produce and shared the costs of shipping to England things that could be grown in England.

'Look at the French,' he would begin.

'Ah, begin about the French again, I would. What difference does it make what the French do?'

'If we could all get together –'

'Who's going to get together? You don't suppose a man with two thousand acres is going to pool his profits and costs with folk like us, do you?'

'I don't mean that –'

'Then what do you mean? One minute you say one thing and one minute another.'

'The land should by rights belong to the people. It was taken away from the people. I remember –'

'What good's the land belonging to the people going to do I wonder? Man, you urge me. You want money for farming. Money's everything. Money breeds money. Unless you've got money you ain't much good.'

'And that's where we're done,' said Jess.

'Quite right, Jess. That's where we're done,' she said.

'You try and put them theories into working and you'll be bankrupt afore you can wink,' said Jess.

They were intensely conservative and he, in a mild, confused way, was a revolutionary, and they had no patience with him. They spoke from experience, and the land, in their experience, had given them nothing.

Mortimer loved the land. On November Sunday afternoons before the leaves had finished falling, when Jess would be feeding and milking early, he and Deborah would walk down the cart-track under the willow-trees and stop to gather watercress at the spring, skirting along the hedgerow where Mortimer laid his snares and climbing the fence into the stubble-field and returning through the spinney again. There would be ears of corn that the birds had not fetched still lying on the dry earth and wood-nuts still in their husks among the pale green catkins already shooting for the spring. The frost had not touched the yellow crabs, and the sloes were still clustered on the thorn, hard and cloudy with the bloom on them. She was like a child. There was so much that was new to her and so much for her still to know.

The future for Mortimer was a dim uncertainty; yet he began already to link it up with her. They would come next year and gather hound's tongue for ointment, and water betony and feverfew, and in the spring there would be nettles and dandelions for diet-drink and cowslips and elder-flower for wine. She had only to say she liked a thing and he would see her satisfied.

They came upon a sloe-bush one Sunday still purple with

59

fruit. The grass underneath the tree was strewn with fallen sloes. She picked one up and bit into the hard flesh.

'Tah!' she spat.

'I knowed what'd happen,' he said, smiling gently.

'Aren't they good for anything?' she said. Her teeth were rough with sourness of the sloe-juice.

'Make wine,' he said. 'Ain't you never tasted it? We'd better take a few and make a drop if you ain't tasted it.'

The waste of the fruit appalled her. It hurt her to see the fruit lie rotting on the grass underneath the tree. He shook the tree and the sloes came raining down from the high boughs. He filled his pockets and she took off her hat and filled the crown. Going home they talked of making the wine, warm and excited and happy.

Mrs. Mortimer was laying the cloth for tea in the parlour. Mortimer found a basin for the sloes and went into the parlour and stood on a chair in order to reach for something in the high cupboard. The clatter of cups ceased and Mrs. Mortimer watched him. He stepped down at last with a bottle of old sloe wine in his hand. Mrs. Mortimer pounced on him.

'And what the 'nation do you want to be fetching sloe wine down for?'

He blew a little dust off the dark bottle.

'Ah! and blow the dust all over the tea-table!' she cried bitterly. 'I would!'

'Shet up.'

He shuffled away into the kitchen. She followed him and saw the basin of sloes on the table. She made a gesture of despair and weariness.

'Here we've had a bottle of sloe wine in the house I forget how many years and nobody drinking it and now if he doesn't bring sloes home again I'll never live. You'll make no sloe wine here, slopping. You needn't think it!'

'Who are you talking to?'

'Who am I talking to? I'm talking to you. And if you don't understand plain English at your age it's time you did. I say you'll make no sloe wine here!'

'The gal wanted some.'

'I dare say! And who put it into her head?' She turned

60

to Deborah. 'You wouldn't like the sloe wine if you had it. It's as bitter as gall and it'll bind you worse than anything.'

The girl said nothing.

'He'll bring home any mortal thing if you harbour him in it!'

She flounced off into the parlour without another word, her face tight and thin with its grievances. The old man picked up a sloe that had fallen to the floor and threw it into the basin with the rest. The girl could not look at him. They stood depressed and silent. She turned away silently at last and went into the parlour. She heard him a moment later shuffle off into the yard.

Mrs. Mortimer met her in the parlour with a confidential and aggrieved whisper:

'The older he gets the sillier he seems to get,' she said. 'Take no notice of him.'

The girl could find nothing to say.

She did not often talk alone with Mrs. Mortimer. Their conversations, short and uneasy, were of everyday things, or they became monologues by Mrs. Mortimer about the farm and Jess.

'You know, the gal as has Jess won't need to be ashamed of herself. It'll be the best day's work she ever done the day any gal marries Jess. And he won't come without a farden in his pocket, I'll tell you that. We haven't always scraped an' slaved. I got me eggs an' hens if nothing else don't pay. An' I allus say to Jess that if he takes good care he won't have no need to be fret about nothing.' Occasionally she would break into a more personal note: 'You know I allus did say it an' I allus shall, farming ain't his line. He's too good for the land. I'm sure he's too good. Don't you think so? He's a fine-looking boy, and think how he'd look in livery. That's what he ought to ha' been – gentleman's servant, groom or something. He loves horses. An' I've been thinking. If ever you an' Jess make a go of it that'd be your tip – you an' him get a place together. You'd be settled for life. You been in service an' you know all about it. Don't you think so?'

The girl would think of Mrs. Arbuthnot's. She felt that if ever she saw the faintest chance to be out of service she

61

would take it and never go back again. But she would say nothing. Gradually she felt herself despising Mrs. Mortimer.

Winter came and she saw the barrenness of the land, stripped of its romance. The yard was under muck and water, the hens dropping muck and muddy straws and feathers over the kitchen floor as they came to peck there. She drifted farther and farther into the life of the farm without conscious effort, paying a visit whenever she had an evening free, lending a hand in the kitchen or helping to fold the clothes or stirring the bran for the hens.

January arrived; and one Sunday afternoon, before she had washed herself and changed her dress in readiness to walk up to the farm, the front house-bell rang. She took off her pinafore and hurried to answer it.

It was Jess. 'My mother's bad a-bed,' he said. 'Come up, can you?'

'How bad is she?'

'I dunno. But I'm frit about her.'

'I'll come. I'll just give my face a lick and change my dress.'

As they walked up to the farm he said again:

'I'm frit about her. I am straight.'

'But what is it?'

'She was drawing water, this morning. She allus will draw the water herself while we're having second breakfast, me an' dad. Just as we were sittin' down there was such a rattlin' and clangin' out in the yard. It must ha' been the bucket rattlin' down the well again. We went out an' there she lay, groaning, I never heard anybody groaning like it. Straight, I'm frit about her.'

'What does the doctor say?' she asked.

'Oh! we ain't had no doctor.'

'Why not?' she said sharply.

'She won't. She won't have a doctor in the house for love nor money.'

'Oh! dear, I don't know, some folks!' she thought.

At the farm the doors were all closed and the place was quiet.

'Hullo, Dad's out,' said Jess.

He listened for a sound of his mother and Deborah warmed

her hands by the kitchen fire. There was no fire in the parlour. She filled her lungs with a great breath of the kitchen wood-smoke, warm like spirit after the raw cold of the wind coming up the hillside.

'She's quietened down a bit,' said Jess. 'Else she's been a-groaning on an' off all day.'

'Groaning?'

'It's her side. When I asked her what it was she said, "Oh! Jess, it's my side. It's like somebody a-stabbin' me." An' every time this groanin' comes on she sweats like a bull.'

'Has she had anything?'

'We put hot bran-bags on her this morning an' that seemed to ease her. You better go up an' see what you think of her.'

They went upstairs. Mrs. Mortimer lay in a half-sleep and she turned her head on the pillow and roused herself and said, 'Is that you, Jess?' as they went in.

'Here's Deborah,' he said. 'Is your side hurtin' you?'

'It don't hurt now. I seem a lot better. I s'll try an' get up after tea.'

Her voice was weak and grievous and her face, always yellow and thin, now looked emaciated and ghastly. Her hands lay outside the coverlet, the fingers gripping the edge of the sheet, and the yellow skin stretched tight over the whitish guides and bones shone queerly like the skin of an over-ripe apple. Her eyes had not lost their sharp piercing stare, but the flesh about them was shrunken and the eyes were sunk deeper under the bony brows. Deborah said, 'How are you now?' She felt her left hand. It was clammy and burning.

'I'm middlin',' said Mrs. Mortimer. 'But I s'll try an' get up after tea. I'd be all right if I didn't sweat so.'

'You'd better stay in bed and let Jess fetch a doctor.'

'I don't want a doctor!' The voice had the old sharp rasping sound with it. 'It ain't the first time I've been bad. I don't want no doctors trapesing up an' down. I don't want 'em!' Her voice was agitated and she was talking desperately. 'Where's Abe gone? I heard him go out. He ain't gone for a doctor? I don't want a doctor!'

'He's out a-feeding up,' said Jess. 'That's all right.'

'I don't want a doctor, anyway. D'ye hear me?'

63

'That's all right. I s'll have to go down now an' milk, but Deborah'll stop wi' you. You lay quiet an' don't fret. Try an' have a bit of a sleep.'

'I'll try,' she said obediently.

Her eyes were fixed on him every second until he had vanished and after he had gone she subsided and shut her eyes and lay again in a kind of half-sleep, breathing heavily. Deborah sat down on a cane-bottom chair at the bedside. It was cold in the bedroom and after a time she got up and moved about softly, trying to keep warm. She stood at the window and looked out over the farm and the bare poplars at the fields bare and rain-swept beyond. There was a raw half-mist over the land and the light was failing quickly.

'Deborah,' said Mrs. Mortimer.

'Yes, I'm coming.' Deborah went to the bedside. Mrs. Mortimer was trying to turn back the sheets and the coverlet.

'Put your hand down here,' she whispered. 'Down my side – lower down. There, that's it. Can you feel it?'

'There's a lump!' the girl said.

'I know, I know. It worrits me a bit. It's been there a good while.'

'A good while? How long?'

'Oh! I dunno justly. Right back in the summer I slipped on them old wet stones round the well one day and I pitched and caught my side on the winch-handle.'

As the girl drew her hand away Mrs. Mortimer shrank and drew her breath in relief.

'It ain't nothing much, is it?' she said.

'I don't know. I think you ought to have a poultice or something before it gets worse. I'll go down and get one hot for you.'

'Don't say nothing whatever you do, will you, will you?' Her eyes were alight with a desperate intensity of fear and pain. 'Don't say nothing to Jess. I ain't said nothing to him! Don't say nothing, will you? I s'll be all right.'

'All right. All right, I won't say anything.'

She went downstairs. She felt cold and troubled. Her mind could not understand the stubbornness and stupidity of a mind like Mrs. Mortimer's, desperately concealing a secret pain. You'd think her own common sense would have told her! she thought. Her own common sense! Half in despair she went into the kitchen. Mortimer had come back. A saucepan of water was boiling on the fire and there was a smell of herbs and earth and roots mingled with the wood-smoke. He was washing some roots in a bowl of water; his hands were red and raw with cold and he moved about slowly and indecisively, as though his mind were stupefied. He brightened a little when she came in. 'Ah! I wondered if you'd come!' She warmed her hands by the fire and tried to think what to do for Mrs. Mortimer. 'A bread poultice won't do a great place like that much good,' she thought. She watched the old man faltering with the roots and herbs and water and she wondered if he knew.

'What do you think is the matter with her?' she said.

'I reckon it's gall stones. But she won't let me touch her,' he said.

She felt relieved. She said nothing and he went on cleaning and scraping the herb-roots and dropping them into the water. About four o'clock Jess came in. He caught the acrid smell of the stewing herbs at once. 'Eh! what the devil?' he said. 'You can throw *that* away afore I throw it away for you. D'ye hear me?'

'This is a cure-all,' said Mortimer. 'It cured –'

'Cure nothing!' Jess shouted.

He suddenly seized the saucepan and strode to the door and hurled the water and herbs into the yard. There was a hiss of steam as the water splashed over the cold mud. He slammed the door. His face was livid with temper and he snatched off his cap and flung it into the corner and then picked it up and hurled it at the dresser. 'I don't know what the hell to make of you!' he shouted. 'Don't stand there gaping! Get out o' my way. Get out!' His voice was hoarse and maddened and his words became tangled up with each other, a torrent of swearing gibberish. His father did not speak. A curious frozen look had come into his face and he looked helpless. Jess knocked him aside. 'Do you want all the sink?' he shouted. He washed his hands and face like a man half-mad, scouring his flesh as though the pain were a pleasure to him. The blood rushed from his face as he dried himself, leaving him white and ghastly. He turned

65

from the sink to the table. 'Can't we have some tea?' he demanded. The question shot straight at Deborah. She stood tense and still. For a moment he did not know her and then as he recognized her suddenly, the last of the colour ran from his face and the strength seemed to leave him. He sobered abruptly and collected himself.

'I never knowed you were down here,' he said. 'I'm all worked up about her.'

She was speechless. In a curious way she felt ashamed for him. She had never seen his temper before and suddenly she felt that she understood him better for having seen it. They had tea in silence and he ate a great deal, washing it down with cup after cup of tea, as though the heat of his temper had burned his body empty.

She left the farm early. She said nothing to Jess about his mother and he walked by her side gloomily. He was coming into Staveston on the following day and she asked him to call on her and tell her the news of his mother. 'I reckon she'll be up and about to-morrow,' he said. 'But I'll call if she ain't no better.'

She left him and went into the house again and then came out again and went straight for a doctor. He would call in the morning.

Jess had gone to town and Mortimer was cleaning up his pigsties the following day when the doctor arrived. He was a tall, oldish man with grey side-whiskers and a tight sardonic mouth. He wore a grey square bowler hat and a black stock spotted white. He rode up to the paddock on a horse and shouted for Mortimer to come and open the gate for him. Mortimer half-ran across the paddock and opened the gate and touched his cap, the muck-fork still in his hand. The doctor rode in and bellowed: 'Well, Mortimer, how's the pig trade?' The doctor's horse neighed as he spoke and he fetched it a crisp blow across the buttocks, making it stamp and wheel. Mortimer had no chance to reply. The doctor got off his horse and tethered it against the stack-yard gate and ran his hand smoothly over its dark brown flank.

'Fine morning!' he shouted. 'Well, let's have a look at the pigs!'

They went across the yard to the pigsties and leaned over

the wall and looked at the pigs. Mortimer had three sties, one housing half a dozen stores, the others each a sow. The sows were lying down in their muck and the doctor leaned over and poked them approvingly with his riding-crop.

'In pig?' he shouted.

'The white 'un is, sir,' said Mortimer.

'What d'ye want for her?'

'Oh! I don't think I want to sell, sir. She's been a good 'un to me.'

'Big litters, eh?'

'She's had three fourteens and a sixteen and a seventeen, and some odd tens and twelves She's been a beauty.'

The doctor poked her again and grunted and the sow grunted too.

'Tig, tig, good gel, good gel,' he muttered. 'Well, what's the matter with the wife, Mortimer?' he shouted.

Mortimer suffered a spasm of alarm.

'I don't know rightly, sir,' he said quietly. 'I reckon it's gall stones.'

'Gall stones! Good God! In pain?' Mortimer had not time to reply. 'Have a look at her in a moment. Stores look all right! What are you going to make of 'em?'

'You never know about pigs, sir. I count I s'll market 'em and keep one back for ourselves for salting.'

'Quite right. Good idea. Salt one for me, too. Salt a couple if you like.'

'Yes, sir.'

Mortimer wondered whether if his wife were ill for a long time the doctor would take the pigs instead of his fees.

'Well, better have a look at her,' the doctor shouted. He gave the farrowing sow a final poke and muttered, 'Good gel, good gel,' and moved away, clapping his legs with his riding-crop.

Mortimer followed him and waited in the kitchen while he went upstairs. He came down again in five minutes. A heap of fallen pears lay on the kitchen table, and the doctor, catching sight of them, chose one and took an enormous bite of it.

'Splendid! Know the name of it?' he shouted.

'No, sir, I don't. It's a keepin' pear, that's all I know.'

'Got a bushel to spare?'

'No, sir. There wasn't a bushel on the tree, sir, altogether. Put a few in your pocket, sir. I wish I had more an' you should have had a bushel an' welcome.'

The doctor took another bite of the pear and then filled his pockets, smelling each pear and rubbing it on his sleeve.

'What's the matter with her?' said Mortimer.

'Wife?' he shouted. 'She'll be all right. Send down and I'll give you some powders. She'll be all right. I'll see to her.'

He walked out of the kitchen and Mortimer followed him to his horse. He wanted to ask the doctor what was wrong with his wife and if there was anything he could do to ease her pain, but before his mind could frame the words the doctor was on his horse and moving away across the paddock. He hobbled after him and unfastened the gate and shut it again after the horse had walked through. The doctor wheeled his horse about and shouted:

'Don't forget that pig! Fatten it well! Good day!'

'Good day, sir.'

In the evening Deborah was folding clothes in Mrs. Arbuthnot's kitchen when the house-bell rang. She took off her apron and went to answer the ring and found Jess at the door. She took him into the kitchen. He shut the door carefully and quietly behind him and she said:

'Come in and sit you down and warm yourself. I've been wondering all day how your mother is.'

She held out a chair for him and looked at his face as she spoke. She knew at once that his mother was dead.

Chapter 7

MRS. MORTIMER was buried on a day at the end of January, in the afternoon. The village was nearly two miles away, and women who had known Mrs. Mortimer casually all her life walked up towards the farm for a last glimpse of her before the coffin was nailed down. On the day of the funeral the house was full of mourners and strangers in black and when the bier was wheeled across the paddock under the bare apple trees a black crowd of people shuffled behind it and another crowd of women who dared not go into the farm stood by the gate and wept and whispered behind their handkerchiefs. The procession shuffled slowly down into the village under a sky full of shaggy grey clouds which the wind hounded low across the land. Sometimes the wind caught the procession and women snatched at their skirts and the undertakers wheeling the bier held on their black top-hats with one hand and pushed the bier along with the other. Deborah walked by the side of Jess, and Mortimer walked with the dead woman's sister Ursula. She was a widow and kept a public-house called *The Falcon* in Staveston. She was a tart, superior woman with a crimson face and an imposing bosom; she wore ear-rings of shining jet and she carried herself stiffly and archly, exactly as Queen Victoria carried herself in an immense picture which had hung for many years in the private bar of *The Falcon*. She snapped at Deborah, knowing she was a servant, and called her 'Miss.' She had taken Mortimer in hand for the funeral, fixing and unfixing his starched collar and dicky and tying and untying his black neck-tie until she felt that he was presentable. He shuffled along at her side with bowed head, miserable and lost, and Deborah walked behind him with tight lips, discomforted but dry-eyed, determined not to weep. The cemetery was cold and dismal and the wind gusted down a few spots of icy rain. She felt cold and unhappy and impatient with the sniffing mourners and

69

the old parson mumbling an extra prayer for Mrs. Mortimer's soul. She wanted to be back at the farm and warm herself and take off her black hat, which was too small for her and was cutting her forehead. She had borrowed it secretly from Mrs. Arbuthnot because she could not afford another.

The tea-table had been laid at the farm before the funeral, and when they returned Deborah and Mortimer mashed the tea and cut the bread-and-butter while Jess milked and Mrs. Ursula Sharp and the other mourners gossiped. Deborah, going in and out of the parlour, heard scraps of the conversation. Mrs. Ursula, who had something on her mind, whispered and made confidential and knowing gestures with her hands, and finally, when Jess returned from milking and they sat round the table for tea she said to Jess:

'Your mother scraped hard for you, young man. I don't want to interfere with nobody, but I only hope you won't go and waste all your mother saved an' put by for you.'

Jess twisted his mouth.

'Ah, wouldn't take me long to spend the few ha'pence there is in this house.'

'You think afore you speak, young man. Your mother took care of her money.'

'Eh?' he said dubiously. 'She needed to, an' all.'

Mrs. Sharp kept silent. When tea was finished Deborah cleared the table and Mrs. Sharp sat by the fire with her hands folded in her lap. She had uttered her first thoughts about Mrs. Mortimer's money and it was easy to go on:

'It ain't no use saying I don't know because I do know. We had a cup of tea together not twelve months ago and she was asking me what I should do with a hundred pounds if I had it.'

'Don't mean to say she had a hundred pounds,' said Jess.

'You don't know what she had until you've looked for it.'

'I've got something else to do besides go foraging in drawers for her few ha'pence afore she's dead hardly.'

'She might have made a will for all you know.'

'She couldn't read nor write, so she made a fat lot o' will.'

Mrs. Sharp persisted. She knew that her sister had left money, and it was right and proper that they should know how it had been left. Jess, sickened and torn by the loss of his mother, derided her bitterly. She grew angry at last.

'I know you think I'm after her money. Well, you can think it! I want nobody's money. But I'll have what she promised me.'

'Ah? And what's that?'

'What's that? That's the picture hanging behind you, that's what that is.'

'Ah, the picture.'

The mourners turned and looked at the picture. It was a brilliant print of *The Virgin and Child* in a massive gilt frame; the Virgin looked anæmic and weak, but the child was wreathed in a wonderful halo of soft gold. There was a hush in the room. The picture was the pride of the house and Mrs. Ursula Sharp had coveted it for many years.

'So that's what you want,' said Jess quietly.

Deborah was watching him. She felt for some reason uneasy and suddenly her heart gave a great bound. The temper was rising into his face and suddenly he shouted furiously:

'Well, want on, damn you!'

He made a movement of swift anger towards Mrs. Sharp that made her cower instinctively. She tried to speak, but the electric force of his sudden words seemed to paralyse her. Finally he gave her a single glance of the bitterest scorn and strode from the room, slamming the door after him.

Mrs. Ursula began to weep. She had been insulted, she had been treated like a dog, and it would be a long time before she ever showed her face in that house again! When finally she rose to go, Deborah, troubled and embarrassed, stood staring at her. Mrs. Ursula suddenly vented her outraged pride upon the girl.

'I'd stare a bit more if I were you, miss!' she cried. 'You'll need to stare. You'll want eyes in the back of your head with a temper like his to look after.'

Deborah tightened her lips and kept stubbornly silent. For the first time she was glad of Jess's temper, feeling a curious thrill of pride in him because of it, her fears about him quietened and her own spirit, hardly ever roused to anger, warmed to a sudden disgust of Mrs. Ursula. She remembered his words 'I'm all worked up about her,' and she understood

71

in a flash the depth of his loss. He came to life suddenly for her. She shared his anger, and to share the strength of such an emotion brought her closer to him than she felt she had ever been. She kept her stubborn, silent glance on Mrs. Ursula, realizing that for the first time in her life she had made an enemy. Mrs. Ursula arched her bosom more imposingly and swept out of the room.

In the evening, by the fire, she talked alone with Jess and his father. The old man spoke falteringly, losing the thread of his speech, like a man with a prepossessing thought driving all others out of his mind. The girl felt that he was afraid of something. She coaxed him at last to tell her what troubled him. 'I don't know what we shall do,' he said. His trouble took shape little by little, unhappily, and Jess put an end to it all suddenly:

'We can't get along here without a woman in the house, that's how it is.'

She understood and waited.

'We'd better get married, hadn't we?' he asked.

'Perhaps we'd better,' she said.

They sat and arranged it. They would give notice at once and she was to tell Mrs. Arbuthnot in the morning that she wished to leave. She was conscious of a feeling of quiet, sober happiness. Her emotions ran deeply, like a hidden spring, and her heart was incapable of any tumult.

'We can manage on a bit o' cold bacon until you start,' said Jess.

He spoke of it all as of something inevitable, the only solution to a problem, and she was satisfied.

'There'll be ups and downs I don't doubt,' she thought calmly. 'But I shall do my best. Nobody can do more than that.'

But for some réason she could not sleep. She lay in bed and ran over her possessions and counted her money over and over again in her mind. She had her clothes, the shawl, the picture of Ruth and nearly ten pounds. When she had exhausted her thoughts about them she passed on to the thought of Mrs. Arbuthnot. Mrs. Arbuthnot had to be told and she dreaded even the thought of telling her. She went to sleep with a feeling that life had become for the first time a little

72

complex. She awoke feeling clearer and calm again, telling herself not to be foolish, and she decided to tell Mrs. Arbuthnot in the afternoon, after she had exhausted her daily suspicions and had written out the fair copy of her poem. She would be at rest then.

At half-past three the following afternoon she tapped on the door of Mrs. Arbuthnot's bedroom and went quietly in. She felt unaccountably nervous. It was cold in the bedroom. She shivered. Mrs. Arbuthnot, having already copied her daily poem into her big black book which lay on the coverlet beside her, was resting. She stirred disagreeably when Deborah entered.

'Well, what is it, girl?' she snapped.

All the words she had prepared to say leapt from the girl's mind like frightened rabbits at the sound of a gun. She stared helplessly and Mrs. Arbuthnot spoke sharply again:

'Well, don't stand there like a dummy! Say what you've got to say and have done with it. Has anything happened?'

'No, ma'am.'

'Then what is it?'

The words which had been so difficult to say suddenly shot out before she was fully prepared.

'I want to leave, ma'am,' she said.

Mrs. Arbuthnot sat bolt upright in bed.

'What?'

'I want to give notice.'

'You want to what?'

'There's a reason, mum. I want to give notice.'

Mrs. Arbuthnot sank back against the pillows again, muttering to herself.

'What did you say, mum?' said Deborah.

'Nothing! Go down and fetch my tea at once. Don't stand there staring!'

Deborah stood still.

'I give notice, ma'am,' she said stubbornly.

Angry at being disobeyed, Mrs. Arbuthnot suddenly shouted in that fanatical voice in which she complained every morning of being poisoned:

'What for, you fool?'

'I'm going to be married,' she answered promptly.

73

'Good God!' Mrs. Arbuthnot shut her eyes.

Before Mrs. Arbuthnot could speak again Deborah left the room and went downstairs to fetch Mrs. Arbuthnot's afternoon cup of China tea. When she returned with the milkless tea on a tray she found that Mrs. Arbuthnot was still lying with her eyes closed. Deborah leaned over and touched her.

'Mrs. Arbuthnot,' whispered Deborah. 'Here's your tea.'

Mrs. Arbuthnot was crying. The girl, astonished, cajoled and humoured her and finally Mrs. Arbuthnot, sick and white, her tears making her doubly hideous and old, turned over and looked up.

'You're not going to leave me?' she said weakly.

'I'm going to be married,' said Deborah.

'I didn't know you had – why is it so sudden? What's happened? Has anything happened?'

'His mother has just died, mum, and we think it's best. It is a bit sudden, but –'

'What is he?' said Mrs. Arbuthnot sharply.

'He's a farmer.'

'A farmer!'

Mrs. Arbuthnot put into the word a kind of sarcastic despair. Deborah stiffened. She looked very proud, a stubborn and rebellious little creature.

'It's my own business,' she said.

She wanted to add 'What's it to do with you? Who do you think you are? You're helpless without me!' but her will was stronger than her anger. The very helplessness of Mrs. Arbuthnot checked her too. The old woman seemed suddenly to divine what she was thinking. An expression of weary resignation came into her face.

'If you want to go you'll have to go, I suppose. There's nothing I can do.'

'Then you take the notice, ma'am?'

Mrs. Arbuthnot had gone off into a mood of reflection, gathering the trail of another thought.

'A farmer?' she said. 'There's no money in farming. Never was! Has he got money?'

'I'm sure I don't know what he's got! Not much, I dare say.'

74

'Then you ought to know!'

Her voice was not angry but level and insistent.

'Money is most important. You know that, I should think, don't you? It's no use entering on married life without money.'

'I don't suppose it is, mum.'

'How big is this farm?'

'Not very big.'

'How big?'

'Fifty acres or so I think.'

'You think! Really, girl! You ought to know! You can't live on dreams and love for ever! You want something to stand on! You'll want to have children I expect, shan't you?'

'I 'spect so, mum.'

'Do you know anything about having children?'

'I know –'

'I dare say! But do you know anything about not having them?'

'I don't know what you mean.'

'I thought not! Well, you'll have to know. Now go down and have your tea and then come up again. I want to talk to you.'

After tea Deborah went upstairs again. It was dark in the bedroom and she put a match to the gas, a single naked mantle, broken, which burned with a bluish flame that hissed and guttered.

Mrs. Arbuthnot struggled up as she lit the gas.

'Get my shawl and prop me up on the pillows,' said Mrs. Arbuthnot.

The girl fetched the shawl from the wardrobe and draped it over the old woman's shoulders and pinned it carefully.

'Well now,' said Mrs. Arbuthnot. 'About money. It's most important. What do you do with your own money?'

'I keep what bit I have got in a bag.'

'There you are! In a bag! You think because I lie here and can't get up I know nothing, don't you? I was young once, don't you forget it. So you keep your money in a bag. Why don't you keep it in a bank?'

'I don't know.'

'Good God! What good is it in a bag? It's just lying idle.

75

Don't you know that if you kept it in the bank they would pay you for keeping it there?'

'Pay me?'

'Yes, girl, pay you!'

Mrs. Arbuthnot began to explain the details of interest given by banks, and as the girl listened she thought: 'I'm just about half-sharp, I am. I might have lost or had my money stolen long enough ago.'

When Mrs. Arbuthnot had finished speaking she was white and exhausted. Deborah went to the chest-of-drawers and poured a little whisky into a tumbler and gave it to her.

Mrs. Arbuthnot drank the whisky quickly. The reek of her breath filled the air, but her voice grew stronger.

'Two things you must be careful about,' she said, wiping her lips. 'Drink and money.'

She began coughing, and the coughing forced her to lie back on the pillows again. She recovered slowly and asked for more whisky. Deborah poured out a little and she drank quickly again, smacking her lips.

'Look in the top drawer of the chest,' said Mrs. Arbuthnot, sitting up again, 'the top left-hand drawer, and give me the box in there.'

Deborah opened the drawer and found a small square tortoiseshell box and gave it to Mrs. Arbuthnot, who unlocked it with a key that hung round her neck on a piece of worsted.

'Fetch me a pen,' she said.

In the box was a cheque-book and under the cheque-book lay a heavy silver necklace, three rings and a piece of amber. When Deborah brought the pen and ink Mrs. Arbuthnot spread out the cheque-book on the coverlet and wrote out a cheque and then put it aside for the ink to dry.

The rings, sparkling purple and green and gold, lay very bright against the reddish glow of the amber. Suddenly Mrs. Arbuthnot emptied them out on the coverlet and gazed at them. There was a ring with a strange green stone set in a twist of gold like a snake curled up in agony and suddenly Mrs. Arbuthnot picked it up and seized the girl's hand and slipped it on. The girl, astounded, tried to speak, but Mrs. Arbuthnot stretched up her hands and folded them about Deborah's neck and drew down her head tenderly and impulsively, pressing her lips into the softness of her cheek. There was a reek of whisky, but there was an agony of hunger and loneliness in the kiss, and tears came into Deborah's eyes. Mrs. Arbuthnot was weeping also and they wept together in silence until Mrs. Arbuthnot spoke again.

'Remember me if ever you want anyone. I've made out a cheque for twenty pounds to you. You must go and put everything in the bank in the morning and keep it there. You hear me? Take care of your farthings. You'll need them. And you can be married with the ring. That will save you something. You won't get rich quick on a fifty-acre farm.'

In the morning Deborah took her thirty pounds to the bank, feeling a little dazed by the possession of so much money.

BOOK TWO

Chapter 1

DEBORAH sat on a wooden bench on the south side of the house, nursing her son. Mortimer had built the seat for his wife in the days when she had wanted to ride in a landau, making it of unbarked hazel stakes which he had cut from the spinney. Now the stakes were splitting and rotting from years of rain and sunshine. Close by the seat he had put up with young larch trunks an archway for roses, which had rambled thick and wild and had grown too heavy for the arch, making it lean drunkenly. In the July sunshine the fragrance of the roses was rich and sweet and the colour of the petals was blood-vivid against the hot blue sky. It was the second summer Deborah had seen them blooming.

Her son was five months old. It was between three and four o'clock in the afternoon and Mortimer and Jess were mowing the grass in the meadow behind the barns. She could hear the swish of their scythes in the grass and the ring of the whetstone on the blades. The land was dry and scorched: a fine day for mowing. At four o'clock she would make big milk-jugs of tea and take across the field to them, leaving the baby to sleep in the yellow wicker perambulator until she came back again. Until then she had nothing to do but sit and stare at the roses and the sunshine and make a soft murmur of conversation to the child. It was not often she sat still, doing nothing for so long. Time went by quickly: she was up at five in the morning, but it was noon almost before the realization of the day had come to her and evening before the dinner-things were washed and the milk set and the hens housed and fed; in summer-time, when there was no difference between evening and night, it was time for bed before she had cleared away the men's supper-things.

The heat of the day had drained her strength. She was glad to sit still. She covered the baby's head with her apron and shaded his eyes. He was a puny, sallow-faced child and he looked as though the heat had drained the life out of his blood too. His eyes were red and drowsy and his forehead was oddly puckered. He was a little like his mother and had nothing of his father about him, and from the first his father had derided him gently and playfully, disappointed in him. 'Ain't much to look at. A little old dillin, that's all he is.' But Deborah defended him fiercely. 'He's lovely, and you know as well as I do the dillin often turns out best. You want to see him grown up before he's born.'

She folded him with a rush of joy against her breast, holding him fiercely and tenderly.

From the first she had accepted the thought of the child with the same stoical resignation as she had once accepted Mrs. Arbuthnot and her accusations. 'If I'm going to have a baby I'm going to have one, and there it is.' Nevertheless she had been glad, too. The farm was lonely; from Sunday to Sunday hardly anyone came up the road and she looked to the child to fill that emptiness. Emptiness! She sat and pondered over the face of the child and wondered how she had ever come to think of emptiness. Life was so full that she had no grievance in it and no unhappiness from it except the faint uneasiness that Jess's derision of the child brought her. If she loved the child, she felt, then she had nothing to fear. She had her strength, she was not afraid of work, and she had her thirty pounds.

She gained a comfort from the thought of her thirty pounds which she could not possibly express. It made her feel wonderfully secure. She had told no one of the money and she had never touched a penny of it. Occasionally she managed to save five shillings and when she had saved so much she took it to the bank and deposited it. While bearing the child she went to the bank more often and finally a week before her confinement her thirty pounds had become a little over thirty-two pounds. She felt strangely happy. The money was the fruit of her unselfishness, her common sense, and her thrift, all the things inborn in her and strengthened by Mrs. Arbuthnot's words: 'Two things you must be careful about, drink and money,' and sharpened by the realization that life at the farm would always be unsure and precarious. She knew that she must save and go on saving, not through any thought of greed or indulgence, but because money was life and because she could not bear to waste either life or money. When the child was born she thought of new ways of saving and she had decided that in the spring she would buy another thirty chickens and a swarm of bees. All these ideas were secret too, and she had also faced in secret the idea that one day the farm might fail or Jess might die and that she must prepare for these things.

The idea that the farm might fail completely often occurred to her. She knew that Mrs. Arbuthnot had spoken the truth; there could be precious little money in a fifty-acre farm. Not that it was even fifty acres: the fallow land had not yet been turned again and its ten acres lay in useless waste. There was always talk of the field being sown, but it never happened; Mortimer could not decide what to sow, or the weather beat him, or some pigs died and he could not afford the seed. It troubled her to see the field lying waste and she tried to think of ways in which to use it, but she was only just beginning to understand the land and she never spoke about it. The land, to her, was an incalculable thing which grew and blossomed and changed and yet never changed; she was baffled by its stubbornness and its strength and she was appalled by the poverty and waste of it. On the first or second day of her married life she had asked Jess what he liked for dinner. 'Meat and taters,' he told her. 'Meat and taters and plenty of suet pudden. You want something as'll wear well on the land.' She made the suet pudding and went on making it, experience making her see the truth in his words.

Jess might have added about the pudding, 'That's what my mother used to make and so you must go on making it.' The loss of his mother persisted; no other woman could make such puddings or air his clothes so well or look after his wants as she had done; the woman who replaced her could only follow her pattern, making the same puddings, baking her bread and ironing her clothes on the same days, even buying his clothes for him as she had done. Deborah, willing to do any-thing for peace and hating nothing more than a quarrel, fell in with his ways and his mother's way. She refused only to pamper him. To her it was 'just about the limit' that a grown man should expect her to buy his clothes. Nevertheless she bought them. It was only once in four or five years that he ever had a suit and when he needed one he gave her the money and told her the colour of the cloth; she tape-measured his legs and waist and arms and shoulders, wrote the measurements down, bought what she thought was a good ready-made suit for the money, secretly thinking that men were babies and that Jess was a bigger baby than most of them. When the suit did not fit she pulled and stretched it over his big body until it would fit and then told him it looked lovely. He wore it after he had milked on Sundays and it was months before he felt at ease in it and ceased to look like an awkward lout.

In the same way as she shut her eyes to the faults of the suit she shut her eyes as much as she could to his own faults. He still looked the same to her, and she felt very little older and different, and if there were subtle differences in their relations she let them pass so long as they brought no pain. She saw his faults as she had always seen them, his temper, his mania for spending money, his occasional churlishness, his utter lack of independence. She saw them clearly enough, though she often pretended to be blind to them. 'He can't help his faults. Nobody can,' she thought. 'And so long as they don't interfere with me I don't care much.' When his temper got the better of him she turned away and left him alone, and his temper subsided like a fire without air. It was part of her natural creed to be sensible, to tolerate, to forgive, never to fly into a panic. What had she to complain about? She had a bed to lie on and a roof over her head and her money in the bank. She had a husband and if he was not perfect he might very easily have been worse. It hurt her that he did not love her child, but even that might be changed as time went on. Who knew what difference time would make?

As she sat on the seat she pressed the child suddenly to her bosom in a spasm of almost defiant happiness and then rose quickly.

'Here, this won't get the tea for your dad, will it?' she said. 'He'll create finely if it isn't ready to time.'

She put the baby into the perambulator and pushed it towards the house. When she moved the heat seemed greater than ever; her underclothes felt moist on her body. She half-reproached herself for not thinking sooner of the men, sweating and parched in the sweltering hayfield.

She pushed the perambulator into the kitchen and roused a handful of faggots to flame under the kettle. She cut bread-and-butter and occasionally rocked the perambulator, hoping the baby would sleep. It was past four o'clock when she had brewed the two jugs of tea and was ready to go across the field, and the baby was sleeping.

The two men were mowing the last quarter of the field. The Mortimers had never possessed a cutter or a reaper. The air was fragrant with the strong odour of the freshly scythed grass drying rapidly in the hot sun, and clusters of fallen flowers, bull-daisies and buttercups and pink-clover, lay shrivelling quickly to brown shreds among the rows of whitening grass.

Jess knocked off as she came across the field. His father finished his bout and then knocked off too, resting his scythe carefully in the grass.

Jess wiped his neck with his handkerchief. 'Thought you were never coming,' he said.

'You'll die I'm sure, having to wait five minutes longer,' she said. She poured out the cups of steaming tea.

'Where's David?' said the old man.

'Asleep,' she said. He took his cup and looked over the sweeping curves of mown grass and waited for his tea to cool. She saw disappointment sharp in his face because she had not brought the child.

Jess blew on his tea and drank it hot, supping loudly. He had laughed a little at the idea of calling the child David. 'I thought David was a strong bloke. This one don't look much of a David.' And she had said: 'We'll call him David Jesse then, and see if that'll suit you.'

With his mouth full of bread Jess said to his father:

'If them rows were turned quick we could carry straight away if the weather holds.'

'They won't get turned to-day,' said Mortimer.

Jess turned to Deborah:

'Better come and turn a row or two,' he said.

'I've got a baby to look after,' she retorted.

'Won't kill him to lay under that ash-tree.'

'I dare say. The hay can wait.'

He drained his cup, swilled out the tea-leaves and held it out to be filled again. She filled it.

'On the land you work when the weather lets you and while you've got the chance,' he said. 'You can't pick an' choose.'

Chapter 2

DEBORAH came up from the hay-field the following evening, pushing the perambulator, which besides the baby held dirty dinner-plates and tea-jugs that clattered together noisily as the wheels jolted over the rough, baked field. She was so worn out that she stumbled as she struggled with the perambulator. She had raked over the hay-rows for so long that when she stopped to rest her body seemed to be going through the motions of raking, spiting her tired mind. Her clothes stuck to her body. Her feet, throbbing hotly, seemed too large for her boots. The sun was going down still brilliant and burning towards an horizon dark with the haze of settled heat. It would be fine again to-morrow. She pushed the perambulator into the farm-yard and looked back over the field. Row upon row of the turned hay stretched feathered-up and ready to cart and already Mortimer and Jess were cocking it. The field would soon be clear.

She took the baby into the kitchen. He was already asleep and she undressed him while he was still asleep and then carried him upstairs. She laid him down in his iron cot and covered him and kissed him quietly. His face, like her own, was moist and wet. She undressed herself slowly and soundlessly in order not to wake him. Her clothes were acrid and moist with sweat and her body was sour with its own dirt. She tried to shake the hay-seeds out of her hair and her garments, but she was too tired to go on. 'I'm fair whacked,' she thought. She half-knelt, half-sat on the floor by the chest-of-drawers, looking for clean clothes – any old clothes so long as they were dry and sweet, she thought.

There were drawers of clothes and linen lying camphored and useless in the room where Mrs. Mortimer had died. No one ever used the room now and hardly anyone ever entered it. It remained tidied and neat, the big bed stark and white,

85

everything unchangeably in its place, the whole room a cold memorial.

It had been a maxim of Mrs. Mortimer's that the moment she threw something away she would discover a use for it, and for years she had thrown away nothing in which one stitch still held against another. The drawers and chests in the room were overburdened with her savings – old frocks and skirts and shawls, out-of-date corsets and hats, lengths of braid and faded ribbons, pieces of print and calico picked up dirt-cheap at market. Once or twice Deborah had looked at them hurriedly. She wondered now if there was some old vest or skirt there still fit for her to wear.

She went into the room. Its windows were fastened and the air smelt stuffy and dead. She swept some dead flies from the window-sill and opened the window and threw out the flies. Sweet air, fragrant with the scent of hay, blew against her face. She began to open the drawers of a big varnished deal chest, turning out unbelievable garments that had lain folded there for years. 'I don't know, some folks!' she thought wearily. Finally, she found an old woollen vest and skirt sweet with camphor and scrupulously folded. She shook them out. The skirt was spotlessly white and hardly worn, but the vest was in holes and on it here and there were patches of dark yellow stain, the stain of Mrs. Mortimer's sweat.

'They'll do, anyway,' thought Deborah. She thought of her own garments stained and stinking also with dirt and sweat.

She put the vest and the skirt aside and began to empty the drawer before replacing the things. The drawer was deep, and at the bottom, hidden by an old plaid shawl and a thick grey cape, she found a box of green plush with a picture of Lowestoft and the words *A Present from Lowestoft* printed on the lid. She took it out. It was very heavy. She rested it on her knees and unfastened the brass catch of the lid.

The box was full of sovereigns. She had never seen so many sovereigns, and she sat staring in wonder. She picked up a few sovereigns and let them drop again. 'My Bible oath!' she said to herself. 'All out of chickens and eggs and scratching and denying herself.'

She took the box to the bed and emptied out the sovereigns

and counted them. There were nearly a hundred and fifty pounds and underneath them lay a piece of pasteboard on which Mrs. Mortimer had pencilled in print the only word she could write, 'Jess.'

She replaced the money and the box and then covered over the box with the old clothes again. She was aghast but cautious. It was not so much the money itself as the means of saving it that impressed her. 'All out of eggs and scratching, all those years. A hundred and fifty pounds. It beats me.'

She changed into Mrs. Mortimer's vest and skirt and put on an old cotton frock of her own. Her tired mind could not grasp the significance of Mrs. Mortimer's savings and she felt troubled by the complexities of so much money belonging to Jess.

'I don't know as it wouldn't have been as well if she had taken the money with her,' she thought.

Chapter 3

As the summer went on she was able to work about the house normally and in the fields whenever she was wanted, but the child ailed. The summer was dry and the harvest ripened quickly. She gave all the hours she could possibly give to the harvest field; there were things that any woman could do and was expected to do. She made the sheaf-bands and tied the sheaves and built the shocks; finally, when the field had been cleared and dragged, she gleaned every inch of it scrupulously and carried the bundle of gleanings home on her head as Mrs. Mortimer had done, storing it in the big barn for the hens. When the harvest days were scorching with unbroken sunlight or heavy with thunder she let the child sleep in the perambulator under the big ash-tree overshadowing one corner of the field. When he woke up and fretted she went over and took him in her arms, soothing him by rocking him or giving him the breast. His cries were low, persistent, grizzling cries, not of pain or sickness, but simply of unrest and fretfulness. There was nothing wrong with him, she thcught, except fretfulness. He was like a young seedling, drooping and slow in finding a place for its roots, and she threw herself wholeheartedly into the task of nursing him and tending him. He was weak, therefore she must see that he became strong. The air of the fields would harden him, the sleep and her own milk would fatten him. It was her whole existence to see that he grew and strengthened; beside him the harvest was a mere incident; she could live without the harvest, and though she never thought of his dying, she could not live without the child. She suffered no panic about him; she fretted as the child fretted, restlessly and persistently, because he was still part of her, and she was calm when he was calm, her moods and ailings a reflection of his. The thought of Mrs. Mortimer's money at first awed her and then worried her, but beside the child it became eventually something quite meaningless. The child was living; it was life itself; the money was dead and a relic of the dead, and while it lay dead and hidden in the drawer it could make no mischief. Against her thirty-odd pounds a hundred and fifty pounds seemed at first vast, but gradually she grew used to it and at last half-scornful of it. A hundred and fifty pounds! It would be thrown away in a week on a new drill and a mowing-machine.

Autumn was late, the elms holding their colour until late October. Jess ploughed the year's stubble early. The weather was quiet and lovely, the sun warm and the dry earth sweet and light for turning up. After the ploughing they pitted the potato crop and thatched the stacks and waited for the roots, expecting an autumn squall day after day. The weather lingered sunny and quiet and the days were easier. Mortimer gathered the late pears and Jess mended the roof of the big barn.

The old problem of the fallow field came up. After the dry summer the field looked rougher than ever, its big clods unsoftened by rain and tangled with pink convolvulus and periwinkle, and the flat grey coltsfoot leaves that Mortimer dried and rubbed up in his hands for tobacco; ripe thistle seeds floated about it in silken transparent clouds and the wind peppered out the ripe red dock seeds. Here and there also tiny hawthorn bushes and wild rose briars had taken root, and were growing quickly.

Mortimer and Jess walked round the fields on the last Sunday morning in October. Every Sunday morning, after feeding and milking, they walked over their land. They detached themselves from their work and stood back, as it were, to review the effects of it. It was on Sunday mornings that they looked to see if the wheat had sprouted or if the mangels were ready or if the wheat was ripe enough to reap. They talked over the things that ought to be done on Monday and they pondered in silence the problems that were too deep to be discussed.

As they walked along the cart-track in silence, looking at the field, the October sunlight, a warm lemon-colour, made the thistle seeds shine silkier and whiter; the willow-trees swayed gently, dropping straw-coloured leaves; the hawthorns in the big north hedge burned a warm crimson and brown. Now and then Mortimer stopped and picked up a withered dock leaf and put it carefully in his pocket. Jess ambled along ahead of him, patterning the bark of an ashstick with his jack-knife into fantastic rings and spirals. He felt bored. To him the field looked as it had looked for the past five years, except that the docks were thicker and that the wild briars and hawthorns had begun to seed. He did not care if the field were ploughed or left to waste. It made no difference to him except that if it were ploughed it meant more work and no more money. If the field had been worth it things would have been different, but he remembered its last crop, a bit of beans that had made him sick to look at.

They came to the belt where the soil, silted by winter rains, dried out into an iron-hard yellow drift. Mortimer prodded the earth with his stick. The earth rang dully and the stick bounced. Jess did not trouble to stop.

They walked on together and at the bottom of the field they became interested in the hare tracks coming down the field and breaking through the big hedge. It was a relief to have something to look at besides the field. They lingered over the gaps. The sun was as warm as summer under the hedge and they walked away and back up the field reluctantly.

The problem of the field remained. It had not upset them. They had grown used to it, almost indifferent to it. Mortimer was too easy-going to trouble himself and Jess was bored.

They stopped for a last time by the gate and looked back across the field.

'Take a lot of cleaning,' said Mortimer.

Jess did not answer and with relief Mortimer followed him into the house for dinner.

Deborah, watching them come in, saw by their manner and knew by instinct and experience what they felt about the field. She felt impatient with them and as they sat down to dinner she said:

'Why don't you try something new in that field?'

They looked up at her.

'Summat new?' said Jess.

'Something you've never tried.'

'What ain't we tried, I should like to know?'

'Well, I'd try again then,' she said sharply. 'I'd never see a good field like that go waste.'

'A good field? –'

'If it was the only field you'd got you'd *have* to make it do.'

'I dare say.'

She thought of the child, an extra mouth to be fed.

'You'll soon have to try something,' she said.

'You know a lot about it. What shall we try?' said Jess.

'You might try sugar-beet.'

They both stared at her, astonished. They had never heard of sugar-beet, but Deborah said she had read about it in the newspapers.

'Ah, the paper,' said Jess. 'Don't you believe all you read in the paper.'

'Well, it's something you've never tried, anyhow. And there's a paper offering free seed and prizes for the biggest beet.'

'Yes, we should get a prize!'

He laughed and Mortimer smiled too in a quiet knowing way. This was a masculine joke, too deep for her. She set her lips in silence until they had finished laughing and then she said quickly:

'You've no faith, that's what's wrong with you. If you believed you could do it you *could* do it and no man alive could stop you.'

She silenced them. Words like faith and belief might have a meaning but it was a meaning too deep for them. There was a faith that removed mountains and doubtless also there was a faith that tilled fields, but they had never tilled a field except by the sweat of their backs.

But Deborah itched to see them tackle the field. It exasperated her deeply to listen to their doubts, their evasions and their spineless excuses. The field had once been cultivated and had yielded a little. If it only yielded a little again it would be something, and nothing was so small that they could afford to scorn or waste it. It was the little things which counted, she thought.

After dinner, when Mortimer had gone out, smoking a pipeful of fresh-gathered coltsfoot leaves, to look at his pigs:

'Your son won't always feed on milk,' she said. 'He's

a right to live as well as anybody. Why don't you think about him and break the field up for something?'

She spoke quietly and insistently, hoping to move him by talking of the boy, but there was something cold and stiff in him, like clay, which would not respond.

'Ah,' he said, 'keep on about it. You and that field,' he added wearily.

'Yes, me and that field, if you like,' she said. 'But if it was cultivated once it can be cultivated again, I know.'

He looked at her scornfully. 'What d'ye think the two of us can do?'

'I know it's hard,' she said, 'but if it's too much why don't you hire a man and buy another horse?'

He stared at her astounded. A man and a horse! What the 'nation was the matter with her?

'Where the devil d'ye think *we* can get money from to get a man and a horse?' he said.

She decided suddenly to tell him of his mother's money. It would relieve her mind and it would be a weapon with which to strengthen her words.

'Well, you might as well know it first as last,' she said.

'Know what?'

'Your mother left you a little money,' she said.

He looked ironical.

'Yes, I know,' he said. 'How much? Eighteenpence?'

She turned away and took the cloth from the table and went to the door with it. She shook out the crumbs and folded the cloth, holding one end with her chin, and put it in the table drawer. He watched her, puzzling his brows, not knowing what to make of it.

She went into the dairy to take the milk-jug. Coming back, she began to wash the dinner things at the sink, ignoring him completely. He went to the door, started across the yard and changed his mind. He sidled back and leaned against the lintel of the door.

'Where is it, anyway?' he said.

'Where's what?' she asked.

'Where's this money you're talking about?'

'Oh! the money. What next? I thought you'd gone across to your father.'

'How do you come to know what she left?'

She did not answer. He waited a moment and then said:

'Ah, it'll be a fat lot anyway. Enough for a pint and a smell, that's about all.'

He walked away across the yard, this time without hesitation. She let him go.

He was back at the door again before she had dried the last dinner-plate. She knew that the money was troubling him and she strove to seem indifferent. He began to ask questions quickly and she answered casually.

'Have you said anything to dad?' he asked.

'I'm sure I haven't said a word to a soul.'

'Where is it?'

'It's safe enough.'

'Ah, let's have a look at it. I don't believe it till I see it. Fetch it out and let's have a look at it.'

'I've got something else to do besides think about money, I'm sure,' she said.

She packed the dinner crocks in the pantry, and rolling down her blouse-sleeves she came back into the kitchen to get the child ready for his afternoon sleep. In her preoccupation with the child she ignored his father, and he stood for a moment impatient and undecided, feeling her indifference acutely.

Suddenly she heard him tramping up the bare wooden stairs. She almost cried out after him, but she let him go again. She heard him tramping heavily from room to room; there was a sound of drawers opening and shutting and of drawer handles clattering metallically. She met him on the landing, coming from his mother's room, as she took the child upstairs.

'Here, show us this money,' he said.

'I've got something else to do besides trouble my head about money,' she said, and took the child into their bedroom and laid him down in his cot. Jess lingered on the landing. She came out of the bedroom and shut the door softly.

'Now just go down and content yourself for heaven's sake,' she whispered. 'He's nearly asleep. Oh! go quietly, man!'

She avoided and ignored him during the afternoon and

finally, defeated, he went to fetch the cows up early. She could tell by the sound of his 'Hoick! Hoick! Up, Blossom! Hoick, Daisy! Hoick! Hoick! Hoick!' travelling sharp and clear over the fields in the quiet afternoon that he was full of impatience.

In the evening Mortimer had to walk down into the village on business about pigs. He petted and kissed his grandson before he went; the child was very sweet to him.

'Ha, old fellow, little old fellow. Good and little,' he said.

As soon as he had gone Jess asked about the money again.

'How d'ye know it's for me?' he insisted.

'It says so. Here, hold the baby a moment and I'll fetch the money once and for all.'

He hesitated, hating to nurse the child.

'Why don't you take him?' she asked.

'I am taking him, as fast as I can!'

He took the child coldly and dangled it awkwardly, holding it from its waist. She was hurt by his coldness. 'Why don't you like him?' she asked. 'He's your own flesh and blood. He won't bite you. Why don't you take to him?'

'There's nothing taking about him.'

'So you think!'

She went upstairs quickly and came down with the Lowestoft box.

'There's your money,' she said, putting the box on the table. 'Now rest yourself.'

She took the baby and sat down by the fire and talked to it softly. Jess opened the box; there was a gleam of gold in the lamplight. He picked up a sovereign and looked at it closely and then picked up another and examined that and then another and another. His actions were slow with astonishment.

'Sovereigns,' he said at last. 'Every jack one of 'em sovereigns. Well, she allus did hate halves. Said she couldn't tell the difference.'

He read the card on which his mother had pencilled his name.

'How much is it altogether?' he asked.

'You'd better count it,' she said.

'How the Hanover did she do it?'

94

'She's the only one who knows that.'

He suddenly tipped up the box and emptied out the sovereigns on the table. The coins rolled and chinked brightly on the bare deal. The baby turned its head sharply, its eyes wide and bright. Jess scooped the money together with his hands and began to count it, stacking the coins in heaps of ten. The baby sat stiff and upright, fascinated by the glitter of the coins and by his father's movements among them.

'He's watching you,' said Deborah.

Her heart was warm with delight as she felt the child's body tense and urgent under her hands. His black eyes were brilliant and she was proud because the signs of life were so strong in him.

'He knows every movement you make,' she said.

Jess counted slowly and deliberately. Up to a hundred pounds he bore himself calmly, but with every ten pounds after the hundred he grew more excited. 'It's a lot of money,' he said once. And she too, seeing the money scattered and piled about the table, felt suddenly the vastness of the sum.

Jess finished counting. There were fifteen piles of ten and one sovereign over.

'A hundred and fifty-one pounds!'

He suddenly saw the baby brightly watching the coins and his every movement. His voice grew suddenly warmer and more excited. He stooped down in front of the baby, holding up the odd sovereign.

'Here, know what that is? Play with that, then!'

He gave the child the sovereign; the tiny hand clutched it and threw it down again.

'Ah, you'd throw it down, would you? Throw it down again then!'

The child clutched the coin and dropped it again. It rolled under the table and Jess crawled after it, searching for it on his hands and knees.

'Oh! you'll lose it,' said Deborah.

'I've found it.' He crawled from under the table and gave the sovereign to the child again. The child kicked and gave a sort of crow and threw it down again.

'You'll keep on until you lose it,' said Deborah.

95

'It's the odd 'un. He can have it. Here, have another throw then, your mother won't know.'

The child threw the sovereign down again, his face radiant. He loved to hold the sovereign and throw it down and hear its chinking and then wait for his father to bring it again. Deborah sat smiling. Every leap of the child's body sent a leap of pleasure through her own.

Jess ran round the room, barking like a dog, searching for the sovereign. He scrambled back with it in his hands and gave it to his son. The child threw the coin at his father's chest and Jess dropped as though a bullet had struck him. His eyes were burning with excitement.

'Oh, Jess, you great fool!' said Deborah.

Jess scrambled off on four paws again. His son kicked and Deborah held him tight against her body. It was a great game.

Chapter 4

THE last days of January tore themselves out in a wild gale.
For three days the wind drove across the land in a moaning
frenzy and rain lashed against the farm-house and the barns
and hissed and roared in the spinney like a stormy sea,
flooding the yards and filling the dykes. The shriek of wind
and rain, the murmur of rushing waters, the whipping and
cracking of trees in the spinney made a chorus of wild and
mournful sound. The ploughed land was beaten into a dead
morass, the furrows turning to dykes of muddy water. The
fallow field was flooded at its shallow end.

At ten o'clock on the second night of the storm a loud
knock at the farm door aroused Deborah and Mortimer,
alone in the kitchen, playing dominoes. Jess had gone
into Staveston. He had got into the habit of going there on
most nights of the week and even a storm could not stop
him. Deborah jumped up, knocking some dominoes down,
and went to the door.

A man stood huddled against the raging blackness of
the storm. She did not know him. He half-shouted at her:

'Your man's had a bit of an accident.'

'Oh! the great loony,' she said at once. 'Where is he?
What's happened?'

'He's out here. We're bringing him in. He got thrown
from a trap.'

'A trap? Whose trap? He never went out in a trap.'

'The horse shied at a fallen tree.'

Out of the darkness came two men and Jess. There was
a white bandage across his forehead and his right arm was
in a sling. The three men shuffled into the kitchen and
Jess stumbled into the chair in which his father had been
sitting.

'Oh, you great half-sharp,' said Deborah miserably.
'What have you been trying to do?'

97

'Nothing. Get me some brandy.' His face was sick and sullen with pain. He spoke to the men. 'All right, Ben, all right, Duff. I'm all right. See you Saturday.' The men shuffled off heavily. Jess leaned back his head and shut his eyes, and Deborah came in from the parlour with the brandy.

She poured out a wineglass of brandy. 'And how the goodness gracious did you come to do this?' she asked.

'Oh! the bloody horse had a fit, that's how.'

He drank the brandy quickly and shut his eyes again.

'You'll be breaking your neck next,' said Deborah. 'Is your arm broken?'

'What the hell d'ye think?'

'You're about half-sharp, that's what I think. You must have been drunk, the lot of you.'

He kept silent.

'You'd better get to bed,' she said, 'come along. What's the matter with your head?'

'Nothing. Shut up and leave me alone. I'll get to bed myself.'

He stayed in bed until dinner-time on the following day. About twelve o'clock he half-dressed himself and came downstairs and tried to eat left-handed, but the inconvenience and pain of it exhausted him. In the afternoon the doctor blustered in and changed his bandages. He cringed and swore with pain, grousing at Deborah when they were alone again. She ignored him. If he was such a fool as to ride about half-drunk in a storm he must put up with the consequences. She had no patience with him.

The storm tore itself out, leaving the sky a bright wild blue, the flooded fields cold and desolate. The young wheat, washed by rain, stood out a brilliant emerald against the sullen brown land. Everywhere there was a continuous whispering and sucking sound, the sound of the land drinking up the rain.

February came in, the weather turning mild and bright, and Jess mooned about outdoors, nursing his broken arm. He had been spending his mother's money fast and life had been good and now when he could no longer spend he felt morose and wretched. Life at the farm was tame and dull even without money, but with a hundred pounds upstairs still waiting to be spent he felt like a beast caged just beyond the reach but within sight of food.

Going into Staveston one afternoon he had a drink or two and bought himself a bottle of whisky. The walk tired him and he uncorked the whisky as he walked home, and every now and then, when he felt weary, he sat on a gate and took a drink and felt better.

At the farm he remained useless. The things that he could do left-handed were not worth doing. He sulked and smoked and lazed about the house, the work that he did not do falling on Deborah. She mixed the bran and swill and fed the pigs; she slushed about the yards up to her boot-tops in winter sludder and she drove in the cows in the afternoon from the half-flooded paddock, where they stood silently awaiting her call, with breath steaming in the cold air; she chopped roots and turned the chaff-cutter and dragged in the firewood. No sooner had she turned from one job than another was waiting. When darkness fell and shut out the farm she did her housework, and when she had done her housework and given the men their supper she was too tired to do anything but crawl upstairs to sleep. When she turned back the sheets her cracked fingers and nails caught the stray threads like thorns catching at sheep's wool. Her body was hardening and toughening and the skin on her hands and face was coarsening.

Coming across the yard with the swill-buckets one February afternoon she saw Jess leading a mare through the gate. The Mortimers had three horses only, two big cart-horses, besides the nag, and she had never seen the mare that Jess was leading.

She set down the buckets and watched him. The light-chestnut mare was saddled and groomed and even she could see the breeding in its light step and high rearing head.

He came within speaking distance.

'Whose horse have you got there?' she said.

'Whoa!' he said. 'What?'

'Whose horse is it?'

'Mine. Whose d'ye think?'

She was astounded.

99

'Why, how's that?' she faltered. 'You haven't bought it?'

'Bought it? What d'ye think I did – picked it off a tree?'

'You'll come to grief one of these fine days, my man,' she said.

'Amen,' he sneered.

'Yes, you sneer!' she challenged him. 'You daren't have sneered me when I first met you.'

'Ah?'

She ignored his sarcasm.

'What made you buy a horse like that?' she asked.

'It was cheap and I wanted to oblige a pal. Satisfied?'

'And what do you think you're going to do with it now you've got it?'

'Ride it! What the blazes d'ye think?'

She picked up the swill-buckets.

'You're well enough to ride a horse,' she said bitterly. 'But you couldn't carry a swill-bucket.'

She walked off quickly and proudly and they did not speak to each other for the rest of the day. She was full of misery. If he had done something wholly foolish it would have been different, but her own sharp sense saw that he had driven a bargain and that the horse was a beauty.

He took to riding the mare about the fields and along the grass of the road-sides. He rode well; it was easy for him to ride with a useless arm. He sometimes branched off and rode along the old green lanes, the forgotten roads of Roman days. Under the high hedges the spring sun was already warm, the dog's mercury shooting green under the budded whitethorn, the sallow buds shining white and fat, like cocoons of silvered silk.

Riding along a green lane one afternoon he passed a girl stooping in the hedge-side, searching for violets. He rode slowly past and looked down at her and she looked up at him, with a violet in her mouth. He waved his hand. She looked at him, startled, and bent her head again. He did not notice whether she was dark or fair; he looked at the white fringe of her petticoat showing under her skirt and the curve of her breast against her costume. When he rode back again she was still there and he reined the mare and spoke to her.

'Good afternoon. Nice lot o' violets I noticed along there by the spinney.'

'Oh! did you?'

'Primroses coming out, too.'

She looked at his arm, lying in its black silk sling under his coat.

'What have *you* been doing to yourself?' she said.

'Breaking my neck.'

They laughed, easier at once with one another. She was a big, fair smooth-limbed girl, she spoke in a semi-refined voice, with a rich tone, a trifle low and half-languid. She carried herself magnificently and her clothes were part of herself, the skirt tight and smooth on her hips and her blouse strained taut on its pearl-buttons by her strong breasts. The violets looked curiously frail and very dark against her big fair hands, covered with beautiful reddish-golden hairs. Her beauty was like the beauty of a great ripe sunflower, burdened with its own luxuriance, her face seemed to be perpetually smiling. Her eyes, large and coloured like the violets she was holding, were full of restless, magnetic life.

They played up to each other, she at moments picking violets as though he were not there and he looking across the land as though he had forgotten her.

'I don't know which are the prettiest,' he said, 'the violets or the one who's getting 'em.'

'You've got a fine horse,' she said wickedly.

'I'll give her to you!' he boasted.

'You will?'

'I said I would!'

It was a great excuse to get off the horse and stand nearer to her.

'There you are,' he said. 'There's your horse. Can you ride?'

'No.'

'Would you like to ride? Come on, I'll teach you.'

She flushed and hesitated.

'Here, put your foot in the stirrup and catch hold of me. Whoa! She don't know you yet. Put your foot in the stirrup. Now!'

It was all over in a moment and she was sitting in the saddle. She sat splendidly, and her limbs, smooth and heavy, seemed at once part of the horse. His hand brushed her leg as she swung up and her skirt was flung back, showing her stocking. She made a great show of smoothing the skirt into place, but she sat astraddle and her long skirts were heavy and awkward and he watched her with a grin on his face as she went from one difficulty to another.

'How do you feel?' he said finally.

'I don't know what you'd think if I told you,' she said.

He smiled inscrutably. 'Ready?'

She nodded and he patted the mare softly and she moved off. The girl jerked in the saddle and uttered a heavy, luxuriant kind of laugh and tugged the reins.

'Sit easy. Don't pull her. Just sit easy and let her take you.' He rested his hand boldly on her heavy thigh. 'I've got you.'

She looked down upon him with ironic amusement.

'So it seems.'

'You wouldn't like to fall, would you?' he said.

'Not yet!'

Every word of their bantering speech was full of significance; they took pains to make their meanings dark, but when their meanings were darkest they managed in some way, by some look or smile or gesture, to make them plain.

They progressed along the lane to where, by a wood, the grass was uncut by cart-tracks. The girl reined in the horse.

'I want to gallop,' she said.

'You'll come off,' he warned her.

'A nice chance for you!' she flashed.

'All right, gallop,' he said. He clicked on the mare. 'Let yourself go with the horse and keep your knees tight.'

The mare moved off and quickened into a trot and the girl rode far up the lane and turned at last and began to return. She could not break the horse into a canter and she abandoned her body to the motions of trotting. Her limbs moved tremulously and her breasts trembled under her blouse and when she finally reached him again she was hot and excited, her eyes brimming with an extraordinary look of pleasure.

He handed her down. He could feel the warmth of her body even before touching her.

'Like it?' he said.

'Wonderful.'

'You'll be stiff,' he told her as he took the bridle again.

She was panting softly. Her brilliant fair hair had shaken itself down a little, her bosom was rising and dropping with great breaths. Her body gave off the faint warm odour of excitement.

'I've lost my violets!' she exclaimed suddenly.

'I'll go back.'

'No, I'll come again to-morrow.'

'You'll come again to-morrow,' he repeated significantly.

'If it's fine.'

'Ah! if it's fine.'

She was picking violets on the outskirts of the spinney on the following afternoon when he rode up. He smiled down at her from his horse.

'Well, well,' he said.

'Well, well.'

He dismounted, the mare began grazing, and he walked to where the girl was stooping in the sunshine.

'Like violets?' he said.

'It's their scent and their colour,' she said. 'So dark. I like dark things,' she flashed.

'Ah? Don't like primroses?'

'Not so much.'

He looked at her fair hair, almost a pale primrose colour itself.

'I do,' he said.

They looked steadily at each other for a second or two. Their eyes put life and significance into their words. They smiled with a kind of ironic innocence.

'Well, well,' he said.

'Well, well,' she whispered slowly.

It was a fine game. They were like flint and steel to each other; the sparks flew easily, never breaking into real fire. It was exhilarating. He had never played this kind of game with Deborah and he was pleased to find that he could play it so well.

'How's your arm?' she said.

'Getting better, worse luck.'

She smiled.

'Like to gallop again?' he said. 'Come on,' he urged.

'In a moment. This time you must hold my violets.'

They went through all the elaborate play of getting her into the saddle again. She smoothed her skirts and sat like a queen and he thought she looked even more striking than on the previous day.

'Tchk! Tchk!'

She rode away up the lane and turned and came back again; she trotted the horse both ways, and when she brought the horse to a standstill again her face was hot and excited and her hair was falling over her face.

He caught her by the waist as she slid off the horse and she leaned heavily upon him.

They walked up into the wood. He kept his hand about her waist. He asked her name. When she told him he did not catch it and she rolled it out again in her rich voice, lingering over its syllables: 'Alma Wolstenholm.' The wood was coming to life; the sunshine filtered down warmly through the spring boughs, lighting up the emerald dog's mercury and the earliest primroses. The scent of earth rose up strong but elusive. She took great breaths of it, filling her lungs until the buttons of her blouse were strained. When the topmost button slipped from its loop he saw the pink woollen string threaded through her bodice; that too was strained over her tight full flesh. She did not button up her blouse and he slipped his hand over her shoulder and touched her neck. She started. He could feel her heart throbbing. She looked superb. 'Ah! Give us a kiss,' he said. She turned and thrust her mouth up to him and kissed him. It was like the tired dry earth sucking up rain; she drank at his mouth, greedily and with ecstasy, as though he were a fountain of blissful strength and delight that she could not leave until the very depths of her soul were satisfied.

Chapter 5

MORTIMER straightened his back and shook the white sweat from his forehead; it was beginning to trickle down from under his hat and into his eyes. Lifting his face to the blazing sun he looked across the half-reaped beanfield and blinked and then bent his back again.

Jess and Deborah and himself were reaping beans in the old fallow field. A spell of hot weather had ripened all the harvest at once. They had not mown the oats before the red wheat was ready and to-day they had left the wheat half-finished because the beans were cracking and shelling themselves. The hot-baked ground was littered with beans. They rattled out like pebbles as soon as the sickle touched the stalk; they dribbled into the great cracks veining the field and were crushed underfoot; they showered from the sheaf as it was banded and laid aside. The whole of the field except one corner, which Deborah had wired off for chickens, had been put down to beans. It was nearly tea-time and they had not mown half the field. Mortimer looked at the acres of black stalks, stretching away down the slope, that they had still to mow. Every pod on every stalk was ready to split in the heat. Another day and every pod would be empty and white.

There would be a moon and they would go on reaping by moonlight. The beans were poor and thin; nevertheless he must harvest enough to see his seed returned. The field had lain waste long enough; they must not waste the crop, however thin, that it did bear.

They worked in a ragged line to the end of the field, towards the spinney. The stifling air was full of the crackling of beanstalks and scattering beans. Mortimer whetted his sickle and wiped his head with his shirt-sleeve; Jess finished banding a sheaf and Deborah dropped her sickle, going into the shade of the spinney to fetch the tea-cans. Jess flung himself down in the dyke and Mortimer dropped in the grass. 'Five minutes,' he said. They drank. The men swigged off the cold tea quickly, but Deborah drank slowly, with cracked and weary lips. Her thin brown face was flecked with sweat and her body was like a great weight in her sweaty clothes. Her arms and hands were raw where the bean-stalks had chafed and ripped her skin. She screwed up her lips in pain. Every scratch on her flesh stabbed her. She held up her arms so that her dress did not brush them; even the thin softness of her dress-stuff could double their pain. She found her handkerchief in her skirt and wiped her face with it. Mortimer was looking at her. She tried not to show in her face that she was in an agony of weariness and he tried to show by looking away quickly again that he had not seen her pain. They finished drinking. They did not speak. There was no need to say that they must go on reaping. They knew that they must go on.

They began to reap again. As they came up the field the sun beat down on their heads and they had the slope to climb; going down the slope it was easier working but the sun was full on their necks and backs. Deborah hardly knew which was worse. After a time she ceased to care. The beanstalks stabbed her flesh eternally whichever way she went. The sun would go down at last, but the bean-stalks would go on stabbing her.

The sun began to drop slowly. She was sick to death, though she did not complain. It was she who had urged them to break up the field and sow it. This was the pain of the change and she must bear it. There were no excuses; there was no hope for it.

By six o'clock it was cooler, but her body was too weary to count the difference. It would be dark by nine o'clock and the moon would be up. She would put David to bed and shut the trap-door on the chickens and then go on reaping again. What she did not reap to-night she must reap to-morrow. After the beans would come the wheat again and after the wheat the barley. Her life was made up of reaping and tying, of sweat and sheaves. She understood more easily why the field, once laid fallow, had not been tilled again. With another man and a reaper they could have mastered it. Now it mastered them. Not that they must let it go again. Having begun to till it she felt that they must go on tilling it. They must fight it and subject it until she had sons big enough to conquer it. She tore up the beanstalks in a frenzy of fresh determination. The field should yield its due and the farm should pay, even though it killed her.

At seven o'clock, without a word of warning, Jess put on his coat. Deborah and Mortimer looked up and stared. He began to walk away. Deborah was dumb with astonishment but Mortimer spoke.

'What's a matter?' he called.

'Eh? I'm off,' said Jess.

He walked on towards the gate. Suddenly Deborah sprang to life. She dropped her sickle and ran after him, stumbling in her haste. She caught up with him and stopped.

'You're what?' she said.

'I'm off.'

'Not if I know it. And I don't care who she is! This bit of beans comes afore any little bitch of a barmaid!'

'Barmaid? Clever Dick!'

'Well, whatever she is!'

She seized his sleeve, trying to turn him back.

'Here, what's your game?' he said quickly.

'You're coming back!' she cried.

'Who says so?'

'I say so! When this field is clear you can do your dirty business, not until!'

She seized his sleeve again. 'Come on!' she said. 'Get that sickle.' He stood rigid, his temper rising quickly, but she did not heed him. 'For God's sake move and get that sickle.'

'Let go my arm!' he said quickly. 'Let go my arm! I'm off. D'ye hear me?'

She clung to his arm, trying to turn him back again. His temper was mastering him quickly.

'It'll be the worse for you!' he warned her, half-shouting.

'You!' she said. 'That's about all you're fit for.'

She clenched his arm. It was as if she had pressed the valve which released the whole boiling stream of his temper.

'I've had about enough!' he shouted.

He gave her a half-blow which sent her reeling. She staggered, half-fell, and by a great effort of will kept her feet. If he laid her dead for it she would stand up to him. He was shaking with rage. She set her lips, ready to lash him with her tongue. He took one look at her and strode off madly.

'Christ!' He came a step back, his rage driving him. 'You'll be lucky if you ever see me in this hole again.'

'You?' she said bitterly. 'You'd turn up like a bad penny.'

'Pah!'

He was through the gate and across the paddock before she had time to realize that she could do nothing. She was sick with pain and humiliation. She went back across the bean-stubble and picked up her sickle. The quarrel had given her fresh energy and determination. She began to work frenziedly and when Mortimer spoke to her she said wildly:

'Ah! let him go. Let's get on.'

She lashed the beanstalks grimly, calling on all the strength and stubbornness and endurance she possessed in order to annihilate her humiliation and pain.

Chapter 6

The following April Deborah bore a second son. There was no argument or sneering about his name. She called him Benjamin. She had grown strong and tough, not only in mind but in body, and the child was a thin, wiry creature, quick and insistent from his birth; he slept little and slipped and wormed in her grasp like a strong young eel, exhausting her. There was never any doubt about him. He fed and fattened where his brother had lingered and fretted. He demanded life and movement, always lusty and fierce and independent. His brows were puckered even in his sleep, as though he were restless and dissatisfied. His weeping was a great insistent bawl, as though he were yelling for all the world to come and do his bidding.

At Benjamin's birth David could walk and speak a little. Very backward, he still moved uncertainly, and sometimes his brain seemed to forget the words his lips were ready to form. He slept heavily for long hours and his eyes wore underneath them perpetually a queer reddish-blue stain; his face was sallow and peaked; the sun never touched him, though the wind seemed to rip through his body as through a piece of muslin; he racked and whooped his way through the winter and was weak against the April winds that tore up the hillside and tossed the boughs of foamy white blossom in the orchard one against another. If he fell and grazed his knee the flesh yellowed to a fester. He ran to his mother a hundred times a day. He woke in the night and fretted for her in fear. Seeing no other children he was full of the terror of shyness at a fresh face.

He sprang to life for two people, his father and his grandfather. Since his father, having no use for him, never spoke to him softly and never stroked his head, the child longed for his words and his touch. After work Jess would come into the kitchen, kick off his boots and sit down before the fire to read the day's paper before he shaved. His big black brows would frown over the print; he would scratch himself absently, lost in the news. The child would stand still at his side and wait, his body tense and his eyes bright with the desire to be recognized. Jess would turn to the racing news and bite his lips, more lost than ever. Suddenly the child, gathering himself, would make a queer insistent noise in his throat and stamp his feet, like a deaf mute demanding something. Jess would lower the paper and raise his hand. 'Here, drop that!' The child would remain tense, his eyes wildly bright, ready to repeat his scream. 'Drop it!' The small eyes would feast themselves on him. 'D'ye hear me? Drop it!' But the child would remain rigid until Jess could endure his sickening stare no longer. 'God Almighty, what's the matter with you? Drop it I tell you! All right then, take that and see how you like it!' He would deal him an open-handed blow on the ear. 'Perhaps that'll cure you! Yes, you can bawl! Now go and bawl to your mother.'

But whenever Jess struck him the boy fled to his grandfather. All the mildness and beatitude and understanding in the world were centred in him. He would never lift his hand or raise his voice against him. The long link of old age and childhood bound them together. When they came together there was no need for blows or cries or fear or distress.

'Come on, let's go and have a squint at the blackies.' They would go into the spinney to see if a blackbird had laid another egg and then out of the spinney down across the old fallow field, planted half with wheat and half with potatoes, to find the skylark's nest that Mortimer had nearly turned up with the plough. The field was big-clodded and the child would fall in the furrows until Mortimer carried him. They would skirt the field and look in the dykes for partridges' eggs, finding a nest of fourteen from time to time and later in the summer putting up the coveys from among the potato flowers. By chance Deborah found a way of easing her burden of him. 'Now button your braces,' she would say every morning. 'Quick! Grandad's found a new flower for you. Off you go,' and he would trudge across the young wheat or roots to where his father and grandfather were hoeing side by side. He would be a little uneasy at the presence of his father, but gradually, picking his sprigs of yellow charlock and speedwell and pimpernel and pink convolvulus he would roam to another part of the field and forget him. When the days were wet he would sit in the barn with Mortimer, perched on a big bran bin, and listen to the stories and songs that his mother had also loved. He loved the gloomy barn, the cracks of moon-white light in the roof, the smell of bran and straw, the murmur of his grandfather's voice wandering on with the tale. The words and scenes and times of a vanished life would sow themselves in his mind and bear him great happiness. He believed in every word that the old man spoke; his words became his gospel, without which he could not live, and the old man his God. If his grandfather was God his father was something like the Devil. Jess could only sneer at the tales that he loved and at the old man who told them. 'Ah, put the kid down and let's get on. I want to be done and off. Don't be so damned pappy with the kid.' Then to David: 'Here, be off, you'll be getting your fingers in that chaff-cutter and then you'll bawl. Go and find your mother and tell her to have the tea mashed in five minutes! Go on! What? You stand and stare at me and I'll give you something to stare for! For Christ's sake get out of my sight!'

Sometimes the boy, backing away, would trip or stumble over a tool or a sack of seed and fall flat. There was something ludicrous in his weedy legs wobbling and sprawling in the muck of the yard and Jess would burst out laughing. His grandfather would set him on his feet again while Jess jeered and laughed and finally pretended to come for him with a bill-hook, making the boy fly in terror.

While the boy suffered and lagged his brother howled and kicked himself lustily from strength to strength. He began to speak very early, his eyes full of understanding; his actions had the fierce independence and vitality with which his mother had borne him. He crawled everywhere, about the house, into the muck-yard across the paddock. He suddenly staggered upright one evening, clutched the chair in which his father was sitting, made an immense effort of will and walked with staggering determination across the room.

His father seized him and threw him with a bound of sudden pride up to the ceiling.

'Here,' he said, 'I'll give ye a sovereign if you'll do it again.'

He staggered off, fell against the table leg, made a noise of rage and then picked himself up and walked again.

'Bloody good,' shouted his father. 'You shall have a sovereign when I put my best trousers on.'

'Bloody, bloody!' said Benjamin.

'Ye young devil! Come here!' Laughing, Jess held him between his knees. There was something vital and bright about the child that he liked. 'Now say it again if you dare.'

'Bloody, bloody!'

Jess lifted him in his arms and chucked him up against the ceiling and shouted with glee.

'Young devil!' he roared.

Deborah suddenly came downstairs, carrying David in her arms.

'That's a nice word,' she said quickly.

'Ah, what if it is?'

Jess threw the boy up to the ceiling and suddenly the boy repeated:

'Bloody, bloody.'

'So that's all you can find to teach him!' cried Deborah.

They stood facing each other, each holding a child, bitterly opposed.

'I'll learn him another if you ain't careful!' he warned her.

'I can well believe it,' she said.

'You can, can you? Here, say "Blast it!" my old cock sparrow, say "Blast it" so's your mother can hear —!'

Suddenly she snatched Benjamin from his father's arms before he could say another word.

'Once and for all,' she said, facing him. 'And listen — I shan't say it again. You may do what else you like —'

'Preach, preach!' he gibed.

'Very well,' she said. 'You know well enough what I'm

trying to say – these children shall grow up a credit to me if they never do to you. Get that into your head!'

She hurried David before her and opened the stair's door and took the children to bed.

Benjamin developed rapidly. He walked fearlessly everywhere, in the spinney, by the pond, far down the road, and among the cattle. Whenever he failed to do a thing he chastised himself until he could do it; he grated his tiny teeth angrily at himself for his feebleness. His mother despaired of him, talked to him desperately, locked him often in his room. When he howled and screamed to be released she was adamant, but he never desisted. Finally she would let him out and whip him. His tears were tears of rage, more piercing than his screams for release. He wore out her strength; he was like a strong fish determined never to be landed. She coaxed and cajoled and reasoned and beat him until her heart ached. At last he grew too strong for her. He could worm from her grasp and flee like a young colt, and when she caught him again he would bite her hands or kick at her until she released him. He kicked once so that the flesh of her leg turned blue and then green, until the bruise crippled her. She hobbled about, sick with pain and with a great ache of doubt and misery in her heart.

She saw plainly that he was like his father; she saw also that his father, in a perverse kind of way, was fond of him. Jess would swing his son high on his shoulder and bear him across the yard and they would look in at the pigs. Jess would scratch the sow.

'Tig, tig, good old gal.'

'Tig, tig!' the child would repeat, struggling until his father set him to earth that he too might scratch the sow. He strode about manfully wherever his father went, spitting when he spat and swearing because he swore.

'Stand over!' he would shout to the horses. 'Stand over, damn you!'

He would frighten his mother's fowls from their laying boxes, chasing them madly about the rick-yard until they squawked into the stacks in terror. He made his father cut him willow-branches for bows and last year's reeds for arrows. The bows were supple and strong and twanged like fiddles and the arrows could be sharpened to a needle point. He lay in wait for sparrows among the stacks, but sparrows were too quick and small to shoot, and finally he made David catch a pullet, climb a stack-ladder and release the pullet when he shouted the word. When he failed to hit the birds he dropped his bow and ran after them, booting them like footballs in his anger.

Sometimes David would climb a stack and remain perched there in terror, afraid to come down. Benjamin would stand beneath him and jeer and shoot arrows at him or wriggle the ladder. The elder boy would turn white with terror, mute and quaking, as though his fear were hypnotizing him. He would try desperately not to show his fear; he would clench the ladder with his hands hidden behind his back; but all the time Benjamin's sickening jeers would go on until he broke down hysterically. Suddenly Benjamin, retreating to a safe distance, would yell for him to come down – his mother was coming. David would scramble down with renewed terror. Above all things she forbade him to climb stacks; she had never forgotten the day when a hay-knife had slipped and fallen within inches of his head. He had promised never to climb again, and he had all his mother's sense of strict devotion to promises.

Benjamin, quick and sharp, discovered this and learned to say:

'Promise you will, go on, promise you will, promise me!'

When once David had said 'I promise,' it was all over with him. Where Benjamin went there he must go. He must conquer his terror and clench his hands until his nails made bluish scars on his white palms. A promise was a promise. He must struggle and fight and do what he had promised even if he perished.

Benjamin, one summer, lashed together two planks and threw them across from the bank of the pond to an islet of osiers and reeds where a moorhen was nesting.

'Promise you'll go across,' urged Benjamin. 'Promise! Promise afore I knock you back'ards in the damn water! Promise!'

David, having promised, stood on the pond bank white and mute with dread. He hated water and he hated heights.

Benjamin was light and quick in his movements. He did everything, like his father, with a swagger of natural grace. He skimmed the plank, keeping his weight light by the speed of his feet.

On the islet he yelled for his brother to come, jeering, threatening, cajoling and flinging his promise at him with derision.

'Run, you damn fool, run, run!'

David stepped on the plank, paused, made another step and paused again. Beneath him the water seemed black and sinister. He was foolishly and sickeningly afraid. His body was clumsy and heavy on the plank and his movements grotesque. He could not even walk in a direct line. He swayed and tottered until the planks quivered too.

At the join by the two planks he made a heavy pause and suddenly the planks slithered apart and he fell into the water.

Benjamin howled with delight. David floundered in terror, struggled and went under. Deborah, coming out to draw water, dropped her buckets in fear, tore to the pond, splashed in up to her thighs and dragged him out. He was unconscious.

'Oh! my dear, my dear,' she moaned.

For the first time in her life she felt the terror of hopelessness. She loosened his clothes and shouted at Benjamin, distracted:

'You stay there until you're fetched off! You've killed him!'

She picked him up bodily, scrambled into the house and laid him down and rubbed him. When he revived at last, she stripped him and wrapped him in hot blankets and staggered upstairs with him to his bed.

Three days later, when pneumonia set in, she drove herself into Staveston and drove back with a doctor, a young locum named Starling. 'I mustn't lose him. I mustn't, I mustn't!' she said. He sat beside her, superhumanly calm. As though taking no notice of her he made remarks about the wheat, just beginning to turn greenish yellow under the

July sun. He was a tall, big-boned young man, his voice calm as a judge's. She answered him distractedly. All at once he said, 'Let me drive,' and took the reins. She felt suddenly ashamed. 'This'll never do,' she said. He smiled and she felt suddenly an immense faith in him. She straightened her hair and laid her hands calmly in her lap, feeling that she had nothing more to fear.

The boy struggled and sank. She sat with him, never sleeping, and wiped the mucus from his lips, all night and for most of the day. Her whole being was an agony of hope and hopelessness. At three o'clock on the morning of the ninth day his temperature suddenly dropped. She flung herself on the sofa in the kitchen, face downwards, utterly exhausted but racked with new distractions and joys and fears, her brain racing like a mad machine. At daybreak she made herself some tea and went up to him again. He was sleeping. She revelled for a moment in the absolute quietness of the room which for days had been broken by his moans and his great agonizing gasps for breath, and then she fell on her knees and slept exhaustedly with her head against the bed.

He struggled on through the summer, coming back to health slowly. Starling, the locum, came often until his time was up. He was calm, laconic, very gentle. She felt at ease with him always. On the last afternoon he came at tea-time and she asked him to sit down and have a cup of tea with them. The pears were ripe in the orchard and after tea she gathered him a basket and he shook hands with her before he went away. She felt that he had been her salvation.

David ailed and struggled on through the winter. He was often in bed, he was never allowed in the barns, and his skin was drawn tighter and yellower than ever over his sharp bones.

Benjamin surged on, never ill or backward, aping his father. His brother, lying in bed with a feverish cold, would often hear his voice crying harshly at the horses as he rode the plough-leader, or the twang of his arrows as he shot at the flocks of winter starlings flying over the farm or at his mother's hens among the stacks.

Chapter 7

On a November afternoon Mortimer had killed a pig and there was great excitement in the evening at the farm. The children had stayed up late, helping to collar the head and cook the jowls and watch their grandfather salt sides and hams in a big lead standing over the kitchen sink. There would be pig's fry for supper and stewed trotters and peas for Saturday dinner. The kitchen was full of the smell of blood and salt and the fragrance of the cooking head and jowls. Benjamin and David took turns to sprinkle a handful of salt on the hams and sides.

Mortimer cut out the pig's tail with a flourish and held it up, calling:

'Who wants it? First come! –'

'Me, me, me!' yelled Benjamin. 'Let me have it. I want it. Me, me! Gimme it, gimme it!'

'Here, here,' said Deborah quietly. 'Where do you think we all are? Out in the spinney? You shall share it.'

'I want it! I want it!'

'You'll do as *I* say.'

She took the tail from the old man and Benjamin made a wild snatch at it. She whipped it behind her back with one hand and threatened him with the other.

'I'll teach you to snatch,' she warned him.

He stood glaring at her, defiant and angry. She set her lips and stared at him in return, her heart cold and wretched and her mind at a loss for the right thing to do or say.

'You shall have no supper, I give you fair warning,' she said at last.

Suddenly he spat at her.

'Here, gently, gently,' said the old man, advancing.

'Leave him to me,' said Deborah quickly.

She seized him in her arms and took him, kicking and struggling, upstairs to his bedroom. Her lips were grim and her face very white; it needed all her strength to hold his squirming and fighting body. She put him into the bedroom, in the darkness, and left him without a word or a blow. As she closed and locked the door he hurled himself against it, calling her bitter names. She stiffened herself into silence and went downstairs.

David and his grandfather were still sprinkling salt on the hams. It was nine o'clock. Trembling, she put the pig's tail into the iron pot with the jowls and went on cutting up the fat for frying.

'Who's coming?' said Mortimer suddenly.

'It'll be Jess,' she said.

'He's early.'

She felt too wretched and tired to trouble and she did not answer.

A moment later Jess opened the door and came in. Instinctively she looked up into his face. When he was angry or moody with drink she knew it at once by the sombre heaviness and the peculiar light in his eyes. Instinctively she looked for these signs.

She saw instantly that something had happened to him. The signs of anger, the sombreness under his eyes, and the queer brilliance in the eyes themselves, were evident at once.

He muttered a greeting, sat down by the fireside and took up the newspaper. As though engrossed he sat silent, his brows heavy.

But he was not reading. He was staring distantly, his anger seething and ready to break out at a word.

'Supper!' he demanded suddenly. 'Come on, I'm hungry.'

The table was a confusion of meat and blood, with knives and salt-pots and saucepans strewn about it.

'I'll clear up in half a minute,' said Deborah. 'Let me just put the fry in the pan.'

She took off the pot in which the jowls were cooking and put the frying-pan into its place on the fire, dropping into it pieces of liver and fat.

'Where's Benjy?' said Jess, looking round.

'He's where he deserves to be,' she said quietly.

'Where's that?'

'In bed.'

'What's up? – what's he there for?'

'He lost his temper.'

'And so you lost yours and took him up? Did he have any supper?'

'Of course not.'

'No?' he roared. He leapt up from his chair. 'No? Well, I'll see as he does then, that's all!'

'You'll do no such thing,' she said quietly.

'Who said so?'

'He'll stay there, food or no food, until he learns not to spit at his mother again.'

'Oh! will he? We'll just see about that.'

He strode straight across the kitchen and before she could move against him opened the door and ran heavily upstairs. She heard him unlock the bedroom door, shout the boy's name, and begin to descend again.

At the foot of the stairs she stood and waited, stiff and determined. Jess came downstairs first, with Benjamin four or five steps behind. As Jess passed her and went into the kitchen she mounted a step or two and said imperatively to the boy:

'Go back! Go back at once.'

Jess gave a roar of fury from the kitchen as soon as she had spoken.

'Didn't you hear me tell him to come down?' he shouted at her.

'And I tell him to go up again,' she said calmly. 'And up he shall go until he's learned manners.'

She advanced a step or two upwards again, speaking quietly to the boy, telling him to go back.

Suddenly she felt herself flung bodily and with great force downstairs. She clutched at the banisters, wildly and vainly, tried to cry out, and fell heavily against the open kitchen door, banging it against the wall with the force of the fall.

'And now come down!' came a great shout.

She struggled to her feet, staggered weakly and clutched a chair.

Weeping and fretting with little noises of fear, David ran across the room to her, and the old man wiped his hands slowly on his coarse apron, gazing in dumb astonishment. Benjamin began to come slowly downstairs. His father shouted in angry triumph: 'And now stop him!' and turned to stride into the kitchen.

He turned quickly, blind with fury. As he turned David, clumsy and fretting and seeing nothing but Deborah in his misery, baulked his way.

Jess stumbled, stood for one moment petrified by drunken rage, and then suddenly seized the boy and sent him staggering across the room. He spun like a shuttlecock and fell with a crash against the fender.

'And let that be a lesson to *you*!' his father shouted.

The boy lay still. Deborah, running to him, picked him up swiftly, with the great strength of terror, and seeing blood on her hands, half-screamed his name. Jess uttered an oath derisively and turned to call Benjamin downstairs again.

Before he could open his mouth he heard his father's voice. He stopped and turned about. Mortimer was white with acute distress. But his tremulous voice had in it something resolute and imperative. He spoke as though he had regained all the strength and courage he had known as a young man himself. Jess had become a child again.

'Get outside that door and don't come back!' said the old man. 'Get outside that door and don't come back. Do you hear?'

He tried to think of other words, but he only succeeded in repeating imperatively and more imperatively the same command:

'Get outside that door and don't come back!'

Jess stood for a moment immobile and astounded. Finally he strode forward past his father with a great swagger of rage.

'Well, I'll go!' he shouted.

He opened the door and in another moment was gone.

'Take no notice,' said Deborah. 'He'll be back. Get some ointment for the boy's head.'

Mortimer found ointment for the wound and together they bandaged the wound and the boy came back to consciousness.

Benjamin stood at the foot of the stairs, watching the door through which his father had gone.

Chapter 8

MORTIMER walked across the farmyard and opening the paddock gate went on down the cart-track under the willow-trees. It was the first Sunday in May, the sun warming the earth steadily, fetching up its rich scents. Mortimer caught the odour of dandelions, the wine-like sweetness of cowslips, the scent of the many grasses. He walked slowly, stopping at intervals to pick a cowslip-head growing in the wet bank by the trickle of water. Among the cowslips little cuckoo-pints waved light clusters of mauve feathers, and gathering a stalk of flowers he put it in his buttonhole, smelling its light fragrance first. The air was still and windless, the songs of skylarks and the odd drowsy notes of cuckoos breaking it gently, the flutter of the thin young willow leaves falling upon it with a light murmur, like the echo of a dim breath.

At the corner of the field was a stile. He climbed it slowly. He hooked his basket on a hawthorn stump, sat on the stile for a moment or two and looked over the field beyond.

The field was a sea of cowslips. Taking long breaths, he stared until his eyes began to water and the cowslips seemed to swim together, surging up and down the field in tawny-golden waves. Finally he climbed slowly down and walked across the slope of the field, into the full tide of the cowslips, like a man wading into a yellow lake.

The land was not his, but for over thirty years he had climbed the stile and picked the cowslips. The immemorial fragrance of their flowers and stalks would cling to his hands for the whole day and would linger about the house for weeks, very faintly, as the petals dried in the parlour-window in readiness for wine-making. In winter he could taste the fragrance again in the wine itself and remember the field, the lake of yellow flowers and the colour of the spring sunlight.

Stooping, he began to gather the flowers, breaking the stems short, working diagonally across the field, leaving behind him a light track of broken cowslip-heads and trodden grass. By and by it tired him to stoop and he half-sat, half-knelt in one spot and gathered every flower within arm's reach, leaving a pool of bruised grass and stems. He moved slowly, picking with extreme care, stopping often to rest and look at the field.

His basket was big and deep and after a long time he stopped and shook the flowers. A thin yellow drift covered the basket bottom, as though the wind had blown the flowers there. He had reached the bottom of the field, when under the shelter of the big hawthorn hedge the air was hot and sultry, and suddenly as he looked at the cowslips he had gathered he felt tired and he sat down, feeling that he could somehow never fill the basket.

He found a heap of old reeds, baked dry by the sun, and squatted on them. After sitting still for a long time he began to rub his hands to and fro across his brow, tilting back his hat. The sun, hotter than ever, made him feel curiously old and tired. His hand ceased presently to move across his brow. His head dropped and he caught it and held it with both hands, feeling suddenly as though even the strength to sit still were ebbing out of him. Quick drops of sweat came out on his forehead and ran cold on his hands. He shut his eyes, and bright stars, like a million cowslip faces from the field, danced bewilderingly in the darkness. He felt a curious cold sensation begin to creep up from his feet and shroud his heart and drive the blood from his face. His flesh went lifeless and white; he let his head sink lower and lower, until it touched his knees. He tried to save himself from falling, but a great wave of weakness came over him and his hands dropped and he felt himself slipping to his knees, the dry reeds crackling faintly, as though at a great distance away.

He came to himself lying on his back in the cowslips. The sky above him looked so immense and over-awing in its breadth that he felt that he had died and that the scent of cowslips was the scent of another world, a world in which he had never believed. But presently he moved. He stretched out a hand and touched the dry reeds on which he had been sitting and then his basket.

Struggling up, he sat looking at the cowslip field, and

slowly he came to life and belief in himself. But the sun struck curiously cold and he was shivering. What the Hanover had happened to him? He got to his feet, tried to walk a few steps and fell down.

He crawled to his basket and leaned against it heavily. The cold insidious weakness spread like poison through his blood. He felt that he could weep. He clenched his cold hard hands in an effort of determination not to fall again into the swooning blackness. A yellow-hammer was chirping somewhere in the hawthorn and he seized upon the sound with desperation, feeling that if he could keep his mind on the bird's song, without letting a note escape him, he would be safe. The song swooned away and surged back in a twittering crescendo. He forced his mind to follow it until it was sharp and bright reality again and he had strength enough to raise his eyes and find the yellow feathers of the bird in the cloud of breaking may-blossom.

He walked back across the cowslip field at last, his hand quavering as it held the basket, his whole body wrecked and full of a ghastly weakness.

Suddenly in his weakness he thought of Jess. Where the Hanover was he? Why hadn't he come back? Jess had been away for eighteen months, not giving a sign or word. He had simply gone out of the door and had vanished like a man stepping suddenly into an abysmal ravine. It was as though something in the darkness had suddenly swallowed him up. Not a word had come from him or from anyone about him, not a word or a sign. It was as though he had never existed.

The old man leaned on the stile after climbing it, too weak to go on. Why had he told him never to come back? His absence had made a great crack in his life and that crack had been widening ever since. His flesh was being riven and tormented by that crack; it kept gaping wider and soon it would split him. He felt old with waiting and the weariness of too much expectation.

He walked up the cart-track wearily, his shoulders stooping, the life in him withered like the cuckoo-pint in his buttonhole. His basket seemed heavy with all the cowslips in the world. He sweated bitterly, feeling his shirt clammy and cold by turns on his back.

'A drop o' brandy,' he kept thinking. 'If I can get a drop o' brandy.'

Unhooking the paddock gate he stumbled across the paddock, too sick and troubled to hook the gate into its place again. Deborah and the children had gone down to the churchyard to put flowers on the grave of Mrs. Mortimer. The house was shut up, but the key was in the lock of the kitchen door. He leaned against the door with all his sick weight and tried to turn the key, but the iron seemed frozen in its socket, and for a while he could do nothing. When the key clicked back at last his own weight forced him into the kitchen with a great lurch. He dropped the basket weakly and it overturned, spilling the cowslips, and he trod on the flowers as he staggered across the kitchen to the cupboard where he kept the brandy, fumbling and groping with his hands like a man coming out of light into darkness.

He knelt in the chair and tried to stand, and with one knee lifted and one hand on the knob of the cupboard door he waited for the strength he needed. Feeling ready at last he made a mighty effort and pulled himself up by the hand on the cupboard knob. For a moment he felt the house was falling down upon him. He shut his eyes and the arm holding the knob seemed to wither, the paralysis shooting down through his body like freezing lightning. He fell heavily to the floor, splitting his temple on the bricks.

BOOK THREE

Chapter 1

THE death of Mortimer meant a revolution; the weight of countless unsuspected responsibilities came down on Deborah, half-crushing her and threatening to annihilate her. After she had buried him on a quiet May afternoon, so still that the creaking of grasshoppers in the warm grass of the graveyard sounded like a chorus of yellow-hammers, she threw a bunch of cowslips on the coffin and went down to the grave on the following day and put another bunch, with a few oxlips, on the clay mound. Afterwards she walked about the farm, quietly ruminating. It was moist warm weather; the grass seemed to grow visibly as she stopped and looked at it. She went about for two days lost in thought, working hard as she reasoned on the future. Always half-wondering if she should give up the farm she worked like a horse, her own bodily determination a contradiction to her thoughts. She rose an hour earlier and half-ran about the place till sunset, foddering the horses, managing the milking, mixing the pig-swill. The land went untouched. The grass was nearly ripe, the potato-tops were darkening and thickening, the wheat was knee-high and strong. It made her restless to look at it all. Work accumulated, leaving her far behind, exhausted. A sow was nearing its farrowing time, the horses were staling for want of work, roots needed thinning, weeds were choking the potatoes for lack of the horse-hoe. In a month or less the hay would be ripe for cutting. She surveyed the grass-land and wondered how long it would take to mow it, single-handed, and she found a scythe and tried her swing at some nettles. She could not keep down the heel of the scythe and the point kept striking earth and finally she gave it up. It was no use. The land was crying out for a man. She knew she would have to

125

face it. She had kept the two boys from school until the schoolmistress was beginning to send her letters, demanding the reason. Sending them back at last she spent a desperate day alone at the farm, working in silence, brooding, the clanking echoes of buckets and tools reverberating about the place dismally and afterwards persisting in her own mind, accompanying all her thoughts. The silence seemed inexplicable, vast. She did not see a soul. As she tried to work things out her mind halted and wandered and everything seemed chaotic and hopeless by the end of the day.

In the morning she got up with fresh determination. Things seemed better, her mind was clear again, and after the two boys had gone to school she had something like an inspiration. She remembered Mrs. Arbuthnot. She put on her hat at once and took her umbrella, cautious even about the morning sunshine, and started off down the lane, hoping she would arrive by the time Mrs. Arbuthnot had finished her daily poem.

At the bottom of the lane a man was mowing grass by the roadside. Instinctively she watched the swing of his scythe. It was effortless and beautiful. His swathe of grass and buttercups was laid across in a perfect line, the sward shorn close, but she watched most of all the distance he could mow, in spite of thistles and the mole-turned ground, without resting to drink or whet his blade. She went up to him finally.

'Who do you work for?' she said.

He was a short, deep-eyed, quick-gestured man of forty or so, his face and his short knotted arms tawny from the sun and weather.

'Me?' he said, feeling the scythe edge with his thumb. 'Nobody. I'm mowing a bit o' grass for myself, that's all.'

She looked straight into his face and said without hesitation: 'Well, come and work for me – old Mortimer's place, up by the spinney. What can you do?'

'Anything.'

'Can you come to-morrow – Rook?' she said.

'Yeh. My name's Baxter. I heard the old man was dead. I'll come.'

She walked on to the main road, hesitated, and then came back.

'You couldn't come back now?' she said.

'Anything,' he said. 'I can pick the grass up when I come back.'

They went up the lane together. They walked quickly, each taking the same habitual, eager, half-running steps.

'Things are in a rare old mess,' she said as she took him from barn to barn, showing him the place.

He said little, but he moved with assurance, understanding things. 'Wants a man,' he said. They went into the house and she gave him some bread and cheese and they talked it over. 'I got hurt a-threshing last November, but I'm all right now,' he said. He worked till dinner-time.

In the afternoon he came back with a young fellow of twenty-five or six, erect and broad-shouldered, a giant beside him.

'My son,' he explained. 'He's been a-soldiering. He's fretting for something to occupy his mind. He'll help us out.'

They took possession of the place. The yard echoed with their voices, creating a new atmosphere, a feeling of practical assurance. From time to time she looked out of the kitchen, where she was baking bread, and watched them going to and fro about the yard, forking clean white straw into one barn and another to replace the old. There was a feeling about the clean straw that she could not fathom, a feeling of something fresh and unspoiled replacing something old and rotten, a feeling of a new life springing up in place of an old.

Rook was married, with a family of eleven, and at haytime he brought the woman and four of the youngest children to work at the farm. While he and his son mowed, Deborah and the woman raked and turned the grass and later the children helped to cock it and drive the carts home. With Benjamin and David helping also the hay was up early. After the hot and dry weather the grass was crisp and light for stacking, every stain of green bleached out of it. Deborah fed the woman and the children in return for the work. The weather kept clear and dry from June till August and the corn was early, the oats white by the end of July and the wheat-crop, though heavy, cleared before September. By autumn there was a feeling of life and improvement about the place.

After harvest she determined to keep accounts, to finish with the old, slip-shod way of doing things, to make sure where she was right or wrong, feeling that the uncertainty of the old way was disastrous. The waste and carelessness of it all appalled her. Autumn after autumn she had seen the fruit of the orchard lie rotting in the grass, no one caring if it were picked or eaten, and day after day the evening's milk thrown to the pigs in the morning. After harvest she began to send her milk to London, pooling the freightage costs with her nearest neighbour Twelvetree, and she made a deal with a Staveston shopkeeper for the late apples and pears, selling the trees as they stood. The accounts puzzled her; she could add and subtract, but the business of profit and loss was confusing. She had to allow a margin for seed which Mortimer had bought and for the bills which had been lost or mislaid. A good deal of money for corn and pigs had never been received and when she found an account of a sale the prices of things were so low that she clenched her hands in exasperation. Deals had been settled over a pint of beer or by the pigsties or in the rick-yard, by word of mouth. Mortimer trusted all men; a man's word was enough. When money was slow coming in he dropped a timid word about it, still trustful, and then kept silent, not daring to ask again. If the money never came he made excuses and in time forgot it. What money he did receive he kept in a little leather bag; when he had been buried and his funeral paid for the bag was empty. She went to the bank and with a curious sickening sense of guilt drew out twenty pounds of her own money and paid the wages from it and made things straight.

In the summer a sow farrowed and a cow calved and in September she had another piece of luck. Starling, the locum, had bought the old doctor's practice and he wrote asking for the lease of the shooting. He came up the following day, a Sunday.

She gathered a few late raspberries and skimmed a bowl of cream and asked him to stay to tea in the parlour. After tea the boys went into the yard and Starling sat and talked to her.

'Why are you in black, pardon my asking?' he said.

'I lost my father-in-law in May.'

'I was wondering where he was – and your husband, too.'

'He left me some time ago,' she said, quite calm. 'He was a bit wild.'

'So you're alone up here?'

'I've got my sons. I don't blame him – his mother left him some money and it went to his head. We can't help ourselves.' He kept silent and she changed the subject abruptly.

'About the shooting. Fifty acres isn't much to shoot over.'

'I'm renting Twelvetree's, too,' he explained. 'I shall drive up the hill and finish at your place.'

'There isn't much, I'm afraid. I see a hare or two sometimes and an odd covey. But nothing much.'

He looked out of the window.

'Perhaps you'd show me your boundaries – I needn't go trespassing then.'

As they left the house the western sky was liquid with changing golden light, the evening full of gentle airs, the pond unrippled except for the little rings made by falling sloe-leaves, the rings spreading and vanishing swiftly. A moorhen ran flustering under the sloe-trees and dropped into the water with a faint splash, making a great swooning ring across the water. 'Last spring we had wild ducks nesting just by the pond,' said Deborah. 'I know it's silly, but if you see them don't shoot them – I should like to see them again.' Promising not to shoot the duck he followed her through the spinney and into the old fallow field. A covey of partridges ran with frightened cries along the bean-stubble, gathering speed for flight, and then rose quickly and swooped over the hedgerow, vanishing abruptly. She showed him the boundaries, taking him back under the big north hedge. The hawthorn leaves were thinning perceptibly, faintly changing to fox-colour and lemon and wine-red, and the summer's magpies' nests hung half-revealed, dead black against the western light. Arriving at the stile below the willow-trees they stood and gazed at the cowslip field where Mortimer had had his first stroke. The field slipped away steeply, the brook below marked clearly by big willow-trees and patches of whitening sedge.

'Any snipe at all?' asked the doctor.

'By the brook, I think. I've heard them say so. Twelvetree's land comes all the way from the village by the brook. You'd see them there if anywhere.'

From the stile she pointed out the other boundaries. Returning up the cart-track they put up a pheasant, a young cock, vivid with blue and scarlet eye, and when the bird had planed away over the bean-field and had dropped from sight, the doctor said:

'So you're keeping on with the farm – by yourself?'

'I want it for my sons. Why shouldn't I?'

She spoke in her old quick downright way, sharp and a little indignant, and then went on, more quietly:

'Goodness, I couldn't do much worse than those before me, I do know that.'

'They're saying there's nothing in the land nowadays,' he remarked.

'They've always said that. What's wrong with the land, I should like to know? It's the same land – the same weather – the same seasons, everything the same except the people farming it. The people have changed, that's all. Take Twelvetree – his land has been known to yield ten quarter to the acre, solid wheat. Now what he gets is often so bad he doesn't trouble to reap it. The land alone can't do much, can it? Look at this field – this land lay fallow through sheer laziness. My father-in-law couldn't make up his mind about it. He'd sow this and he'd sow that – and in the end he sowed nothing. He thought he was saving money on seed, so he let it go completely – and now look at it. It's poisoned. Look at the weeds and twitch. Five years won't see it clean again. It's always the same – always has been and always will be. If you're not master of the land, the land will be master of you. Nothing's so sure as that. I only wish it could be.'

Before he had time to speak again she went on:

'Nothing worries me much except accounts – and they frighten me rather. Do you know anything about them?'

'A little.'

'If it's only a little and you can tell me what it is, I shall be thankful,' she said earnestly. 'I want to do things properly. I must. A farm is a business, like anything else. If it isn't run properly there's no hope for it.'

Back in the parlour they sat together at the table with pencil and paper and he made out trial columns of figures, explaining how a balance was worked. Afterwards he made her understand the system of percentages and he did explanatory sums for her, taking old bills as examples. She grasped things easily, her brain quick, her habitual stubbornness of mind filling her with a determination to understand even the obscurest things. Twilight came on and she brought in the lamp and they began to work on actual accounts, striking off bad debts, allowing margins for seed, gradually setting things straight. He handled figures with a kind of smooth delibera-tion, as she would have liked to handle them herself, his large, pink, fair-haired hands very masterly and reassuring in the fall of the lamp-light. 'Figures aren't so terrifying,' he said, 'if you keep to date with them. You must keep to date.' Steadily her figures were put down, checked and balanced until she felt a curious sense not merely of gratification but of power too. She had gained fresh knowledge. Her eyes had been opened. It was the state of mind she loved, hating as she did all blundering and indecision and falsity and blindness.

'I'm so thankful. I don't know what to say,' she said.

He got up, smiling, and held out his hand, ready to go.

'It's enough to say you are thankful.'

She went into the kitchen and came back with a bottle of wine and glasses.

'Before you go,' she said.

She poured into the glasses a pale, greenish-yellow wine, clear as spring-water, the colour of half-opened cowslips. It tasted of the flowers and gave off the dim scent of them.

'A happy wine,' he said, and then setting down the glass hurriedly he exclaimed:

'I almost forgot the shooting. I'll pay you now.'

'Oh! no, that doesn't matter. In the spring.'

He made an insistent gesture and counted out ten sovereigns and set them in a heap, making a candle of gold, by his wine-glass. 'I think that's what we said.'

She made a sound of protest, but he had opened the parlour door and was through the kitchen and into the twilight, tawny with the afterglow of the sun, before she could frame her words. She heard him call back something about 'The boys can beat for me – Good night!' followed by his retreating footsteps and then silence.

Afterwards, from time to time, he would call in after shoot-ing on the darkening afternoons of winter, quite early if rain began to fall or if the birds were shy, and warm his bloodless hands by the kitchen fire and drink a cup of tea if she had time to make it. Catching her sometimes on baking days he would sit and watch the sponge rise in the big yellow-and-brown panchion, the white dough, pinked with firelight, swelling gently upward like a woman's breast. When the bread had been baked and came hot to the hearth, against his feet, he would let it cool a little and then break off some crisp morsel of crust and crack it with his teeth, smiling curiously. It began to snow one afternoon as she went out to fetch the cows up, her voice brittle in the air, still and sharp, without a wind to break its echoes. As she drove up the cows the snow was beginning to fall like whitest thistle-down, settling on the black steaming flanks of the beasts, melting as it fell. As she turned the cows into the paddock gate she saw the doctor coming up by the willow-trees, carrying nothing but his gun. The snow was thickening the air to the east and north, the sky, sombre with the burden of it, sagging low over the horizon and obliterating the farthest trees. When the cows had gone in for milking she found the doctor sheltering under a bramble-hovel, leaning on the old landau. The land was dim under the dance of illimitable snowflakes. She called to him to come in.

In the kitchen he stood against the window, watching the snow. She asked if he had shot anything, and he told her how shy the birds had been, as though scenting the snow, and how nothing would come within range – not even a rabbit. She began to lay the cloth for tea, setting out cups and saucers for the two boys and herself and then one for the doctor. Suddenly, still at the window, he said, without turning:

'Come here.'

His voice was so imperative and soft that she felt her heart give a bound of dread and wonder. She stiffened her breast, quietening herself, and then went to look.

'It's only the snow – but very wonderful, the transformation. I wanted you to look.'

She stood by his side, catching the strong masculine smell of his body and his damp tweeds, and looked out at the snow. 'It falls on everything differently,' he said, and she saw how the grass was already more white than green, but how the elms and the spinney and the apple-trees were still dark, catching only a rare flake here and there, like a petal. Beyond the spinney she saw the ploughed land barred black and white, the lands like great striped scarves roughly dyed, and farther beyond still the ghostly effect of falling and fallen snow under the twilit sky. The snow was coming faster, driving a little. A flock of starlings flew low over the barns at a fretful speed, travelling with the storm. 'There will be sea-gulls up if the weather gets bad,' he said. The land began to look strange and startling in its whiteness, and as one thing and another lost its old character he talked of it, making her follow the beauty of the changes until she began to see things as he did. The earth was a veritable wonder of darkness and light, the air a white madness of swooping and dancing flakes. Shortly the rugged forks of the apple-trees gathered whiteness and the snow spread along the twigs and clung to the storm side of the rain-green trunks. Darkness and snow and the silence of the world seemed to increase together, the silence great and strange, the darkness bit by bit swallowing up the snow, the silence finally swallowing both the snow and the darkness.

She went back to the table to finish setting the tea and as she put out spoons and plates and coaxed the fire to flame under the kettle he went on speaking, still discovering light and beauty, a drift of flakes on a barn-roof or a fence, the slow painting of a tree, flake by flake. Having been accustomed to people who saw nothing like this she could not grow used to it. She felt stiff and unreceptive, like parched earth unable to drink in a sudden fall of rain. His thoughts and his words haunted her strangely, odd words and images flaring up and dying in her mind like distant fires.

When presently the two boys came in he was still standing there. The kitchen, except for the red firelight, was nearly dark, and not seeing him at one window David ran to another and began to rhyme:

'Snow, snow faster, else I'll tell your master! Snow, snow –'

'Ah, shut up,' said Benjamin abruptly.

'That's nice talk!' said Deborah.

'He's been saying that all the way up from school – all the way up,' he said. 'Snow, snow faster,' he began to gibe, his voice derisive and taunting. 'Dah, dah, dah, dah!' he mocked.

His voice, small and ugly, destroyed suddenly all her dreamy illusions.

'Just mind what you're saying! The doctor's here,' she warned him.

The two boys started, seeing him at the window simultaneously. David stood timid and startled, and his brother shifted his feet, uneasy but unsubdued.

'Don't quarrel,' said Starling, mildly.

'I ain't quarrelling – I ain't quarrelled with nobody,' flashed Benjamin.

'Hush, hush, boy, do!' said his mother.

'Well, I ain't quarrelling, am I?' he half-shouted.

'All right, all right, you're not quarrelling. That's enough.'

She brought the lamp in and put a match to the wick and as the ring of light dropped murkily over the tea-table she called the three of them to tea.

'Come, doctor, you sit between them.'

When the lamp had burned up and the light, brighter and stronger, spread beyond the tea-table to the corners of the room the doctor saw the younger boy gazing at something under the window. A great light of interest was driving the sombre, ugly gleam of temper from his eyes. His mother saw it too and said:

'What are you staring at so, boy?'

'Your gun,' he said to the doctor, ignoring his mother.

'Then get the gun out of your head,' said his mother.

She turned to pick up the kettle from the hearth, and thinking her back was turned he pulled a face of ugly derision at her, but she was too quick and she caught him full in the act.

'I'd be ashamed,' she said, in hard, level tones, 'I'd be ashamed, I know!'

'What? What did he do?' said David.

'Ah! you shut up!' flashed his brother. 'Mag-mag-mag-magpie!'

Deborah set her mouth tight, keeping herself reined, but she could not hide the conflict nor the shame in her face.

'I want a gun!' said Benjamin suddenly, as if challenging her.

'Indeed?' she said, archly. 'And is that the way to ask?'

'Why can't I have one? Why can't I have one?'

'Ask the doctor.'

'Why can't I have one? – one like that!' he demanded quickly.

Starling told him abruptly.

'Because you're not old enough, and because they cost more money than you dream, and because you must have a licence, and because you could never lift it –'

'I could lift it!'

The doctor drank his tea, ignoring him.

'I could lift it!'

The voice was half-angry with whining persistence, and suddenly the boy leapt up from the table and made for the gun. Starling, with one movement, wrenched him back and forced him into his chair. The boy sat rigid, without a trace of humiliation, his body tense and full of hatred for the doctor, his whole soul rankling with the bitterness of a defeat which he could not bear. He picked up his bread and tore at it sullenly and then drank his tea with loud gulps, making a half-muttering, half-snarling noise as he swallowed, his brows never lifting out of their blackness of hatred.

Afterwards, as the winter went on, Starling would sometimes take the boys shooting with him, letting them beat the bushes. But Benjamin would never beat for long. Hanging back he would walk with a dogged worship at the doctor's side, his eyes fixed on the gun, his mouth open with a kind of surly admiration. David walked on ahead, dutiful, beating the bushes with all his mother's methodical care. The land was poor in game and the birds were getting shy. When the doctor came in Benjamin would follow him everywhere, trying to touch the gun when it was set down, always furtive and stealthy, never daring to ask. From the afternoon when he had first tried to touch the gun the boy and the doctor had been foreign to each other, the boy sullenly hating the man but loving his gun, his hatred increasing as the gun became more inaccessible. The doctor remained aloof from the boy, hardly ever speaking, and the fundamental antagonism between them became absolutely established before the winter had ended and the shooting was over. In the spring the doctor, instead of shooting, rode a little, hiring the mare that Jess had bought. Benjamin's longing for the gun gave way to a desire to ride the horse. 'Why can't I ride that horse? That horse was my dad's! Why can't I ride that horse? Why should he ride it?' He was growing up loud-mouthed, with a strident, animal voice, and large, unshapely hands and a derisive, bullying strength. It made him happy to shout and jeer and fling his strength at something. It gave him a gleeful satisfaction to call David into the muck-yard and point to the sky, as though at a bird, and while the boy was looking to push his knee into his back and send him sprawling. The doctor painted a little and when the summer came he walked out to the farm with brushes and paints and a little canvas and sat on a box with the canvas on his knees, and painted a stretch of corn-land still green against the sky or the line of willows by the dyke or a bit of the spinney, pale green and yellow with elm leaf and oak-flower, with the pond overhung with may-blossom in the foreground. When the land itself no longer interested him he turned to the house, painting it towards the end of a hot afternoon, picking out the lichen like a drift of mustard-flowers on the roof, painting the shadows of the eaves heavy and blue across the pale stone face. In the foreground he would put in a group of hens, mere blobs of black and red and white, with Deborah feeding them from a blue corn-bin held against her hip or David rubbing the nose of the mare. Benjamin was never painted. Standing apart, infuriated or morose, he hated it all, venting his rage and dis-appointed vanity on the elder boy, going about for the whole of another day with some mocking gibe on his lips, making it intolerable by its very repetition and monotony. 'Davy's in a picture! – painted in a picture! – painted in a picture! – dah-di-dah-di-dah-dah! – Davy's in a picture!' The elder boy began to lead a confused and wretched existence. Finally he begged one day not to have to sit. To his mother's questions and entreaties he simply shook his head, stubborn as she her-self would have been. The doctor talked warmly, but the boy set his lips. His mother despaired and wondered. Benjamin was nowhere in sight, but as the doctor was sitting down to paint he unexpectedly appeared from the spinney and the old intolerable gibing began again, striking with a stab of ice into the consciousness of the other boy. 'Davy daren't do it, Davy daren't do it! Dah-di-dah-dah! Davy daren't do it!' When his mother advanced upon him he entreated to the spinney nimbly. Leaping over the fence he stood there in defiance of her, ready to frame the old gibes when her back was turned again. Her heart sank and blackened and she felt herself become helpless. Seeing him slipping away from her, out of reach of her influence, she began to take the problem of the boys about with her, devising means of peace and framing words of conciliation, soothing the bitterness of one against the other in her own mind. She gave up her sleep for them. They were poles apart, but they were also the poles of her existence, making the very axis on which her life must revolve. Without them there was no life. She could sit down and die from the sheer uselessness of living. When she looked into the future it was them that she saw, two great men, the fruit of her own worn body. Nothing else mattered.

The summer was wet and the hay lay swamped and finally they carried it hastily, risking the damp. In May the wheat had turned a sickly yellow and in the humid spells of June weeds sprang up in armies. She kept the hoes working until the wheat was too high. Towards the end of July a short dry spell pulled up the corn quick and straight, and the stalks, shoulder high, began to ripen. At the beginning of August the oats had whitened and the wheat looked healthy, the ears reddening and beginning to droop.

She decided one morning to cut the oats on the following day, and Rook promised to bring his family. In the night two thunderstorms came up, and lying awake she heard the rain smashing to earth and running away in the dykes like a torrent. In the morning the land was a swamp. The oats, on their light fragile stalks, lay beaten to earth in great waves, mud-splashed and broken. In dread she went to look at the wheat. Her heart sickened even before she came near it. The weight of rain on the ears had flattened it to earth in great sheets. Only the barley was saved; it was short and the wheat had broken the storm before it. As she went back to the house she felt the air warm and oppressive, stifling everything. In the evening the storms rolled back again and she lay awake listening to the waters rushing past the house, not daring to think of the morning.

The harvest lengthened out into late September. Having mowed the corn they could not shock the sheaves and when finally the shocks had been built the rain returned and sagged them to earth again. The land was sodden with rain and the corn ears began to sprout afresh. She cut open the sheaves and spread them out for the fowls and chickens. As the best of the remaining corn was carried she knew that she would scarcely see the return of her seed. It seemed like a mockery to thatch the stacks against the weather.

Looking in the glass one morning she saw a vein of grey in her black hair. When she turned to the light the grey hair shone almost white. She folded and smoothed the black hair across the grey and covered it. Her face had begun to show a faint ageing too. Her skin, thin and tight over the bones, was brown with the sun, and her lips seemed thinner. Her dark eyes were sunken a little under her brows. Everywhere ran little wrinkles, faintly darker than the rest of her face, little soil-coloured veins against the sun-colour of the skin.

The doctor took the shooting again and the winter went on as before, Benjamin full of the same gibing and the same intolerable jealousy. 'I want a gun! Why can't I have a gun? Why can't I ride the horse? Why can't I do what I like?' And with it all the same 'Davy's in the picture! Pretty, pretty picture! Dah-di-dah-di-dah-dah! Pretty, pretty picture!' Finally one winter morning Deborah heard a report from the spinney, and running out, found Benjamin with Mortimer's old shot-gun in his hand and a pigeon fluttering crookedly, wing-shot, among the trees, the boy chasing it with a kind of angry delight.

'Where did you find that gun?' she cried. 'Give me that gun at once!' she ordered him.

She mounted the stile. Suddenly he left the pigeon and pointed the gun at her. She felt one moment of mortal dread. Then she turned on her heel and walked across to the barns, where Rook was strawing the pigsties.

'Benjamin's found his grandfather's gun from somewhere,' she said to Rook. 'Go and take it away from him. Take the gun away and then do what you like with him.'

Back in the kitchen she heard his cries of rage and his sobs of defiance as Rook thrashed him in the spinney and her hands quivered as she peeled the potatoes. Before it was all over she felt weak from the anguish of not knowing whether she had done right or wrong, and later when Benjamin did not return for dinner her silly, womanish fears resolved into bitterest reproaches against herself. When supper-time came and he had not returned, she was beside herself with self-hatred and helplessness. When David and Rook went to search for him she sat and told herself miserably: 'This'll be a lesson to you,' and long before he returned she was ready to forgive him anything if only he did return.

He came back on the following morning, about ten o'clock. When she first saw him coming across the paddock her heart seemed to bolt suddenly across her breast like a frightened hare. Unrepentant, he sat down and ate ravenously, while she hovered about him silently, trying not to show her thankfulness. After that they suffered each other for a long time in silence. She sold the gun and only afterwards saw the folly of what she had done, knowing that the absence of the gun could only increase his desire for it. For a time he was quieter. Then he broke suddenly upon her with a fresh shock.

'I'm going to join the Yeomanry,' he announced one day.

'You're not old enough!'

'Well, when I'm old enough!'

'What next, I wonder?' she said, treating it lightly.

'Can't I do what I like?' he half-shouted.

She met him with silence. If he began the subject she counter-talked of crops and pigs, or she treated it with the old common sense, almost derisive of her fears. David wanted to drive a threshing-engine – why shouldn't Benjamin want to join the Yeomanry? They meant nothing. They were mere boyish longings. She was a fine mother not to know that they would grow out of these longings as they were already growing out of short trousers. Yet she was so stupid and fretful and afraid, and at the back of her mind, in spite of anything, she had only one destiny for them. Often she tried to pretend that it was not so, that she was willing to let them go wherever they themselves wished, to do what they liked and to shape their own lives, but in secret she knew better.

As the year ended she straightened the accounts. It was a poor year, but there was a thin margin of profit, even though she had not threshed her corn, and she felt satisfied. But looking out one night before bolting the door she caught the smell of smoke and running into the yard, found herself full in the yellowing drift of it. She knew in a moment what had happened; the hay-stacks had heated and the heat had found air at last. The smoke was thickening as she ran back to hurry the boys into their boots. A big flame shot up and died and shot up again as they ran down the road. She ran backwards and forwards from the pond to the stacks, throwing buckets of water into the heart of the smoke until she was half-blinded and half-suffocated. The smoke began to envelop the farmhouse and the barns, drifting into the spinney and down the fields. She went on running to the pond, stumbling and staggering and drenching her skirt and legs with the icy pond water. Finally a great flame shot up from the stack with a roar. The throwing of water became more and more futile, like a man spitting on a furnace. When she could no longer throw water she ran hither and thither frantically and then half-way down the road to meet the villagers and the boys returning.

The stacks blazed all night, throwing up a great crimson light against the black winter clouds. In the morning the firemen, in little black round caps, were still forking over the ruins, spreading the thick damp hay about the yard to burn itself out. The black heaps smouldered for a week. The queer unpleasant acrid odour of the fire lingered about the house and the farm-yard and in the fields. Even when the ashes had been carted away on the land Deborah still caught the smell, bitter and unpleasant, as ever, and it still hung about the yard on windless spring days and after rain.

Chapter 2

DEBORAH and her neighbours, the Twelvetrees and the
Sharmans, did their threshing communal-fashion. The
tackle arrived at Sharman's, moved on to Twelvetree's and
finished at Mortimer's, the farm-hands from the first two
farms shifting with it to the third. The Sharmans, who had
the largest farm, a place of eighty acres, were energetic,
go-ahead people, with two grown-up sons and a shrill-voiced
daughter of eighteen who swore like a soldier and handled
her father's bull like a lamb. They reaped with a horse-
reaper which felled their corn in one day and they owned a
horse-mower which rattled away and slaughtered their grass
in no time. Their farm was a model place, with water laid
on in the cow-houses and special hygienic coops for the hens.
They ploughed with a team of three, and if necessary four,
where Deborah ploughed with one and a nag. They worked
like demons; to them the land was like a kind of horse which
they must keep whipping. At threshing time they all drove
up in a light cart, the sons dangling their legs behind, the
man and wife scotching on the splash-boards, with the
daughter driving as though she were in a race, standing up,
her strong legs apart, curling and cracking the whip as she
swore and tugged at the horses. The sons dropped off as the
cart entered the yard, Sharman and his wife leapt down
nimbly and Sophie, the daughter, drove the horse away
with more oaths, scattering the terrified hens, and stabled
him. When she returned the Sharmans gathered in a group
about the stacks and the threshing engine, sized up the
stacks, seemed to laugh at the idea of threshing such a
paltry harvest and then flung themselves into the work as
though they had pressing business elsewhere in ten minutes
or so.

The Twelvetrees had neither reaping-machine nor
grass-mower. Their farm stood over on the hillside to the

141

north of Mortimer's, a straggling place of sixty acres with a long tongue of meadow-land that came down to the Mortimers' boundary, ending in the cowslip field, and a farmhouse of red-brick surrounded by poplar-trees which sighed and fluttered languidly even on the stillest days. It was the poplar-trees which seemed to set the tune and pace for the whole farm: nothing troubled to move faster or make more noise. Nobody ever shouted or hurried; the cows were silent, ruminative beasts, and pigs seemed to be altogether too gross for the Twelvetrees to keep. It was enough to plough and sow and reap in their own leisurely, silent way, the way in which they had done things ever since they could remember. There was more noise in their one day of threshing than in all the rest of the year together, and the coming of so many people, the Sharmans especially, half-terrified Twelvetree and his wife and two daughters. The man moved about the threshing-drum with air of wonder and stupid timidity, a small, plump, cherubic person, more like a monk than a farmer, and he looked at everything and everybody as though all the time he were thinking of something miles or years away. His wife shut herself in the house or went to town with the two girls as soon as the threshing started. She would take one look at Sophie Sharman driving the cart into the yard and then shut the door of the house hastily and bolt the windows. Every year she begged her husband to thresh alone and every year he promised to do so if only he had money enough. Every year, however, he found himself on the verge of bankruptcy. Nothing ever went right: his cows fell sick and morbid and died off, rabbits devastated everything, the fox fetched chickens from under his bedroom window, a winter flood swept his young corn down the hill or someone who owed him a hundred pounds went bankrupt too. His wife had a legacy and each year she nibbled a piece off the capital in order to save the farm, but the next year the same thing happened and the threshing had to be done communally again for cheapness.

For nearly twenty years she had nibbled off this yearly mite of her capital and in order to make up the loss she practised all the economies she dared. She wore the same dresses until they could be worn no longer and could only be cut up to make little dowdy ill-sewn garments for the girls. She denied herself and screwed and schemed and fought desperately to keep up an appearance of gentility. She was a tall, bony, colourless woman and in her long, sweeping old-fashioned frocks, always pale cream, she looked like a thin, almost transparent shaving of wood. The two girls, also pale and yellow-haired, were shorter. They had their mother's pride and some of their father's dreamy, timid manner. She had named them Prunella and Anthea. She was so afraid for them that she seemed to sweep her long skirts about them as though to hide the world from their faces as she shepherded them away from the farm on threshing days.

In the winter the Twelvetrees acted plays in the big farm kitchen. They generally acted Shakespeare, choosing more often than anything else *Twelfth Night*, because their father as Malvolio was so droll and dreamy and funny that all the dreariness of the farm itself could be forgotten as they watched him. The girls, who admired and worshipped their father, had proud, lofty-eyed faces and by contrast soft, timid voices, and they walked on and murmured their lines inaudibly and walked off again without a change of expression, like pale marionettes badly manœuvred. Their mother moved like a ghost and spoke like a ghost, solemn and dim in spirit and movement and speech. When the girls grew up they were sent to a High School in Staveston and in their straight-cut cream frocks and big flat straw hats with the white elastic under their chins they looked more than ever dowdy and dreamy and simple-souled. They suffered continually. Whenever they tossed their heads loftily in pride or faded away on their own dreamy thoughts they were teased or sneered at. They wept often, and as they became older they seemed to become prouder and more reserved than ever, a strained, untouchable virgin hardness about them.

Prunella, the eldest girl, was the same age as David Mortimer. They knew each other distantly. At seventeen they were of the same height, rather stocky in body, the girl as pale as a stone even in her deepest moments of embarrassment, the boy dark, and red-skinned from wind and sun. He behaved like a rabbit before her, scuttling away to hiding, and she would stare after him blankly, white and expressionless as an egg.

At seventeen he was at last beginning to feel his strength. It gave him pleasure to run his fingers down the smooth tight muscle of his thighs, to harden the sinews of his arms and feel the power of his voice deepening in his chest. He was quick, hard and compact, like his mother. Benjamin was already taller, his frame looser, all his limbs swaggering and easy.

The threshing had been delayed till March. A strong west wind drove up the hill to Twelvetree's, whipping the young-budded poplars and churning the chaff to a thick yellow fury and sweeping the black smoke away over the fields in surging coils. The sun broke out intermittently, lighting up the bright cups of daffodils bending and tossing and fluttering in the grass in the Twelvetree orchard.

After dinner Mrs. Twelvetree shepherded the youngest girl across the orchard and vanished hurriedly. David was on the stack with Sophie Sharman, throwing up sheaves to the drum. The wind caught the sheaves and tore them from the fork and caught the skirts of the girl and whipped them about her waist. As the mood took her she smoothed the skirts back quickly or she stood in the gust of the wind and let them balloon still higher, laughing and shouting at him, her words half-lost in the wind. In a furious gust she let herself be blown against the boy and he felt the smoothness of her skirtless legs pressed against his own. She laughed and looked at him with a gay light in her eyes and he felt himself quicken and laugh in return.

During the afternoon he looked up and saw the elder Twelvetree girl in the orchard, gathering daffodils. Unconsciously he ceased throwing up the sheaves and watched her half-kneeling, half-stooping among the wind-blown flowers, breaking off each stalk with a slow, dreamily methodical air, her mind only half with the daffodils. He saw her sometimes stretch out her fingers for a flower and grope for it like someone blind, the wind tossing it again and again out of her reach, her slow hand always too late. Her long skirt, which had swept a pale path in the grass, was of

144

some heavy dark-blue stuff, so that the wind could never bluster it or toss it higher than her ankles. She broke the daffodil-stalks finickingly with her fingers, and now and then he saw her wipe her fingers on her handkerchief and he knew that she was wiping the stalk-slime from her hands. She moved absently, hardly increasing her bunch, and he felt sometimes that he must rush to her and break off the flowers for her instead, severing them with quick clean snaps of his fingers in his own impetuousness.

'Now, dreamy!' said a voice. He turned and saw the Sharman girl laughing at him. He began forking sheaves quickly, tossing them hastily to hide his confusion at the girl's laughter and her soft gibing words.

When he looked up again Prunella was crossing the orchard towards the house. As she mooned along, a daffodil or a daffodil leaf would slip from her fingers and she would go on, too dreamy and strange to notice it. But at the white orchard gate a daffodil dropped at her feet and she caught sight of it. Stooping to pick it up she let the gate slip from her fingers and it swung back and caught her unbalanced. She stumbled to her knees, the daffodils scattering in the grass.

A voice on the threshing-drum laughed out. At once all the threshers were watching her, amused at her slow-moving form groping for the fallen daffodils. Finally she went mooning off to the house, too dreamy even to know that the men were laughing at her.

On the stack the boy felt suddenly a great rush of pity and then of anger for the girl. She was at once so pathetic and stupid that she touched and infuriated him. He stood blushing and setting his teeth for her at the same time, pitying and hating her awkwardness. It would have been so easy to hold the gate with her foot and gather up the flowers lightly and easily, and long after she had disappeared with her mud-stained skirt he was still picking up the flowers himself, the act so light and simple in his imagination, that she seemed more pitiable than ever.

At three o'clock he was to go back across the fields to home and drive up the cows as he went to do the milking. As he came off the stack the Sharman girl slid down too, ruffling up her skirts. 'I'm off to do our milking,' she said.

'I'll drive you along home. Come and help me get the horse in.'

As they were driving away the girl said:

'How many cows've you got now?'

'Five,' he said.

'You come and help milk ours and then I'll come and help with yours and we can drive back together.'

'Ah, that's all right,' he said, 'I can milk ours.'

'It'll be quicker and we can drive back,' she persisted. He shook his head, and watching his face she said quickly: 'You daren't, that's all it is.'

A flame of denial sprang up in him at once. He hated the insinuation. For years his brother had taunted and dared until out of habit he flared up in instant denial.

'Who says so?' he demanded. 'How many cows have you got?'

'Ten,' she said. 'We can do them first and then go back to your place.'

'I'll give you daren't,' he warned her.

They drove to Sharman's farm and he tethered the horse while the girl opened the cow-yard gate and let in the waiting cows. The cow-stalls were white and clean, smelling of new whitewash and disinfectant.

'Take Hetty,' said the girl, 'the black one, there. She's easy.'

He sat down by the black one and shifted his seat and leaned his head against her flank. Not knowing him the cow was uneasy and he felt unsettled for a moment or two, her teats strange in his hand and the milk running fitfully. On the other side the girl was working easily, and he sat looking at her quick brown fingers and the white soft stream of milk squirting into the bucket and sometimes trickling over her hands. The black cow began to give more easily and when he rose and went on to the next cow Sophie came and looked into his bucket and remarked:

'She seems to like you. That's nearly three gallon. You must have a way with you!'

She laughed, and her words warmed him, and her laugh ringing through the cow-house filled him with some of its own boldness and strength.

The girl drove fast up the hill to Mortimer's, her cheeks shining in the wind. In the cow-house the cows were flanked against each other, two by two, and he took the inner flank, not thinking, and Sophie brought her stool and sat next to him, her shoulder touching him as she leaned back. Used to his own cows he milked quickly and smoothly, the milk running fast, and after every cow the girl looked into his pail and said:

'Your cows are giving well – or else it's you. It's you, I believe. You must have a way with you.'

He began to like her. She was broad-mouthed and downright, but there was no nonsense about her and there was a curious languorous grace about her strong heavy limbs as she let her body rest on the flank of the cow, her tawny hair ruffled upward and catching the light, every stray strand of it bright against the dark cow's hide, her eyes quick and bold and challenging, her full lips quivering with the weight of their own ripeness and life.

They finished milking and he took the buckets into the house, calling back to her as she stood sucking the milk from her fingers:

'There's an old hen lays in the loft – go up and see if she's laid while I get the milk in.'

When he came out of the house again the girl had vanished and he called: 'Where are you?' two or three times before she answered from the loft:

'Up here, still. She's laid, but I can't get the egg. Come up.'

Going up the ladder into the loft he found Sophie lying full length on a heap of old hay stretching her fingers behind an old orange box full of chitting potatoes. 'Move the box,' he said. 'She'll lay anywhere. She laid in the chaff-cutter last week and the egg got smashed.' He stooped beside the girl. 'My fingers aren't long enough,' she said. 'You try. Bend down and look and see if you can see it. No, wait a minute. I can touch it.' He was half-lying beside her and suddenly she gave her body a sinuous movement, heaving herself face upwards, and he saw the buttons of her blouse break loose under the strain, showing the white rise and the shadowy channel running softly down between her breasts.

147

'Give me your hand,' she said, and before he could obey she had taken his hand in her own quick firm fingers and was guiding it along behind the orange box. 'I can't reach,' he said. 'She must have laid a thin egg!' and she burst out laughing. When she laughed she opened her mouth wide, showing her fine milk-white teeth and her quivering red tongue, and now she flung her head back, swelling her lungs and her breast with the strong sound of her laughter until the boy was laughing also. She held his hand firmly still and when her laughter had died down a little she lay panting and said: 'Oh! you should just feel my heart – it's going like that old threshing-drum,' and she guided his hand and laid it quietly on her breast about her heart. He felt the lace of her bodice and the heat of her breast and then also the shape of the breast itself as she guided his hand down the long curve of it, her eyes shining strangely and her voice whispering, 'You won't feel it beating there – don't you know where a girl's heart is? Lower than that,' and suddenly she slipped his hand lower still and instinctively he felt his hand spread its fingers and form a cup to hold the heavy beauty of the breast from beneath, the nipple firm and soft as a March bud against his palm. 'Now can you feel it?' she whispered. He nodded quickly and his hand half-unconsciously began to caress her, making her murmur as though in pain in a dream. The invisible beauty of her body was too much to resist at last. He could not rest until he burst the pink ribbon of her bodice and was looking down at her nakedness, white except for the rim of sunburn just touching the breasts. She lay smiling wonderfully at him. 'Look, look,' she said. 'You can see my heart beating now if you like.' He saw the blood pounding up as though it would burst her throat.

A sound in the yard below made them start violently, and he scrambled up and looked out of the broken window. 'I shall have to go,' he said. 'It's some children come for milk.'

'Don't go, don't go,' she begged, and when he said: 'I must!' she entreated desperately:

'Come here, just for one moment – then you can go.'

'I must!' he said, and he turned and went down stubbornly.

At the threshing next day he was uneasy at the constant laughter quivering in her eyes. Her boldness and the way she seemed to take him already for granted, disquieted him. He wondered at himself too. She wanted him to meet her in the evening. In the roar and moaning of the threshing they could not speak to each other except by shouting and all day her lips mouthed at him single isolated words: 'To-night' and 'Seven' until it became a kind of game between them, and he mouthed promises in return.

In the evening he waited for her behind a blackthorn scrub down the road. The black twigs were just breaking into blossom, half-flower, half-bud. He had washed his face and hands but he had not changed his threshing clothes and they were still covered with scraps of chaff and a fine settling of corn-dust. As he leaned on the fence and waited he could smell the dirt of his clothes, a rank mixed odour of oil and earth and sour milk and corn, and he broke off a spray of blackthorn and tucked it in his buttonhole, half-hoping its scent would drive away the dirt-smell of his clothes.

When she finally appeared from behind the blackthorn bushes he stood transfixed and foolish, hardly recognizing her. She had put on her best clothes, a pink-striped blouse with puff sleeves and a long grey skirt with a narrow pink belt of shining patent leather buckled so tight that her body lost all its natural poise as she walked. She had corseted and pinched her waist until she could have spanned it with her own large hands almost, and even before she came close to him he could smell the crisp shop-smell of the garments and the strong scent of mignonette she had spilled on them.

'Well, don't you like me?' she sang out. He did not know what to answer. The fine stiff new clothes were out of place on her wild, lusty body and he felt embarrassed. He looked down and began kicking the soft spring turf with the toe of his boot.

'You might show you're glad if you are dumb,' she said.

He looked up and stretched out his hands and tried to take her in a clumsy embrace. But he had no sooner touched her than she pushed him away violently.

'I should like!' she said sharply.

'What's the matter?' he said.

'You haven't even changed your clothes!' she accused him. 'Who do you think I am? Don't you touch me with your mucky old clothes. This blouse and skirt are clean on. Why didn't you take and change your clothes?'

'They were good enough yesterday,' he said.

'Yesterday! You don't know how to treat a girl.'

He did not know what to say, and he stood looking at her, prim and stiff as a doll, remembering her all the time as she had lain in the loft with him.

'I like you best as you were,' he confessed stupidly.

'I like that!' she cried.

'I can't help it,' he said.

'I can just believe it. You wouldn't know when a girl was well dressed if you lived to be a thousand.'

'I dare say.' The words came out with some of his mother's arch coolness, as though he were utterly indifferent.

'And don't you dare say me!' cried the girl. 'Why didn't you put a collar on? And what's this in your buttonhole – you needn't think that makes you look any better!' She threw the blackthorn away and brushed the chaff and dust from his clothes, straightening and turning him and re-turning him about until suddenly his pride leapt up.

'Leave me alone!' he demanded.

'Well, that's a nice way to speak – after yesterday an' all!' she cried.

'What do I care about yesterday?'

'Whatever's the matter?' she asked. 'I hope we aren't going to stand here nagging all night?' The tone of her voice dropped and quietened. 'Let's walk along – and if you're good you can put your arm round me.'

'I don't want to put my arm round you!' he half-shouted. 'I'm going!'

He swung himself from her hands and pushed roughly past her and was out of the blackthorn scrub, proud and disgusted, and down the road in a moment. Half-way down the hill he turned and saw her standing in the road, watching him, but she tossed her head and walked away as soon as she saw him turn.

He had all his mother's impatience of show and falsity. Nothing could stop him once his mind had set itself. His youth was furious and humiliated, too, and he hated the girl in her shop-new clothes scorning the clothes in which she had loved him the day before. 'What do clothes matter?' he thought. 'What good would they be if I had good clothes?'

Skirting the village he walked to the brook, intending to walk back beside it and so up through the cowslip field and home again.

At the bridge a figure was trying to climb the stile, and as he came near he saw Prunella Twelvetree with parcels and a basket, fumbling and floundering awkwardly as she tried to swing her heavily skirted legs over the stile without dropping the parcels. He walked across the bridge to her and at the sound of his footsteps she turned and blushed and stumbled awkwardly, as she had done with the daffodils, and the basket tipped, spilling tea-packets and tins and bags of groceries. He was down in a moment, picking them up before the girl had found her balance again, his movements quick and final, never bungling. A packet of rice had burst and spilled a white heap of grains, and as he put the packet carefully in the basket he again said:

'That's all right. Put it in so and your mother won't know.'

'Oh, dear, but the rice!' she complained.

He saw her drop to her knees and begin to scoop up the rice and empty it with great care into the bag again. Grain by grain she gathered it up from the grass, searching short-sightedly in the twilight and asking him at last, 'You can't see any more, can you? I think I've got it all,' and he felt all the fear and horror of poverty in her voice as she spoke.

'Ah, a few grains won't matter,' he said, picking up the basket.

'Oh! Don't you think so?' she said timorously.

'They might now, this minute, but in ten years they won't.'

'Don't you know Robinson Crusoe?' she said suddenly.

'Yes, I read it once. What about him? What's he to do with it?'

'Don't you remember how he found a few grains of corn and sowed it and then sowed again and went on sowing until he had acres of corn?'

'Not on *this* land,' he said.

'But it happened.'

'In a book.' And he persisted further. 'You don't sow rice, anyway. You only eat it.'

She did not answer. Were they so poor that every grain mattered? He had heard his mother say that they saved the very salt and mustard left on their plates. 'I've no patience with such folks,' she would say.

He carried the basket as they walked by the brook together. The evening sky was cold and clear and the sharp yellow light of the west lay mirrored brokenly in the running water of the brook, bright and cold as running ice. Against the sky the March twigs were black and sharp, their buds invisible, even the sallow buds washed out by the falling darkness. The cold came up from the meadows and the water, chilling his hands a little. Thrushes were still singing and a peewit rose up and cried madly, followed by another, the pair swooping away on the wind into another field, then back again, always decoying and returning and screaming mournfully.

The boy stopped and looked up, and involuntarily the girl paused too.

'Ah, you old fools, keep quiet!' he said. 'Who wants your eggs? Peewit, peewit! Go it! Who wants your eggs?'

'Silly birds!' he told the girl.

'What are they?' she said.

He turned on her quickly.

'You don't know? You don't know? Don't know a peewit when you hear one?'

She shook her head in a dumb, stupid way.

'But you can *hear* them! They say it! They call their own name. Listen to them – all the time – peewit, peewit. It's as plain as cuckoo. Don't you hear them in the night sometimes? And you see them in the winter – great flocks high up. Plovers if you like – haven't you ever eaten a plover's egg?'

'No.'

'Good Lord! I'll bring you one. In London d'ye know what they charge for a plover's egg? – What should you think?'

'I really don't know!'

'Well – a guinea! And I'll bring you one. A guinea for one

egg, that's what they charge.' The sound of his excited voice seemed to awe her and she kept silent, and he suddenly went on:

'Don't you know birds at all! – any birds?'

'A few,' she said weakly.

'What sort? How many?' he challenged her at once.

'Oh! I really don't know – blackbirds, I suppose, and sparrows and thrushes.'

'Not starlings? You know starlings? – and crows?' – his voice twisted to faint sarcasm – 'and linnets and robins? You're born knowing birds like that.'

'You know a lot,' she said. 'Tell me some birds.'

'What? – now? They're abed and asleep, except owls and peewits and that old thrush back there. It's no use unless you see 'em – pinks and writing-larks and magpies and all of 'em – you must see 'em. Don't you ever go nesting?'

'I don't!'

'Then I'll take you! You don't know A from a bull's foot.'

'What *are* you saying?'

'Lord! – you never heard that? A from a bull's foot?' He shrugged his shoulders very slightly and kept back a mouthful of astonished words, swinging her basket at the same time with an arch indifference.

'Don't swing my basket!' she said peremptorily.

Obeying instinctively he walked along in silence, not speaking again till they had climbed the stile into the cowslip field and had paused at the footbridge which took the path over the stream and up to Twelvetree's. She halted then and thanked him for carrying the basket. Her words had a queer copy-book order and coldness about them, as though she had learnt them off by heart, like words in a play. He stood and listened to the coldness of her words against the cold prattle of the stream on its stones, and then he stared at her face, attracted even against himself by its pallor in the half-light, forgetting her clumsiness and his own anger against it the previous day.

'I'll bring you that plover's egg sometime,' he said. 'Else you can come and help me find it. How would that be?'

'I don't think so.'

'Do as you please,' he said bluntly.

She was silent, looking over the darkening fields, her face stiff and averted.

'I come down in these meadows every Sunday morning, fishing or nesting or something,' he said.

'I go to church on Sundays!' she said.

'Ah! You'll never learn nothing at church,' he said.

'You know a great deal,' she said.

'I never learnt it at church if I do!' he flashed. 'We ain't church folk – my old grandfather stopped that. Learnt me about birds instead.'

She was gazing at the last yellowish-green light hanging cold above the hillside, as though she were not listening to him.

'If you went to church till Doomsday you wouldn't know what a pudden-bags was, I warrant,' he said.

'You know everything. What *is* it?'

'It's a nest – a nest like a pudden-bag – the funniest nest out. Ask your dad. It's a long nest all fur and moss and horse-hair, and there's a bit of a mouse-hole at the top for the bird to go in. The bird's a tit, no bigger than a mouse, not so big – and she lays eggs like peas. You ain't seen nothing if you ain't seen a pudden-bags.'

'How do I know you've seen one yourself?'

'Seen one? I find one every year – down here, in these meadows. You come down and I'll show you one in May-time.'

'Bring me the plover's egg first,' she said.

Suddenly out of the darkness a girl's voice called down the hillside, 'Prunella! Prunella!' dragging the final syllable, the echo travelling faint across the hillside.

'My sister,' said Prunella. 'I must fly. Good-bye and thank you!'

'I'll bring the egg,' he said. 'So long.'

She turned and walked away across towards the farm with stiff dignity, and after watching her for a moment he turned and walked home also, thinking of her, wondering if he could find an early plover's egg by Sunday.

April came in with sleet and fierce showers of icy rain that slashed the plum-bloom and made the earth bitterly wet and cold again, and it was Good Friday before he came upon a plover's nest in a cup of earth on a bit of unploughed land, among yellow-flamed coltsfoot flowers. Of the three eggs he took one, the birds crying and swooping down at his head as he walked away across the field with the egg in his cap. In the afternoon they were still wheeling skywards and down to earth again in distress, their mournful cries cutting the sharp April air as he walked down by the willows and over the brook to take the egg to Twelvetree's.

When he knocked on the farmhouse door nobody answered, and after a time he turned away and searched the farmyard. Finally he found Twelvetree himself dreamily turning the chaff-cutter in the biggest barn. His wife and daughters had gone to the Good Friday service, he said, and would be out to tea. 'I'll come up again,' the boy said, and back at the farm he wrapped the egg in a handkerchief and laid it in the drawer with his Sunday clothes. The following day he drove his mother in the trap to market and did not remember the plover's egg till Sunday morning, finding it as he searched for his clean shirt. He changed into his best suit, thinking of taking the egg to Twelvetree's again, and then remembered that Prunella went to church on Sundays.

The idea of going to church himself in order to give her the egg came to him with a gust of laughter, and he was laughing quietly all the way down the hill and through the village to the churchyard. There he stopped behind a yew-tree and took the egg from his cap and put it in his pocket. He had arrived early and he mooned about the churchyard, and looked at the graves of his grandmother and grandfather, tombless, grass-grown mounds, each with a jam-jar half-filled with greenish rain-water and dead flower-stems. Prunella and her sister appeared at last, dowdy and dreamy in grey, long-skirted costumes of their mother's making.

He went up to them as they came up the path. 'I hoped I should see you,' he said, and held out his hand. Politely Prunella held out her own and like a shot he dropped the plover's egg into it and half-ran into church.

He sat on the opposite side of the nave to her and all through the service he would turn his head and take sly, solemn looks at her still-set face, knowing she was furious.

As soon as the service was over she left her sister and came up to him, her voice, arch and offended, pouring out a ready torrent of words about behaviour and respect and decency.

'And in the House of God,' she finished, frigidly.

He wanted to laugh and he tried to frame some quick reply, but she began to hurry off and he felt suddenly small and foolish. He hurried after her, intending to apologize, but as he was ready to speak he saw the plover's egg still in her hand and he knew that it must have lain there all through the service, and he saw her kneeling and praying and singing and making responses, all with the plover's egg still in her hand. He burst out laughing.

'Exactly what one would expect of you,' she flashed.

Half-ashamed, he walked on in silence and they had reached the bridge and were walking along the footpath before he spoke again.

'I'd better say I'm sorry,' he said at last.

'You'd better!' she repeated. '*Aren't* you sorry?'

'Yes.'

'Then you should say so!'

'I did say so, Good Lord!'

She quickened her walk, and as they were going through the next meadow they saw her sister waiting at the bridge.

'Are you going to say you were sorry before we catch up with Anthea?' said the girl.

'I said it once,' he said stubbornly. 'That's enough.'

They reached the bridge and Anthea stared at them: 'What's the matter with you two?'

'He knows!' said Prunella, and suddenly she turned and put the egg back into the boy's hand, flung up her head and said, 'There's your egg!' and scrambled across the bridge and half-ran up the hillside.

'Don't be ridiculous!' called Anthea. 'Come back, Prunella!'

The boy stood stubborn and grim, like his mother, hating the fuss of it all.

Anthea turned to him and smiled. 'She's a bit dramatic and ridiculous.'

'She wanted the damned egg!' he said.

'It's father's fault – we're always acting in plays. It's second nature.'

He looked at the warm brown egg in his hand and she looked at it too.

'Ever tried one?' he asked. 'It's a plover's.'

She shook her head. Her dark hair was still in plaits and her whole being was softer and more tender than Prunella's, her eyes shining and full, ready at any moment to spill their laughter, the noon light brilliant and quivering in them. Standing there with the egg in his hand he became suddenly shy and silent. He tried to think of something to say, but his mind felt dazed and empty, and he lowered his eyes and looked at the girl's grey-gloved hands, finger-locked, resting on the bridge, and then at the first soft green tassels of early cowslip buds growing down the brook bank, and then back at the hands and from the hands to the cowslips and then to her face again.

'Cowslips are pushing through,' he remarked.

'Yes,' she said, but he felt that she did not see them.

He looked again at the tiny, stiff, insignificant buds, knotted and tight, and as he looked up again the girl also raised her eyes and they broke into a smile at each other, a quick, unpremeditated smile, and the girl spoke with a sly, quiet air which captivated him at once.

'She dropped the egg in the Lord's Prayer!'

'Dropped it?'

'It rolled down her skirt and fell on the hassock and she caught it.'

He burst out laughing. 'Why didn't she drop it in the collection-box?' he roared suddenly.

The girl broke into quivering laughter and he leaned on the bridge, half-choking until the tears ran down his face. The girl leaned her head on her hands and laughed with a lovely, merry sound, high and low, stamping her foot now and then when the laughter took her breath away.

'We're a pair of fools,' he said at last, drying his eyes. 'You'd better have the egg and see if you can drop it.' He put the egg into her hand.

'*You* know a plover when you see one, I should hope?' he said.

'A black and white bird that cries all the time and swoops down at you?'

'With a tuft on its head. First bird on the game list,' he said, at ease with her at last. 'I like it best of all birds I know, except one.'

'Which is that?'

'Guess,' he said.

She screwed up her eyes and half-raised her face to the sky, trying to think of the birds, while he watched her expectantly, a strange pleasure in his heart because she was baffled.

'A kingfisher,' she said at last.

'How did you know?'

'Ah.'

'It was luck and just luck. Admit it. Just luck.'

'It's my own favourite,' she said.

His words sprang out like joy: 'Did you ever find a nest?' he asked her. 'A kingfisher's?'

'You can see us nesting, can't you – Prunella and I?'

'Prunella!' he scorned. 'She wouldn't know a starling from a robin. And every kid knows that.' And suddenly, his voice shyer, he said: 'I go nesting every Sunday afternoon – you come down and I'll show you any amount o' nests, any amount. A kingfisher's an' all.'

'This afternoon?'

'Yes.'

'I'll try,' she said.

He went home turning her promise over and over in his mind. He scrambled his dinner and was back by the stream at two o'clock, waiting for her to come. Under the shelter of the willows and hawthorns the sun struck warm on his face. A lovely spring light lay over the meadows, the air very still and clear, the quietness broken only by birds' songs, and by a warm hum of bees working the lemon sallow-bloom by the water. He sat on the bridge and picked out the bird-notes one from another, half-consciously, half-instinctively, black-birds' from thrushes', yellow-hammers' from finches', the larks shrilly-sweet above all others. He heard the clock in the church strike a quarter. A water-rat dropped into the stream and swam over to the other bank and he watched it working its way under the shelter of the reeds until it disappeared. He kept looking up the hillside for the girl, and when another quarter struck he began to walk about, looking among the

158

sedge on the chance of a wild-duck's nest. The cuckoo flowers were opening, slender quivering heads of mauve, and in the watery places an early king-cup or two, breaking yellow. Another quarter struck, and a hare strained into sudden flight from under his feet and bounded away up the field.

When three o'clock struck he walked dejectedly away up the brook, half-angry with the girl. Trying to quieten himself by searching for nests he found a blackbird's bare and exposed in a hawthorn crook, and then everywhere he began to find nests in just such silly, easy places, half-woven magpies', an early finch's, a moor-hen's beginning by the root of a willow, a three-egged thrush's in an elder. Back at the bridge he waited again, watching the young brook-trout making vague flickers of shadow in the sun-clear water.

When four o'clock struck he walked away up the field, alternately angry and wretched, looking back at intervals across the hillside and thinking of all the nests with regret. In the evening he sat about the house fretfully, always half-angry and half-regretful, his mind restless.

On Monday there was a letter for him. He took it away into the cow-barn to read. 'No chance to come. We are not allowed out on Sundays, except with mother. I tried to slip away, but it was no good. Awful row with Prunella. She hates you. I can come next Saturday if you still want me to come. I am writing this in bed.'

He read the letter again and again, baffled and overjoyed, until he could repeat it by heart.

Chapter 3

HE began to meet the younger Twelvetree girl by the brook-
side on spring evenings. From one meeting to another, not
knowing until he saw her grey figure hastening down the hillside whether she would come or not, he lived in suspense.
When they parted, she could never promise to come again.
She could only scheme and lie and trust her luck, hoping that
her mother would not see and that Prunella would not tell.
Gradually he became aware of the extraordinary life the
Twelvetrees lived. Aloof from the rest of the world, they led a
strange stiffly ordered, dismal existence, like the life of some
sort of genteel prison run by charity. Anthea was sixteen, a
year younger than Prunella; the girls had left school the previous autumn. The day began with breakfast at nine o'clock
and their father came in punctually at two minutes to nine
from the morning milking, which was always late, and stood
at the table with his little fat red hands clasped together under
his belly and said grace in a mumbling voice as though he
were playing the part of a country clergyman in one of their
plays. The girls and Mrs. Twelvetree made a thin, mincing
breakfast of tea and porridge, with a slice of bread and butter. Their father had an egg and bacon. The girls, as children, were each allowed to take a thin finger of bread and
butter and dip it briefly into the yolk of the egg, first saying
'Please, father,' and afterwards 'Thank you, father,' their
voices small with a tone of prim duty. As they grew up they
gradually ceased dipping into their father's morning egg.
'You are big enough now to have an egg for yourselves,' said
Mrs. Twelvetree. 'You have only to ask.' But something
about the tone of her voice seemed to insinuate that it would
be lady-like and well-mannered and considerate and better
altogether if they were not to ask. When very occasionally
they did ask the egg was always given them. But as the eggs
were cooking or as they were eating them, Mrs. Twelvetree

would remark in a detached voice that eggs were fetching four shillings a score that week at market or that too many eggs were not good for growing girls or that eggs were very much overrated as a breakfast dish. The girls, Anthea especially, would detect at once the miserly, forbidding tone of her voice, and for a long time they dared not or would not ask for eggs again. At the end of the meal Twelvetree would return thanks for the food they had eaten, his voice lugubriously fervent, and after breakfast the girls would take up knitting or embroidery. Anthea also painted a little, making copies on boards of woodland scenes or sunsets. In the afternoon they sewed or they painted again if it were wet or they paid calls in the village if it were fine. In the evening they read or learnt speeches from Shakespeare or acted plays in the kitchen, going to bed the instant nine o'clock struck.

Twice a week Anthea or Prunella went down to the village for the groceries and lamp-oil. Anthea, by leaving the farm early and running down the hill, could manage to be away an hour. She met the boy in an uneasy, half-frightened mood, constantly turning and looking furtively back at the farm. Oppressed with responsibility, she seemed half-fearful of enjoying the pleasure of the quick walk along the brook. The nests the boy had found and the birds singing brilliantly by the water in the spring twilight did not seem to touch her. They would walk for long intervals in silence, trying to interpret each other's thoughts. There was a feeling of uneasiness and secrecy about every moment. Anthea could hardly look into the nests; she would simply stretch her hand through the leaves and touch the eggs, counting them with some vague part of her mind, all the alert part of herself thinking of the time and listening for a footstep or some indignant voice calling her back. It was not until they arrived back at the bridge that she felt safe again and the tension of their minds relaxed. They talked even then in whispers.

She had never hinted at what might happen to her if she were late home. He had often wondered, however, and one evening he asked.

'Mother would question me and try to make me cry and then she would question Prunell nd probably Prunella would let the cat out of the bag.'

He felt furious.

'She hates you,' said the girl.

'Let her.'

'She'd love the chance of telling on you. And she'd do it. She's always saying she'd do it.'

He raged against the elder sister in silence. They stood for a moment looking at the water, listening to their own silence again. Suddenly, looking casually up the hillside, he saw a figure coming down the path. 'Talk about the devil!' he said. The girl turned and uttered 'Prunella!' in a startled voice. A moment later she had climbed the stile and was hurrying up the field. 'Thursday?' he called in a whisper. She merely waved her hand.

On Thursday he waited a quarter of an hour past their time. Half-angry and half-dejected, he wandered off among the sedge. The cuckoo flowers were fading and dropping, but the cowslips made a great shawl of yellowy-gold over the slope of the field. He picked a cowslip and tore out the yellow cups and sucked their sweetness. Stooping to break off a second stalk his eyes wandered up the field and he saw suddenly both girls coming down the hillside.

He waited by the bridge, mute and stupid with disappointment and resentment. The girls climbed the stile and he looked up.

Prunella sailed past him as though he had never been there.

'Oh! Prunella, don't be ridiculous. We can all walk together!' Anthea called.

Prunella let herself turn very slightly and then stopped as though surprised.

'Oh! I'm sorry,' she said sarcastically. 'I didn't see anyone.'

'Don't be theatrical!'

'Of course some people are like that. You don't see them first time.'

'Oh! do shut up.'

'Don't let me intrude,' said Prunella. Her voice had a kind of thin sweetness, mocking them. 'I'll walk on.'

'We'll all walk together!' flashed Anthea. 'You wanted to come.'

She was silenced and they walked on together. The boy

said nothing. The silence was antagonistic, pregnant with unspoken jealousy and bitterness. Prunella walked with a stiff-bodied, condemnatory aloofness, half-ludicrous, half-intense.

Farther along the brook, in a low, unblooming bush of hawthorn, David had found a yellow-hammer's, three-egged, the evening before. Coming to it, he spoke for the first time:

'Here, there's a writing-lark's in this bush,' he said.

'I don't think we've time to waste on birds' nests,' said Prunella.

'Some folks wouldn't know a bird's nest when they saw one!' he flashed.

Prunella stopped involuntarily; her face turned crimson and she gazed at him with her old awkward, pathetic look of helplessness. He felt a kind of exultant, wicked pleasure in hurting her. She gazed at him mutely, defeated. He thrust his hand in the bush and found an egg for Anthea. With the egg in his hand he said: 'I call 'em writing-larks – you see the lines like writing on the egg? They're yellow-hammers by rights. Some folks call 'em scribbling-larks.' He gave the egg to the girl to hold and she rolled it softly to and fro in her hand, as though trying to read its brown scribble.

'You're trying to read it,' he said. 'Everybody tries to read the writing on a yellow-hammer's.'

Suddenly he turned and saw that Prunella had come quietly up and was standing behind him, trying to catch a glimpse of the yellow-hammer's egg over his shoulder. His desire to hurt her sprang up at once. He took the egg from Anthea's hand and put it back into the nest.

'Now you'll know a yellow-hammer's again,' he said.

He saw the pain in the face of the elder girl as they walked along. She tried to walk with serenity, with a proud, un-touchable aloofness. They all walked in silence, the sense of the elder girl's coldness and suffering, like an awkward pain itself, making them wretched.

When they came back to the bridge again the elder girl went on ahead serenely and climbed the stile and walked slowly up the field, looking at her feet, as though preoccupied. Anthea spoke quickly:

'If she tells I'm done for.'

He nodded moodily. The girl half-turned away her face to look at Prunella going up the field. Her face, watchful and pale against the dark hawthorn hedge, had a soft, intangible beauty about it. He suddenly laid his hand on her bare arm and tried to say something. She turned at the touch of his hand and he stood foolish and mute, unable for a moment or two to think of a word.

'Isn't there somewhere else we can meet?' he said finally.

Before she could answer the high-pitched cold voice came down the hillside, calling half-accusingly:

'Anthea! Anthea!'

The younger girl spoke hurriedly: 'I don't know. I'll think of something. But I'll come here on Saturday. Good-bye.'

'Don't bring her,' he entreated.

On Saturday he brought a message from his mother, asking the girl to come to tea on Sunday.

'On Sunday?' she repeated. 'Oh! I don't know about Sunday. They wouldn't let me come. You've no idea what my mother is. If you knew you'd see how impossible it is.'

'Nothing's impossible,' he said. It was a phrase of his mother's. 'If you tell her it's my mother inviting you, won't that be all right?'

They discussed it for a long time, the girl apprehensive and full of doubt: he always insistent and determined. They arranged at last that if she could come she would wave her handkerchief from the orchard at ten o'clock on Sunday morning; he would see the white flash across the hillside.

In the morning at ten o'clock, he sat on the gate of the cowslip field and saw the flutter of white by the Twelvetree house, a double flutter like a white pigeon turning in its flight in the May sunshine.

Until she came in the afternoon he fretted as though in a cage. His mother watched him, half-amused, half-suffering for him. When he had asked her if he might bring Anthea Twelvetree home she had flashed at once, hardly thinking: 'They're a queer lot, my boy.' He looked at her instantly in pain, and his voice was small and strained as he said: 'But she's all right. She's not like the others.' And she caught his desperation so clearly that she softened her voice to reply: 'All right, my boy. Bring her. You know I want you to do what's right. That's all.' He had the last word. 'It is right. I know it's right!' he declared. 'I know it's right.'

He gathered a jar of cowslips for the table and a spray or two of honeysuckle buds to scent the room. The girl was to come at four o'clock and for a long time previously he would go out and pretend to look at the sky or the wheat or the thickening grass in the hayfield, only to see if she were already coming. At a quarter to four he went down the track under the willow-trees to meet her and she came up the hillside at last in a mauve-coloured frock, long-skirted and tight-bodiced, so queer and old-fashioned that his heart ached for her. Her waist was pinched and it was a pain for her to walk. But her face was radiant. She was proud at having broken away. 'I did it!' she said. 'Don't ask me how I did it. I did it, that's all.' As they went up the track he gathered a sprig of honey-suckle for her buttonhole. 'Let me thread it,' he said. The stalk was thick and woody and she was afraid of tearing the buttonhole. 'In your hair then!' he said.

'No!' she was vehement, shaking her head. 'No, young man,' she mocked gently.

'Why? Why not?'

'You'll see why not!'

Though he kept insisting she would tell him nothing, and it was only when she came into the parlour that he saw what had happened. She had put up her hair, bringing her two long gleaming pigtails of black silk round above her ears and over the crown of her head in a thick cross, weaving the ends into the plait again.

After tea he took her about the house and barns, showing her the place proudly. The farm was beginning to prosper. His mother now kept a girl as house-help and dairy-hand, and Rook's son, who had been a soldier, worked regularly for them. The farm and the ricks and the stock were all insured. His mother had learnt wisdom. She was paying her sons men's wages, schooling them in independence. She was keeping more cows and soon she hoped to begin with sheep, things they had never troubled about before. She was thinking of thinning the timber in the spinney, which had never been touched within the memory of man. She was tightly waiting for the right offer to come.

They came into the house again. His mother was sewing in the evening sunlight by the parlour window, her spectacles half-slipping from her nose. Benjamin had gone out. Deborah looked up from her sewing.

'There's no call for you to be staying in on a fine evening like this,' she said. 'Take Anthea along with you down the fields. And while you're there you might see if the cows have trampled that gap again.'

The meadow-land was divided in half by a wire fence, one part for grazing land, the other down for hay. The cows were grazing in the pasture after milking. The fence was unbroken. David and Anthea, coming down on the pasture side, slipped through the fence into the hayfield and walked along by the hedge where the grass was coarser. The evening was quiet and lovely with falling sunlight and in the corner of a field, in a bog sycamore, a nightingale was trying its note, breaking off for long intervals of silence between one phrase of singing and another.

'Let's sit and listen,' he said, dropping in the grass.

'Is it damp?' she said.

'Sh! He'll hear you. Sit down.'

She came and sat in the grass, pulling her skirts over her ankles and clasping her hands about her up-crooked knees. 'Take your hat off,' he begged. She took off her hat and laid her head sideways on her knees, the slanting sunlight catching her eyes like the dazzle from a mirror. The nightingale trilled and broke into a long thin note of sustained sweetness and then was silent. The boy lay full length in the grass, wondering where the nest could be, and looking at the pensive, drowsy, listening head of the girl.

'No more,' he said at last. 'He must have gone.'

The girl opened her eyes to find him gazing straight into them, intent and dreamy.

'We'll listen again as I take you home,' he promised.

The girl looked over the field. A lark, breaking its song, fell like a stone into the grass. The boy broke off a head of pink clover and sat looking at the flower.

The clover made him think of her breasts, soft and round as clover flowers under the prim stuff of her dress, and he sat looking at her white neck and the curve of her bosom, stifling the flame of his own ecstasy until he could stifle it no longer. Leaning forward he put one hand on her breast and ran the other along the thick silk of her hair, tracing the plait about her head as he pressed it gently down to him. As he did so he thought suddenly of Sophie and the great white breasts she showed him after the milking in the barn and he brought the girl to him and began to kiss her with awkward, ecstatic lips. She resisted him gently. Her body was stiff in his arms. Breaking away from each other they sat half-smiling at themselves, the light of happiness shining out from their eyes wonderfully, the girl smoothing back the stray strands of hair he had stroked out of place.

As they were walking back to the farm he picked another clover-bloom and pulled out a pink tube and sucked it. 'Try it,' he said. 'There's honey in it.' He picked a clover-bloom for her quickly.

She took the flower and began to do as he did, picking and sucking the honey from the pink flowerets.

Presently he began to gather other flowers for her to suck, white-nettle bloom and cowslips, a cluster of honeysuckle and a late primrose here and there, and they went up the field drinking in the sweetness of them excitedly. Sometimes they came upon a bloom of extra sweetness and shared it, sucking it in turns, drawing the last drop of its nectar, pulling it from each other's lips in their eagerness to share. She took turns at taunting him, pretending to have found some exquisite flower, making soft sounds of pleasure with her lips as she ran off invitingly. As he chased her she ran in circles, laughing and panting, swerving her body swiftly, twisting and turning and letting herself be caught at last. Holding a white-nettle flower in her lips she slipped and stumbled and let herself fall in the grass and he half-knelt and half-lay by her, his arm touching her body, tracing the shape of its soft firm curves under the tightened dress. She was laughing and panting, but he saw a spasm of fear and wonder come into her face at the touch of his fingers. She stretched out her hands and begged to be pulled up and he pulled her to her feet, baffled and excited by her small, lovely face glowing with happiness.

Afterwards, as Deborah watched the changes in his manner, never questioning him, careful never to talk of the girl except when he did, she felt him become warmer and closer to her.

He began to go off every evening, polishing his boots in the kitchen and struggling with his collar and tie first before one mirror and then another. Benjamin, who had joined the local volunteers and went off for drill twice a week, cleaned his service rifle while David cleaned his shoes. The training was broadening and straightening him and there was a kind of defiant pride in the way he held the rifle. Standing at the table, snapping the bolt in and out of place for the sheer pleasure of the sound, he would gibe softly:

'Bit o' courtin' like? You wouldn't think some folks could do it, would you?'

The elder boy had learnt to say nothing. Sometimes he would throw the face-flannel or lift a boot – no more.

Deborah stood apart from them, never interfering. They were already men, strong-bodied, deep-voiced, proud and sensitive of their manliness. She stood apart and watched them, hoping so much.

Chapter 4

AT the beginning of August, 1914, the oats were ripe, red and strong in the stalk, and by the second of the month they were cut and tied. The men were setting the shocks as Deborah harnessed the mare to the trap and drove off to Staveston to bank some money and do her weekly shopping. She could hear the bantering voices of her sons in the oat-field as she drove down the lane.

In the town the streets were crowded. She sensed an electric atmosphere of trouble the moment she drove in. Leaving the trap in the market square she walked to the bank, wondering at the gabbling knots of people and the newsboys running hither with placards flapping at their excited knees like blooded aprons. She read the word 'Ultimatum' on a placard, but she had no idea what it meant. People were holiday-making; girls in fine long summer dresses were walking arm in arm with young men in yellow boaters, and farmers' wives had driven to market in cotton frocks, with ribbons on their whips and sprays of green ash leaves fluttering on their horses' heads to keep away the heat-flies. It was like an election day. But the air was apprehensive, faintly troubled. She walked into the bank and as she handed over her money to the clerk she stood listening to a man farther along the counter banging his fist on the wood, saying to the cashier: 'It's got to come, I tell you! A question of honour. All the deepest principles of honour are involved. There'll be war before you've eaten your Sunday dinner!'

Deborah turned to the clerk with a scared face, repeating quickly, 'War? Did he say *war*?' The clerk answered in a low voice. Hadn't she seen a paper? She shook her head in dazed, frightened fashion and hurried out. In the street she bought a paper, flapped it open, and read. Every word of it seemed hot with war.

She drove home in a wretched state, the reins slack in her

hand. She let the horse trot as it would. She thought always of Benjamin, she tried to fashion the course she must take with him if the moment came. She hated the thought of war as she hated hypocrisy and cruelty. Thinking of Benjamin she felt frightened too. When she arrived home she was glad to find Ada, the girl-help, making the tea for the men. She poured out a cup of tea for herself and drank it hot and strong, feeling better before the girl came back with the empty tea-cans. Afterwards she went across to the oat-field and she felt almost wildly joyful to see that the field was only half set-up. She could make them stay and finish it, pleading fear of rain.

'You'd better stop and finish,' she said to Benjamin. On Saturdays they knocked off at five. 'There's a storm about.'

'All night?' he groused.

'You'll stay until it's finished. I've seen enough corn laying soaked in my time.'

He groused again. 'Saturday an' all.'

'For once you'll do as I tell you,' she said calmly, 'big as you are.'

He snatched up a sheaf in each arm and shocked one against the other savagely. She went off to the house, taking no notice, knowing the field could not be finished before eight o'clock. Later, when the field was finished, Benjamin came in to wash, grousing again because David was first at the sink. 'Courters can be off,' he muttered sarcastically. When he had washed his mother asked: 'Aren't you going out, too?' and he grumbled, 'At this time o' night?' and went off to smoke his pipe in the orchard.

In the morning he was cleaning his volunteer's rifle in the yard, whipping the oil-rag through the bore and then looking down the barrel at the clean pink of his thumb in the breech. As he was slipping the bolt rapidly in and out Rook came through the paddock excited.

'Cleanin' up, like?' he said.

'Ah.'

'You'll need it.'

'What's that?' he said quickly.

'War! – that's what. A humbuggin' war. My son's off like a blood-hound.'

Benjamin leaned the rifle against the house and ran indoors, shouting for his mother. She was in the dairy, skimming milk.

'Leave that old milk!' he said excitedly. 'Help me get my kit together. There's a war! A war, d'ye hear? I'm going.'

'What the 'nation are you dancing round for?' she said quietly. Her heart was pounding with dread.

'There's a war! Didn't you hear me?'

'I heard. What war?'

He poured out the news for her, telling her again and again that he must be off. As she listened and grew more frightened she tried to appear more calm.

'Your place is here,' she said at last.

He grew angry and tried to bully her into seeing his views.

'I shall *have* to go! I shall *have* to go. I'm a volunteer. That's what we're for – in case. We go first! Don't you see. I shall *have* to go?'

She kept up her proud, deprecating, almost scornful manner.

'You're only one,' she told him.

'A few ones soon make an army,' he flashed. A moment later he tried to rush upstairs but she barred his way. They stood defiantly facing each other, the boy pushing her in his excited anger.

'You wouldn't like it if you hurt your mother?' she said, as he struggled to get past.

Her words cut him and humiliated him. She entreated desperately:

'Wait till after harvest. Wait and see what happens – it may all be over. The harvest is everything. You must wait till after harvest.'

He acquiesced at last, consoling himself with the thought of the morning drill. At noon he was back again, more excited than ever. He sat down to dinner without troubling to change his khaki, his sunburned face shining with sweat, the collar of his tunic unhooked, a dull red rim across his forehead where his cap had pressed. He ate hurriedly, talked with his mouth full, hammered his knife-handle on the table like an orator driving home his points. 'Ah, the parade-ground was crowded – crowded. Everybody talking about war. Fifty chaps 'listed straight off.' He would take a savage mouthful and declare: 'And I'm going – I'll stop until we've carried unless things are bad – but I'm going, sooner or later.' And at last:

'What about you, Davy?'

'His place is here!' flashed his mother quickly. 'If you go he stays.'

David was silent.

'If things are bad he'll have to go!' Benjamin said.

'Things won't be bad. It'll be over before we've ploughed,' she said.

'That's what they're all saying – but you wait – you wait!'

During harvest there was no rest. The temperature of war leapt and quivered. There was a corresponding tension and restlessness at the farm, the conversation on that one topic day in, day out, the air full of war. Benjamin fretted for harvest to end. His determination never wavered; his whole being was on edge. His anxiety to be a soldier welled up into a passion, breaking out at times into the old half-bantering, half-bitter feud with David. As they carried the barley he would rush at the sheaves with the pitch-fork, sticking them madly, and toss them lightly up to the wagon. Each of them was a stricken enemy. He was full of a blind, unshakable war-lust which his mother feared and hated. As the last wagons came up she sickened with dread. As she lay awake at night her mind worked as clear and quick as day, her fears aggravated into a fever of wretchedness. By day, as he swaggered about the rick-yard, he seemed to her so like his father that when she met him unexpectedly her heart stopped, thinking Jess had come back again. Sometimes he seemed, however, merely a boy again; and then her anguish dribbled away, thin and silly, and she felt her old sensible, hardheaded, phlegmatic self come back, reproaching her for fears and weaknesses.

When the last wagon had come up he stripped off his shirt in the evening and stood at the sink, naked to the waist, to wash. He threw out his chest like a wrestler before plunging his hands into the water, knotting his sun-brown arm muscles and smacking his chest, dark with a deep triangle of curly black hair.

'Well! the last time I wash in this old sink for a good while,' he announced.

'The last time?' said his mother sharply.

'I'm off to-morrow,' he said, soaping his hands.

'To-morrow?'

He swilled the water up his sun-warm arms, catching his breath with pleasure. 'Call me early, mother dear!' he sang in a mocking bass, looking at her over his shoulder. 'For I'm –'

'What a row!' she said tartly. 'Folks'll hear you in Staveston. Be quiet for goodness' sake.'

'To-morrow,' he teased her, 'you'll be saying "Oh! if only that boy was singing at that sink" –'

'If you weren't so big,' she said, her heart quickening in spite of herself with fear, 'I'd give you something to sing for, I know.'

'You can't keep a good man down,' he teased on. He plunged his face suddenly with a shout into the water and she went out of the kitchen, trying the old trick of indifference she had so often tried on his father.

But at supper-time he would not let her rest. When he had grown tired of teasing her impassive face he turned on his brother.

'We'll get up afore it's daylight and be off, won't we?' he said. 'I'll give you a knock.'

David did not answer.

'No more courtin'!' Benjamin made a sound with his lips, a half-kissing, half-sobbing sound.

'His place is here,' said Deborah. 'And so is yours – if you could see it.'

'I see – said the blind man.'

'You're stubborn – if that's anything,' she said.

'I said I was going, and I'm going.'

'*When* are you going?' she said. 'You talk about going – but *when*?'

'Early in the morning before the sun was rising,' he said, half-singing the tune of the words.

His tone was so light and careless that she could not believe him.

'Very well then, if you want to go you must go,' she said.

'But don't come grizzling home to me when your shirt isn't ready to put on – *or* when your dinner isn't ready – *or* when your socks want darning. I shan't be at home, my lad.'

Something in the ironical gaiety of her words seemed to alarm him and he got up suddenly and pushed back his chair and knocked out his pipe on the heel of his boot and left the kitchen, smarting at her taunts and restless under her warnings.

Knowing she had touched him at last she slept better, not waking in the cloudy September morning till nearly six. She dressed hastily and went downstairs, buttoning her blouse.

David was lighting the kitchen fire, a thing that Benjamin always did while David fetched the cows and did the milking. The boy turned his face to her and turned it away quickly again.

She knew at once that Benjamin had gone.

Chapter 5

UP at the Twelvetree household the patriotism was intense.
A feeling of lofty, outraged, suffering dignity was mingled
with a proud hatred of the enemy. It was the old creed of
Right against Might. At the outbreak of war Anthea was
eighteen and she began to bring David home in the evenings,
and during the dark winter nights he sat in the Twelvetree
parlour while the family talked of war. They discussed the
wrongness of war as fought by the enemy and the Divine
Rightness of war as practised by their native land. His
mother had schooled him to a hatred of war and a contempt
of patriotism which she in turn had learned from his grandfather, and the talk of the Twelvetrees, night after night, put
him in an inward rage. He sat there staring at the fire, gripping his hands in his pockets against the flesh of his thighs,
while the nightly ritual was performed. A vast map of Europe
had been pinned on the wall of the room, and a snake of little
red, white and blue flags curling across France and Flanders
showed the points to which the forces of Right had advanced.
During the day Mrs. Twelvetree studied the newspaper and
compared the map in it with the map on the wall, and every
evening the family gathered together for the moving of the
flags. It was like a play, with William Twelvetree in the lead
and Mrs. Twelvetree the heroine. She read from the newspaper the details of advance and retreat, her voice dramatic-
ally triumphant or tragic, Twelvetree moving the flags backwards or forwards with flourishing or dreary gestures. Ad-
vances were applauded; great victories were even cheered;
there was groaning or silence for defeat. All the time Mrs.
Twelvetree and the two girls sat knitting scarves or comforters
or socks in a greenish, khaki-coloured wool, the needles clicking without pause, the faces of the women, strained with
determination, repeatedly uplifted to the line of flags that
justified the desperation of their needles. After the flags

Twelvetree read aloud from the paper the day's war news. As he read Mrs. Twelvetree gripped her hands together and turned her face upward with the same look of suffering innocence as she had seen twenty years before on the face of a Lyceum actress playing Desdemona. When the reading was finished she rose and laid supper, and when supper was ready she turned to David.

'Would you join us at supper?' she asked. 'It's very frugal. But we have no right to eat when others are suffering.' And when they were all seated: 'And where is your brother now?'

'He's at Gillingham.'

'In Kent? How proud your mother must be of her son!'

He could say nothing, seeing only his mother's bitter, pensive eyes as he saw them across their own supper-table. His mother had no conscious pride in Benjamin; she only waited stoically, suffering in silence, for this fool's business to end and for her son to come back to the land again.

'And when you go, too!' said Mrs. Twelvetree.

He did not answer. He only knew that he was not going. He had made up his mind, knowing without any falseness of pride that without him his mother would be like a plough without a horse. As the war went on Mrs. Twelvetree began to talk of his going more pointedly, a forced significant smile on her lips as she said the words. He never answered her, knowing he could not be responsible for the fierceness of his words against her if he did speak.

He longed for spring to come and free him from that false, forced atmosphere of patriotic pride. As the March evenings lengthened and thrushes went on singing in the cold, primrose paleness of twilight he suddenly refused to go to the farm any longer, and Anthea, afraid of her mother, told lies again in order to meet him by the stream.

He stayed away from the Twelvetrees until one Sunday in April Anthea brought an invitation for him to go to tea. Hating the idea, he nevertheless went, afraid of hurting her. An April wind was blowing sunlight and shadow swiftly across the hillside, the apple-blossom in the orchard tossing and showering a fall of fragrant petals on the grass. In the Twelvetree parlour the varnished walls, the frugal tea-table and the war-map, crinkling up at the edges, all seemed drab and life-less in the spring light.

'Ah! here you are, stranger,' Mrs. Twelvetree greeted him. And then:

'We thought you had gone. But of course you'll come and say good-bye when you do go.'

'When I go.'

At tea Mrs. Twelvetree talked pointedly of men in the village who had enlisted. The war was growing desperate, and young men, younger than himself, and middle-aged men, older than Twelvetree, were going off every day. Mrs. Twelvetree called enlisting 'making the sacrifice.' There was a strange tension in the house. He sensed it quickly and saw also that all Mrs. Twelvetree's remarks were addressed to him, directly or indirectly, and that Prunella, who usually never spoke to him, made occasionally some detached, significant remark, looking out of the window at the apple-blossom as she spoke. He ate and drank uneasily, glancing furtively at Anthea, but she sat quiet and pensive, as though in a day-dream or as though she had deliberately cut herself off from it all, anxious simply to remain neutral.

After tea Mrs. Twelvetree read out the war news and Twelvetree pinned the little flags solemnly backward or for-ward along the battle-line. After he had pinned the last flag she turned to Twelvetree and said in a queer detached voice, hard with significance:

'Now read us the leading article, Daddy. I do feel it's so good and so important. Mr. Mortimer would like to hear it, I feel sure.'

'I feel sure he would,' said Prunella.

The boy sat stiff and silent. He reddened with anger as Twelvetree opened the Sunday paper and began, in a solemn, almost ecclesiastical voice, to read the appeal for men that the leading article contained. As he listened to the empty, bom-bastic words he felt his body sicken, his bowels turning to water as he saw why Twelvetree was reading. The minutes while he read seemed endless, and bitterness of every moment intolerable. He tried to look calm and quiet, but both anger and misery rushed with the blood to his face, and he could only clench his hands against his thigh and wait desperately for the voice to end. When Twelvetree had finished he sat as though petrified, waiting, too sick to move or speak.

'Oh! I think that's so noble!' said Mrs. Twelvetree. 'It's what we should all do if we were able. If I were a man that would send a thrill through my heart.'

'People are not all so easily stirred as you, mother,' said Prunella.

Twelvetree walked to the window resolutely as she spoke and stood looking out, thinking. The boy sat with a fixed, negative stare on his face, the tension of the room pressing on his mind. Suddenly Twelvetree turned and strode to the centre of the room and put his hand on the boy's shoulder. Every movement was false and theatrical; the boy felt the touch of the hand like an irritating pain. He felt himself become stiffer, as though to harden his flesh against it. He did not look up. Twelvetree, with a sudden increasing tension of his hand, burst out:

'I'll go if you will!'

'Oh! Daddy!' said Prunella.

'Yes, I'll go if he will go. I mean it.'

'William,' murmured Mrs. Twelvetree. 'Oh! William!'

'Look up, my boy,' said Twelvetree. 'Will you go if I go?'

The boy's body felt cold, like stone, and his words had a kind of cold quietness about them.

'Why should I go?' he said.

'Ah,' said Prunella.

The word was spoken as quietly as his own, but it flashed at him with insult and pain. He felt his body surge suddenly to heat again, full of hatred and defiance.

'Who spoke to you?' he said quickly.

They faced each other with all their former antagonism, the girl very white, her thin neck quivering. Before she could speak he flashed at her:

'No one asked you to speak. Your father asked me a question. And I'll answer it when I've made up my mind.'

He turned from her to Anthea and spoke with a kind of savage quietness:

'Come out and talk with me. Whatever you say I'll do.' He made the promise in the desperation of the moment, ready to say anything that would take him quickly out of sight of that drab room, the war-map and the inquisitorial faces of the three Twelvetrees staring at him.

'May I go, mother?' said the girl.

'I have nothing to say,' said her mother. 'Ask your father.'

Twelvetree nodded. The boy strode to the door and opened it and followed the girl out without another word.

They had crossed the bridge and were walking along the brook-side before they could speak to each other. They walked at a stiffly even pace, unhappy. A crab-tree was breaking into fat pink buds of blossom by the water-side and the king-cups, open flat and wide from the day's sun, shone gloriously in the dark marsh earth among the watercress and brook-lime and bits of sedge. Among the marsh and sedge the boy walked distantly from her, miserably anxious not to touch even her dress, and at the stiles and fences he stood back and let her climb first and walk on and wait for him.

At a place where the path divided he turned on her suddenly:

'Which way?'

A pain at the hardness of his speech shot up in her eyes, accusing him. She pointed miserably to the left-hand path and they followed a backwater of the stream, where crab-trees were tangled also with lovely webs of pink-white blossom.

He could endure it no longer.

'Do you want me to go?' he said in a hard voice.

He stood still and involuntarily the girl stopped too, but without speaking.

'You want me to go, don't you?' he demanded.

She stood there for a moment in a dazed, half-lost fashion, as though dumb. She turned away her face, ready to break down, and the gesture accused him, making him ashamed and miserable underneath his defiance.

A moment later she turned on him.

'Why should I want you to go?' she said quickly. 'Do you think this is the first I've heard about it? Don't you know they've been talking about you for weeks – for weeks and weeks – nothing but you and the war and why didn't you go? Prunella wouldn't let me sleep for talking about you. She's never forgiven you for what you did to her – and it's her way

179

of revenging herself. It must have been her who thought of what happened this afternoon,' she finished wearily.

'Like a damned play,' he said. 'Just like her.'

He stood tense with exasperation and helplessness. He wanted desperately to do something.

'I'll go back and have it out with her,' he declared.

'It's no use,' Anthea said. 'I know them too well – you'll never make them see otherwise.'

'I'll tell them something!'

Her voice became very quiet. 'What about me?' she said. 'Afterwards?'

The very quietness of her words made him suddenly afraid of the situation. He felt anger and defiance leave him. And suddenly the thought of the promise made him go limp; a promise was a promise; nothing could alter that. The inevitability of it sent him suddenly coldly sick, with a kind of involuntary cowardice, and the thought of being disloyal to the girl finished him, plunging him into a final gloom.

'If your father goes, what will you do?' he said.

'I don't know. He talks of selling out. Mother has money, but we lose it in the farm. We were the last people who ought to have been farmers. If father goes we shall sell up perhaps and go into lodgings or rent a house somewhere. I don't know. I don't care much.'

'Does he want to go?' he said.

'He thinks it right. They all think it right.'

'Must I go?' he said.

She did not answer.

'If I go,' he said, 'will you marry me? My mother would have you to live with her.'

She looked half-frightened, half-puzzled. There was no joy in her face. To marry him meant a revolt; they would never allow it otherwise. She tried to think of something to say in answer, and automatically the fear in her mind broke loose:

'They'd never let me!' she said in misery.

He held back his anger. In suspense she waited for him to speak, but he looked away over the fields mutely. The sun had set, the wind was dropping and overhead the last of the clouds, yellow and grey, were sailing east, leaving a clear cold blue sky. Something in the pitiful muteness of his face drew her suddenly to him and she put out her arms quickly and embraced him, and he opened his arms in response and they stood together, their bodies tight against each other, in anguish.

He knew suddenly that he would have to go; the agony of leaving her was already beginning. He sensed in the desperate strength of her embrace a corresponding agony, but sharper and more feminine, a more conscious emotion, without illusions.

They broke from each other at last in mutual relief and began to walk back along the backwater to the main stream.

'When will you go?' she said presently.

The first agony was past; they could talk of it as a simple, accepted thing.

'I'll stay a week.'

He was thinking of his mother. The girl knew and was silent, and again, for a long time, they had nothing to say.

At last he spoke: 'If we got married my mother might buy your place and put us into it – one big farm,' he said. The prospect was distant and wild, but it brought them relief.

'One big farm,' he repeated. 'All your fields, right down here, and all ours, right up to the road. Think of it.'

'Would she do it?'

'She'd do it if she could.'

'But could she?'

'You never know about her. She's deep. She's got her head screwed on right way, don't you fret. Since my father went off she's *had* to use her head.'

'Don't you hear of your father?' said the girl.

'Never.'

'Doesn't she speak of him?'

'She told us about him and then it was finished. Once she's said a thing she's said it. She's never said another word.'

As they went back along the brook they talked of the farms joining, the big sweep of land, like a switchback, that would sweep between the two farm-houses. They worked up their joy in it more intensely in order to forget the thought of his departure. But the anguish came back as they were ready to depart and they clung to each other in a tenseness of pain and happiness again.

'Tell them I'll go,' he said at last.

At the farm he sat and ate his supper in silence, eating with a false eagerness of appetite that aroused his mother's suspicions. When she addressed him he looked away, unable to meet her gaze. When she saw him at last trying to force the last of a slice of bread down his throat as though his gorge were sickened, she began to understand.

She said nothing, and soon, very quietly, he told her everything. She sat drawing her darning-needle through a sock-heel with her fist clenched hard beneath, listening with apparent tranquillity. When he told of the war-map and the flags and Twelvetree's offer to enlist if he would enlist she clicked her tongue quietly in impatient disgust. 'I've no patience with them. You're not beholden to them for every step you take.'

'Well, I promised,' he said at last.

It was the end, for her equally as for him. Against that she could say nothing. Her heart contracted, sending a chill of fear through her. She went on darning, drawing the needle through and through mechanically, not seeing the sock.

'I'll stop a week,' he said. 'The roots want hoeing.'

'They do, bad,' she said.

'That wheat ought to be rolled as well,' he said.

'It ought.'

'I might do that, too.'

'I should.'

'A week's a long time,' he said. 'You can do a lot in a week.'

She was silent, waiting for him to go on speaking. But suddenly she turned and found he had gone and she heard him climbing the stairs to bed. She went on darning the socks, dropping one and picking up another and drawing the needle through them mechanically, not seeing them.

Chapter 6

SHE hired an old man from the village to take his place, and she struggled on as she had struggled when her sons had been too small to help her, rising earlier and going to bed much later, taking her hand with the milking and hoeing, the potato-work, the thinning of roots, the spring planting. At the end of the day's work, utterly exhausted in body, she sat down and wrote laborious letters to her sons, telling them all that she did and planned to do. She wrote in one long unbroken sentence without stops or commas, ending with some trite phrase expressing her regards or loving wishes; it seemed embarrassing and strange to write the words of her love nakedly on paper. Timber was urgently in demand and she had sold fifty trees from the spinney to the Government and the price was so absurd that she went about for days half-stupefied, unable to believe it. To David and Benjamin she wrote 'Have sold a few trees in the old spinney the young ones will grow up again so do not mind and am thinking of buying a grass-mower being short of hands like the one Sharman has.' From Benjamin came a letter of great joy; the grass-mower, he wrote, was what they had always wanted, the identical thing; he was trying to get leave at haytime to come and drive it for her. He had joined the artillery; he believed that this was the age of the machine and the machine alone. Why didn't she get a binder for harvest? he wrote. He would ride the forrardest, showing her how he rode the horses with the guns. Curiously it was from Benjamin that she received the most living letters – letters full of bantering and wit, with stories of his officers to make her laugh and army rhymes that made her blush. They were letters which, as she read, brought him with a shock of vividness before her eyes. The letters from David were short and halting, and she read into them a kind of gloomy dread of something; he found it hard to express himself and after a single page he

183

would give it up, penning the last formal wishes to her with panic of relief; she read his letters again and again, trying to read into them some fresh, light-hearted, living meaning, but his words were too veiled or brief and she felt nothing except his mute unhappiness. Once he wrote to know if she had sown sweet-peas and a second time to remind her to plant marrows on the old muck-heap in the orchard. She had done neither and she drove off at once to a seedsman and brought the pea plants and the marrow seedlings, planting them herself and watering them every day until they were root-strong and flourishing. She remembered then how pink and apricot and purple sweet-peas, with their lovely fragrance, and the big golden trumpets of the marrow flowers, had pleased his father.

In June she wrote asking them to get leave for haytime, but only Benjamin came, large, stiffly upright, with a foreign twang of certitude in his voice and a more lordly and swaggering attitude than ever. When he changed from his sleek tunic and elegant riding-breeches into his old jacket and corduroys, his limbs filled them to bursting point, like ripe seeds in a pod. He spent the days cutting the grass for her with the new horse-mower, halting the horses at frequent intervals in order to tinker with some loosened nut or to shift the knife.

'All you want now is a binder – cut and tie and throw it out afore you can wink. You're all behind. You'll be the last farmer in England to have a binder,' he teased her. On the last day of his leave, the hay having been carted, he spent the day tinkering with the mower again, lost in a world of screws and bolts, emerging with a new machine-given dignity.

A week after he had returned she received a letter one morning and was carrying it into the house, trembling quietly with the apprehension and pleasure that a letter from either of them gave her, when she saw that the writing on the envelope was strange to her. Afraid, she tore it open and read the typewritten letter it contained, her brain heavy with astonishment, her eyes staring incredulously. She sat down in the kitchen and read the letter five or six times. Mrs. Arbuthnot had died, leaving her more than nine hundred pounds.

She drove off that morning to Staveston and saw the

solicitors. Her mind was too dazed to frame any other thought than 'And I didn't know she was dead even!' which she kept repeating both to herself and to the solicitors as they talked with her in their dingy, colourless office overlooking the market square.

Leaving them she went to the post office and sent a telegram to David, urging him to get leave and come home immediately. The framing of the telegram and the sending of it excited her more than the letter about the legacy had done, and when she drove home again her hands quivered foolishly as she held the reins.

He came home in the late afternoon of the following day, tired with travelling all day in the July heat, his nerves stretched with the uncertainty of not knowing whether her news were good or bad. Her telegram had been nothing but a stilted request to come. His body was moist and itching with sweat under his thick tunic, and his forehead, sun-brown except for a bleached rim just under his hair where his cap had made a shadow, was golden-white with beads of moisture that trickled down warm and bitter into his eyes.

'It's good news,' she greeted him.

He was relieved. 'Can I wash my feet?' he asked.

As he sat in the kitchen soaking his tired, sweat-stale feet in the little round bath-tin of steaming water, she hurried about the kitchen and laid the table for tea, telling him her news to the accompaniment of her old incredulous 'And I didn't know she was dead even!' while he luxuriated in the hot blessed water and said 'Ah!' and occasionally 'Well I never, it's a licker.' She did not tell him the amount of the legacy and as he dried between his toes he said, 'But how much?' and she pretended not to know or to have forgotten, adoring the puzzled incredulous look in his eyes. It was Saturday, and the men had knocked off and there was a clean, quiet, almost hallowed Saturday-feeling about the place, the sun blazing hot on the silent yard, the smooth kitchen bricks scrubbed and shining red as apples, his mother clean-aproned and prim, her Sunday brooch flashing silver against the black throat of her dress.

He drank his tea in long deep drinks, with sighs of unconsciously heavenly pleasure, talking little.

'When I worked for her,' prattled his mother, 'she gave me five shillings a week and all found, and I was satisfied, too, I tell you. It was a good job in those days. And I saved nearly every penny. She must have known that – ah, she was artful. I never knew how artful she was until I was leaving her.'

'Well, how much *is* this money?' he persisted.

'If I told you, you wouldn't believe me.'

'Twenty or thirty quid, I expect.'

'Who *said* it was twenty or thirty pounds?' she flashed. 'My goodness gracious! I'll give you twenty or thirty quid.'

He loved her look of pretended outrage, and for the sake of teasing her he made a wild guess, watching her face solemnly as he spoke:

'Twenty thousand!'

'Do you think she was a millionaire?' she cried.

'Well,' he said, shrugging his shoulders, full of strategy, 'if it's not twenty thousand it's not worth having.'

The words sprang from her with involuntary pride and contradiction: 'Then you don't think one thousand is worth having?' she cried.

'A thousand?' he said slowly.

'Cash and securities.'

'A thousand,' he marvelled softly. It was a colossal sum. 'The old tit.' He revolved the amount in his mind and passed his empty cup to his mother in silence, and after taking a long drink he said:

'Now you'll *do* something with that, I should hope?'

'Do something?'

'Buy some land – a bit more pasture, some more cows. You want more cows, don't you? Milk! – it's all milk nowadays.'

'We'll see, we'll see,' she said, tight and cautious.

'You've got to strike out!' he said. 'If we're going to farm, let's have a farm – not a mole-hill. What can you do with fifty acres?'

He was thinking of Twelvetree's, a vision in his mind of the land sweeping from farm to farm, all belonging to her. She sat thinking too, wise, meditative, cautious as ever; and then, changing the subject abruptly, she said:

'Are you going up to see Anthea?' and when he nodded, 'If she'll come, bring her back to tea to-morrow.'

He changed into his civilian Sunday suit and went into the orchard, standing for a long time contemplating the great golden convolvulus-like marrow flowers on the muck-heap; in the garden the first sweet-peas were in flower, blossoms of pink and blue and cream on tall stiff vines climbing a row of hazel sticks, and he nicked off a four-flowered bloom and threaded it into his buttonhole and then lifted the lapel of his jacket to smell the sweetness of the wine-dark flower.

Up at Twelvetree's he found the two girls at their knitting in the hot, airless parlour; the map with its snake of union-jacks was still on the wall, its edges curled up like cankered leaves and the three women sat silently beneath it, melancholy, pale, weary, persistently knitting with the same greenish-khaki wool as though they had never ceased doing so since he had seen them last. They greeted him with a strange quietness, smiling spiritlessly, their old anger against him used up, as though they had knitted it away with their unceasing needles. Prunella, he noticed, stooped a little, only a shadow of her old haughtiness remaining in the way she sometimes tossed the hair away from her eyes, and when he looked at Anthea his heart sank. There was something about her grave, thin face that hurt him and a brightness in her eyes that was too bright; when she smiled it was as though she had smiled in order to drive away a sudden pain.

He asked about their father.

'We heard to-day that he was drafted to France last week,' the mother told him. 'We are expecting to hear at any time.'

They were all very frightened; and he felt their fear acutely as they questioned him. Their words were put to him indirectly so as to conceal both the depth of their fear and their eagerness for enlightenment and comfort.

'A battalion often doesn't go up to the lines for six weeks,' he said. 'He's a small man, too,' he went on. 'There's a lot in that.'

'Yes?' They snatched at that hope like hungry dogs, and presently some of their old hope and pride returned. 'Naturally we wondered a little – but we're very proud of him – we're very proud of him, of course.'

All through his visit he kept looking at Anthea's face, troubled by its thin, sharp, underfed look and his heart ached at the sight of her colourless, almost transparent skin, and the queer brightness of her eyes. He stayed on to supper, a dim meal of war-bread and cheese and water. The women ate so frugally that in the end he gave it up, ashamed of his own appetite before them. Out in the orchard, saying good night to Anthea, he was glad of the twilight, which lessened the peaked whiteness of her face, but as he pressed her very close to him he felt her ribs standing out as sharp as knuckles under her thin dress. He thought of asking her to dinner on the following day, but he changed his mind, not wanting his mother to see her until the colour had come back to her face, and he suggested instead that they picnicked on the back-water.

'My mother'll pack things – she's got a ham hanging that's a disgrace, and she'll boil eggs and give us a loaf and butter.'

'I must bring something as well,' she said. 'What can I bring?'

'Nothing – don't bring a crumb. If you bring a mite of anything I'll eat *you*,' he threatened.

They were to meet at eleven, when the church-bell had finished, and they were to go back to the farm for tea. The morning was hot and brilliant. The path by the brook was a parched brown line, the last of the dog-roses were withering on the hedges, the grey willow leaves drooping in the heat, the birds quietening down for noon, bringing a quivering silence. Up on the hill the corn stood stiff and straight, still green, the ears unfolding from the curving sheaths, ready to swell and yellow. David had brought a peck-basket of food and his army haversack full of knives and cups and a billy-can for tea. He kept looking furtively at Anthea; her face was fresher and brighter and the sunlight had enriched the light in her eyes, and he liked her thin cotton dress with a flower pattern in it. She was carrying a small paper bag. They turned away from the stream and followed the backwater. The day quietened as they went, the water too gentle and slow to make a sound, the midsummer sky an intensely bright blue with heat. In a deep green pool a mass of water-lilies covered the whole width of the stream with snow and gold, the pale flat leaves gleaming with sunlight, the fat buds pushing up among them like cool water-roses, half-green, half-white.

Within sight of the lilies, under a big alder, they sat down and made a fire of old reeds and dry, dead wood, the smoke curling straight up through the tree to sunlight. They boiled the billy-can, full of spring water, and Anthea laid out the food he had brought. The noon silence was intense, the meadow quivering with heat, the water-lilies blazing under the perpendicular beat of the sunshine.

As they ate he told her of the legacy. He raged softly against the force of circumstances:

'It would come just at this time – just when she needs us and money as well.'

'But the war can't last for ever,' she said.

'Can't it? Can't it?' he said. 'That's what my mother said when it began. I've got no faith at all. Tell me when peace is declared and I'm driving plough in our fields again and I'll believe you – not until.'

They had eaten all the ham and he was sipping a last cup of tea when he remembered her paper bag.

'What are you nursing there all the time?' he asked her.

'Something,' she said distantly, half-teasing.

'Tell me something I don't know,' he said.

'Will you have it?' she said. 'It's for you. I made it.'

She stretched out her hand and gave him the paper bag and he unscrewed the mouth of it, looking inside. His heart sank with pity as he saw the little hard flat cake she had baked for him, a brown burnt-edged cake with cinder-like plums that was heavy in his hand. He did not know what to do and she said:

'I baked it myself. I got up early this morning.'

'I'll leave it and eat it as I go back in the train to-morrow,' he said. And almost deliberately he said in a quick whisper: 'Look, look – over there, just under the water, look at it!'

'What?' She turned sharply and looked at the stream.

'A pike. Sunning his old self,' he whispered. 'See him go off when I make a noise.'

He clapped his hands and the sun-yellow fish struck off with the swiftness of a swallow across the water, vanishing in a single second into the deeper reach under the willows on the opposite bank of the stream. 'Did you see him?' he said.

She nodded, watching for the fish to return.

'He won't come back,' he said. He put the cake away into his haversack while she was still watching the water.

As they lounged and lay under the alder-tree the shadow of the tree moved, and the sun, fiercely hot, began to blaze unbrokenly down upon them. After lying a little while in his shirt and trousers David sat up and took off his boots and stockings and paddled into the stream, picking his way along the stone-strewn bottom, gasping with the cool pleasure of it. He called at last for the girl to come.

When she shook her head he paddled to the bank and urged her softly, standing there with his trousers rolled to his knees, the water gleaming in pearl-drops on his legs. 'It's fine,' he said. 'You wouldn't believe it.' She smiled and shook her head, but he persisted:

'Come on! Come on! Why not? The Lord knows when you'll have a chance to paddle with me in this brook again. Not this year, you bet your life.'

'You won't push me,' she said, 'if I come?'

'Push you?' He laughed at that. 'We'll paddle up the other side and look for a kingfisher's. Come on, my sweet.'

Very timidly she lifted her dress and unfastened her stockings, peeling them off slowly and then folding them carefully to tuck into her shoes. Her legs were very white and slender, the toes long and pink, and as she stepped slowly down the bank her feet sank into the hot, red sand, making soft footprints. He stretched out his hand and led her into the water, looking down at her feet and her beautiful, slim legs, and then up into her face as she laughed and gasped with the sudden sharp coolness of the stream after the hot sand.

They waded about up to their knees, in and out of the sunlight, laughing and calling and sometimes flicking an arch of water over each other, until the girl's limbs were faintly goose-skinned with the coolness of the running stream. Standing on the bank David lifted her bodily over the sand and set her down on the sunlit grass and with his big army handkerchief began to dry her legs and feet, rubbing her soft flesh gently, his hand quivering at the touch of her. He dried her feet first and she drew her skirt above her knees so that he could wipe the splashed beads of water from her thighs. For one moment he let his hand pause and rest on her flesh, feeling the sun already warming it softly again, and she sat staring at him with an expression of rapturous, yet almost frightened intensity. He drew his hand away, tortured by the memory of the touch as soon as he had done so. His heart began to beat wildly and he looked with sudden beseechment at Anthea, and she looked back with a flash of understanding that turned suddenly to fear. A second later they could not look at each other for timidity and the frightening power of their longing, and she stretched out her hand and began to pull on her stockings. As the white beauty of her legs was covered up by the coarse, heather-coloured stockings he did not know what to do with the anguish of his love for her, and suddenly he embraced her, kissing her with all the strength of his longing. One hand was laid as though by accident across her breast and when the kiss had ended she looked at him with a strange, almost ethereal happiness. He moved his hand away from her breast involuntarily. They seemed to remember suddenly that it would be a long time before they could see each other again and all at once she hugged him to her desperately in order to kiss him with all the deep and painful fear of losing him. For one moment she felt inexpressibly old. She hugged him tightly to her breast as though she must protect him. When the pain of it was too much for her she loosened herself gently, and without releasing him, stared with dreamy contemplation at the sunlight beating with brilliant silver on the water.

When he came back from Twelvetree's that night he sat at the open kitchen door to talk with his mother. The air was hot and oppressive, and in the still half-darkness he could hear a meadow-crake's cry somewhere over the fields towards Twelvetree's. His mother listened with him to the bird's cry and then said at last:

'What's the matter with Anthea? She's so thin and white. I don't like it, my boy.'

'I know, I know,' he said. He had hoped desperately she would not notice it.

'She looked so fine and healthy when you first brought her home.'

He was silent a moment and then broke out:

'They're starving themselves. The three of them don't eat enough to keep a mouse alive.'

'Starving? But why, why?' she cried.

'They think it's patriotic.'

'Patriotic!' she cried with disgust. 'Oh! I've no patience with such folks. I've no patience with them.'

He fumbled in his pocket and took out the cake which Anthea had given him and showed it to his mother.

'Look at that,' he said. 'She baked it for me – and that's something special. They're just starving. The farm's going to ruin – they've got no cattle and the wheat's never been hoed since it was drilled in. And they're frightened to death,' he added.

'Frightened?'

'Twelvetree was drafted to France last week. I tried to tell them it was all right – but they're scared. They seem to know something'll happen.'

'Ah,' she said, half-impatient, half-pitying them.

They were quiet again, listening for the corncrake, but it was silent and finally he said:

'What are you going to do with this money?'

'The money? The money's all right where it is,' she said.

'Why don't you buy their farm – Twelvetree's?' he said impulsively.

'Twelvetree's?'

'Yes, buy it. I'll marry Anthea and she can come here and live until the war's over and then we can live at Twelvetree's and I'll farm that side and you this.'

'They don't want to sell, do they?'

'They'd be glad to sell. They can't farm – they know that. They'd be only too glad to sell.'

'But they can't do anything with Twelvetree's not here.'

They went on arguing into the darkness, he eager and insistent, she always calm and shrewd and cautious, always putting him off. Yet secretly she was glad that he felt for the land as he did. Inwardly the idea appealed to her and as she argued and reasoned against it with him, merely in order to make him sane and level-headed again, she half-saw herself mistress of the two farms, one son on one hillside and the second on the other, they and their children growing up for the inheritance of the land while she grew old and mellow upon it. Finally her conscious mind asserted itself and she said in her calm, habitual voice:

'It wants thinking about. I should want to be clear about the rights and wrongs of a big thing like that.'

'Yes, I know,' he said, 'but I want you to do it. If anything happens to Twelvetree you must buy it – promise you'll buy it – promise,' he insisted.

She was silent for a long time and then to his surprise he heard her murmur quietly: 'All right. I promise.'

It was enough; and he got up a moment later and kissed her and went to bed. Knowing she would not fail him he lay awake, his arms clasped behind his head on the pillow, for a long time, thinking of the future, the land, and all that he could do with the other farm. The night kept hot and oppressive, and when he shut his eyes to sleep the heat conjured up at once a memory of the day, the brilliant stillness of the backwater, the lilies, the girl's white slender limbs in the water, and all the fragrance of the summer day.

In September, after harvest, he received a letter from his mother. Twelvetree had died of wounds at a base hospital and Mrs. Twelvetree was selling up. In reply he wrote the longest letter he had ever written her, urging her to buy the farm. By the same post he wrote to Anthea, a short, awkward letter of consolation. As he wrote he imagined her, with Prunella and her mother, sitting in the farm-parlour, mute and grief-stricken but still proud, their needles clicking eternally in their hands, and the map of Europe, with its line of blood, still hanging on the wall beside them.

A month later his mother wrote that she had bought the farm and he wrote at once to Anthea, asking her to marry him. There were rumours of his battalion being drafted to France before the winter and he asked her to telegraph her reply. She telegraphed one word: 'Yes.' He went home to her in late October, having received a leave for one night and a day. The countryside was wonderfully green, a wet autumn having kept the leaves green and late on the trees and honeysuckle was still blooming on the hedgerows and sweet-peas were still a tangle of pink and cream and blue among the hazel sticks in the garden. The land lay quiet and lovely, the stubble silvery-yellow and the ploughed land warm and red in the soft sunlight.

He arrived at four o'clock in the afternoon; he was to report back at ten the following night. He saw Anthea for an hour that evening at Twelvetree's; the three women were dressed in black and they sat there under the map in the parlour just as he had imagined. He felt he could not bear their mute, strained, half-broken look and their tragic air of unhappy sacrifice.

They were married at twelve o'clock on the following day. There were no guests except his mother and Mrs. Twelvetree and Prunella. Benjamin had been drafted out of England, to a destination unknown. It was a silent, awful wedding. The joy as they sat in the Twelvetrees' parlour was forced and tragic. Not even his mother's hearty, sensible talk could drive away the strain and the gloom of the house.

After tea he walked with Anthea along the brookside and they stood by a fence beneath an old crab-tree and tried to talk to each other. She had on her wedding dress and it was made of some stuff that was crisp and stiff to his touch and she stood like a ghost, dim and white, in the falling October darkness. He put his arms about her tenderly and kissed her lips and as he did so, aching for the fulfilment of his love, she burst out crying. She leaned against him and cried with deep agonizing sobs of despair. Her breast was a torrent of gasping and great fluttering breaths of anguish. He could do nothing. He stood like a fool, in pain for her but helpless, his words of condolence not touching her. It was beyond him. As she ceased crying he hugged her closely in a fresh torment of tenderness and she drooped in his arms like a flower in the sun, all the life and youth gone out of her. It was all he could do to keep her from falling. He held her quietly until she was calm again and they walked back to the farm as the first stars were glowing like lanterns through the trees. 'This time next week,' he said, 'I shall be in France.' Her face was white and deathly, and suddenly torn with love and anguish and pity for her, he stopped and kissed her desperately, first on the lips and then on her breast, burying his lips in the warm fullness of her body. She stood curiously aloof and resigned, in another world from him, her body spiritual and cold after its grief, the last spark of passion dead in it.

She drove him to the station that night in his mother's trap. Twice he made her stop the cart so that he could kiss her and once he laid his hands full on her breast, imploring her love mutely, but she looked at him strangely like a child, and in a moment they drove on again.

As he leaned from the window, waiting for the train to move off, he remembered something.

'I meant to tell my mother something. Tell her for me, will you? – It's about time she gave that field down by the willow trees a rest. Tell her I say it could do with a rest. She could let it lay fallow for a bit.'

'I'll tell her.'

A moment later the train began to move. He had only time to touch her hand before she retreated and vanished into the darkness.

Chapter 7

PRUNELLA and her mother left the farm in November and took lodgings in Staveston, and Anthea came to live at the farm with Deborah.

'If you'd like to help with the chickens and the milk you can, and welcome,' Deborah told her. 'I'd be glad, in fact. And I'll pay you wages same as I should other folks.'

'I'd love to help,' said the girl, 'but I don't want any wages. I don't really.'

'Now come – work's work and it's worth money.'

'Oh, no!'

'There's nothing wrong about working for money, is there? If it's right for a man it's right for a woman I should think?'

'I suppose it is.'

'No suppose about it. It's just give and take. Now, what can you do? Can you feed-up an' milk?'

'I could feed, but I can't milk. We never did a thing on the farm.'

'You do what you can, then. You'll pick things up,' said Deborah. But to herself she thought: 'I don't know! Some folks! – all her life on a farm and can't milk. The humbugging nonsense of some folks and their children.'

The girl helped with the hens and made the beds and dusted the house. She sat down sometimes on a laying-box in the hen-house or on the stairs in the house, curiously tired out, weak from head to foot. All through the winter she went about pale and wistful, frail as a scrap of thistledown. In January she was ill with influenza. When she came downstairs again she was like a sick ghost about the place. She coughed her way through February and March. The cough made a small, fretful, troubled grating noise in her chest. She kept indoors till April, watching with dejected envy Deborah's small, swift, electric figure half-running about the yard from cow-house to pigsty, in and out of the stables, working in the fields, hanging out the washing between the apple-trees in the orchard, gripping the pegs in her strong, bared teeth, never resting for wind or weather, never tired out, the whole life of the farm whipped into energy by her tireless body and spirit.

Deborah, never saying much, watched the girl in return, troubled by her. When she did speak to her she spoke in her old downright, deprecating way, seeking to drive away the girl's morbidity and weariness by the sharp clear sense of her own words.

'You're not worrying about that boy, are you? If I catch you worrying one minute about him I'll warm you. If he's in the line he's in it, and all the fretting in the world won't make it different. You must take things as they come – you can't help them on or keep them back.'

The girl would smile and try to pull herself together, but the smile was faint. Nothing could drive away her thoughts. She wrote to David once a week, posting her letter never less than three days apart from Deborah's, thus hoping that he would hear at different times from them. They sent him also parcels of cake and chocolate and tobacco and occasionally woollen scarves and socks which she had knitted. In return he sent them the same brief, halting letters as of old, bare of all but the most trivial news. They read the letters aloud to each other, only to find that he had told them the same things, written often in the same words. He seemed cut off, imprisoned away from them; his letters left them, as it were, in air, waiting for some contact with him which never came. In the autumn Benjamin had been drafted to Palestine, and from there he wrote, once a month, long sprawling letters, full of the old liveliness, the old jocularities that made his mother laugh and blush. As she read his letters aloud in the kitchen on dark evenings she felt his presence in an amazing way, half-hearing his old blatant swaggering voice drawling out its jokes or grousing or complaining about a button on his shirt. 'I've got so fat,' he once wrote, 'that I look like an old sow going to have seventeen. Sorry can't enclose photo but see picture in margin,' and there, in a corner of the note-paper, he had drawn himself, a great fat balloon of a soldier, firing off a piece of toy artillery. Again he wrote: 'The folks plough here with a bit of wood and an old cow. All the chaps laughed, but I said laugh, show your ignorance. My old mother still ploughs like that on our old farm, all behind, like the cow's tail. Well, missus, when I come home we'll have a tractor and I'll drive it. Get the work done in half the time and jam on it as we say out here. Well, I'm going to wash my feet, they're a disgrace to the war. Don't forget what I say about the tractor.'

His letters cheered them greatly, but the girl was still thin in the spring and the cough persisted, and when Starling came up to the farm one afternoon to sketch the willow-trees yellow with blossom Deborah spoke to him about her as he was about to drive off in his car.

'I want her examined,' she said. 'She's my daughter-in-law and it's my duty to my son.'

'It looks like under-nourishment,' he said.

'I thought as much,' she said. 'And that's patriotism – patriotism! What can I do for her? Is it serious – very serious?'

'It could be serious. She's at an awkward age.'

'And it's this humbugging war, too.'

'Does she worry?'

'She broods and thinks – always having presentiments about something. She used to go to church; now she won't go near. She says she can't bear the singing. If she would work the garden it might occupy her mind, don't you think?'

'The garden? – of course!' he said at once. 'Let her sow things – more of those lovely sweet-peas and marigolds and poppies. I'd like to paint the garden this summer.'

'She paints a bit herself.'

'Does she? Then she could come sometimes with me and we'd paint the same bit together. Don't ask her – drop a hint, quite off-hand.'

He stepped into the car, and sitting with his hands on the steering-wheel, he looked at the spinney. Only the thin saplings and brushwood had been left standing by Government men; the floor of the wood was strewn with the wreckage of dead tree-tops and splintered boughs and axe-chips; here and there were white circles of fine wood-ash and through the heart of the spinney a deep-rutted lorry-track ran, the black

198

earth churned to mud. In isolated corners the last primroses still showed and stretches of bluebells shone like pale blue corn.

'I shall always be sorry you let them cut down the trees,' he said.

'The young things will grow again,' she said. 'Things can't go on for ever. We're not so young as we used to be.'

He smiled at her, relishing the quick, almost tart twang of her words.

'And that reminds me,' she went on. 'My country paid me another cheque for the wood to-day. It's not the first time – this makes three cheques. I've already returned one.'

'Keep them,' he said. 'They'll make you pay in the end.'

As the summer came on Anthea took an interest in the garden. She put in a double line of sweet-peas and stuck them with hazel sticks, as she had seen them the year before; she sowed a drift of marigolds, black-and-gold suns which blazed against the wall of the farm-house, patches of pink and purple candytuft, with fragrant lines of mignonette and evening-scented things, white tobacco plants and night-scented stock, with beds of ten-week stock and China asters to follow for harvest-time. Hours of sowing and weeding sun-burned her face and she felt her limbs harden and strengthen. With the contact with earth itself soothing her mind, lessening her fears and redoubling her joy in living, she lost the old melancholy brooding attitude; in the garden the war could seem infinitely far away, almost non-existent, obliterated by the richness of earth, the summer, the blaze of blossom.

The first pink buds of the chrysanthemums were breaking raggedly as she stooped among them one September afternoon, pulling up great roots of marigold full of green seed, and the last of the candytuft. Taking an armful of plants to the rubbish heap under the hedge she saw the postman leaving his bicycle in the lane. He crossed the paddock to the house.

She dropped the plants and watched him tensely. The coming of the post, until the letter had been opened, was a time of agony. She left the garden and crossed the orchard to meet him.

Suddenly the old dreadful coldness swept up through her

body. She began to walk mechanically but weakly. A terrible presentiment filled her mind. She stumbled across the orchard.

She took the letter into the house and sat in the empty kitchen, looking at it, not needing to open it. A queer numb ache seized her body and she sat staring, gripping her own fingers, her teeth set with terror.

Deborah, coming in from driving the drag over the barley field, found her sitting like a white, vacant-eyed statue. She hurried to and fro with calm deliberation and gave her brandy and rubbed her hands, not asking what had happened. As she knelt by the girl, chafing her icy wrists with her own harvest-rough hands, she saw the letter lying on the table. She half-stopped and then knew with absolute certainty, like the girl, what news it contained. She went on rubbing the girl's hands, her lips tight and bitter, trying to get the life back, her own heart deathly with dread.

She took the girl to bed and came down and read the letter. When she had read that David had been killed she mechanically put back the letter into the envelope and pushed the kettle into the red embers of the fire. Her face was white and immobile. Once or twice she ran her fingers across her brow, a bewildered gesture, feeling the cold sweat breaking out among its wrinkles.

She made herself some tea and drank a cup, as though nothing had happened. After drinking the tea very hot she went out into the orchard. As she walked under the trees she crushed the first fallen apples under her feet as though she could not see them. She skirted the pond and stood staring at the empty spinney. The frost had touched the sloe leaves, turning them a beautiful pink, and she saw the sloes themselves shining in misty purple clusters as she leaned on the spinney stile. She stared on, her eyes dry, as though her tears were frozen. She felt dimly that she must weep, that grief ought to break from her with a wild moaning, but she felt stunned and strangely elevated, without feeling or pain. With her right hand she kept passing her fingers to and fro across her sweating brow, and when at last her mind began to work again it worked with all the old deliberation of thought and she found herself half-reproachfully thinking 'It's happened – you can't change it. All the fretting in the world won't alter it.' She found herself walking away from the spinney to the paddock and down to the barley field with the same griefless deliberation, as though stunned.

The sun was shining brightly in a sky empty of clouds. She had left the drag by the hedgerow. The horse, as she came up, stood browsing the hawthorn, the bit tinkling and flashing silver. Seizing the horse's head she turned him about. Within herself she felt suddenly a wild groping as though she had lost something and must find it quickly. A moment later she felt the old calmness return, so ominous and quiet that it was worse to bear than grief itself.

With a half-savage motion she seized the reins and climbed up into the drag and sat in the iron seat. The horse moved off and she began to drive up and down the field, lifting and lowering the lever and leaving the draggings of barley in straight, perfect sweeps, driving on and on with all her old implacable determination, staring ahead.

Chapter 8

By winter-time she felt broken up. She went about with a silent, indomitable expression, working as usual, wrestling more bitterly with the land. Her grief, imprisoned by her own fortitude, wormed into her very being deeper and deeper, like a weevil into oak, hollowing her and breaking her to dust. Outwardly she looked hard and strong and untouched. Inwardly she felt broken and desolated. She began to go greyer and she suffered an everlasting pain in her chest, a little physical gnawing pain about her heart.

She sometimes wondered if she would not have suffered less alone. The presence of the girl aggravated all her pain. She went about with her desolation and agony as plain on her face as though she had just been struck. She had no power to hide her grief. Her body had become thin again, her face grievously narrow and white. They spent hours of silence with each other. Their own pain was sharpened and embittered through each other's, and the dreariness of time was an agony itself. In November they tidied the garden, working one Saturday afternoon; the air was mild and still and the sunshine apricot-coloured and warm on the wall of the farmhouse. Pink roses were still blooming on the arch that old Mortimer had built long ago and a marigold or two, late-seeded, blazed against the sun-bleached wall. The two women pulled up the summer plants that the frosts had nipped, piling up tobacco plants and stocks and evening primroses and the things that were dying or dead. The sweet-peas were past their beauty, but here and there a stiff stalk of pink or purple still blossomed, and the two women debated a little about uprooting them, afraid to speak much. Deborah picked off a stalk of pink blossom and twisted it like a feather in her fingers. A moment later the girl suddenly began to tear up the vines and hazel sticks in a kind of frenzy, as though angry against something, hardly knowing what she did. Slowly Deborah began to uproot the plants also and together they cleared away the still-blossoming vines that secretly they had wished to leave, every wrench at the summer-deep roots a wrench at the strength of their own hearts. The girl began crying quietly. Deborah, too weak to comfort her, pulled up the plants as though it were the last thing she could ever do, feeling that something vital within her had died.

They spoke of the war rarely. The war did not touch the land. Seed was sown, corn sprang up and ripened and was reaped, and the land still slipped from summer to autumn and from autumn to its dead, rain-beaten winter, just as it had always done. Nothing changed. But finally a Government Commissioner drove up one day in a large car and stalked about the fields and sniffed and hawed and told her to plough up the fifteen acres of pasture by the brook, the field where the cowslips grew.

'How am I to plough it?' she asked sharply.

'A plough, woman,' he said satirically.

'Will you drive it?' she snapped. 'A plough wants a man behind it. I've enough to plough now without turning fresh land.' She felt herself grow bitterly angry: 'You take the men away from us and send them to their deaths and then expect the land to plough itself. What do you know about the land? Nothing! You've sat on your backside in an office all your life and in five minutes you think you can learn what it takes a lifetime to learn. Who told you to come ordering here, anyway?'

'It's my duty.'

'Duty! If you want to do your duty, come and strip yourself and plough this fifteen-acre field. I'll pay you well.'

'What do I know about ploughing!' he said, angry too. 'I'll send you some German prisoners. They'll plough for you.'

'Prisoners?' She stiffened.

'Yes, woman, prisoners. How many shall I have sent?'

'None! I'll neither plough the field nor have the prisoners. While I can stand up I'll run this farm myself and when I want prisoners and advice for it I'll ask, not until.'

'My good woman, it's a Government order and if you don't obey you'll suffer.'

'Suffer?' she cried. 'Suffer?' She laughed in his face at the irony of it, the bitterness of all her suffering coming out in her voice. He turned and strode off, indignant, threatening obscure penalties.

In January the prisoners came, three humble, almost servile-looking men in bluish-grey uniform and little round caps of the same colour. They tramped up to the farm every morning under guard, their gait stiff and militarized and yet in some way crushed and soulless. In the dead of winter she was puzzled to find work for them, but after a rain-storm which flooded the yard and the gateway by the spinney she set them to clean and re-cut the dykes. They worked as though some unseen force were driving them. She went about marvelling, her distrust and suspicion of them changing to wonder as she saw the beautifully cut dykes with the blue clay shaved as though with a great razor and the perfect draining away of the brown water.

After watching the prisoners trenching one afternoon late in January she came up the cart-track under the willow-trees, looking at the field, which was lying fallow again, at every step she took. The furrows, beaten down with the winter rains and overgrown with autumn weeds, looked desolate and dead. She leaned on the gate after shutting it and gazed at the field in meditation. It was in her mind to let the field lie fallow for one year, as old Mortimer had done. The land, like all things, must rest sometimes. She would let it rest, perhaps, until her own vitality came back.

Still reflecting she crossed the paddock to the house. The sun was setting bleakly and cold spits of rain were beginning to drive across the fields from the south-west, the wind making a level moan in the farm-house. At the doorstep she turned and looked back. The prisoners were downing tools and were lining up ready to march away, bending their heads against the driving rain. A dark twilight was deepening rapidly and suddenly she felt overcome by desolation and loneliness of the winter land, the empty fields, the falling rain-swept gloom. The absence of life and light half-frightened her.

She entered the kitchen, where Anthea was setting out the cups and saucers for tea. The girl moved listlessly. Deborah, glad of the warm fire, the shifting and flickering light of the fire on the ceiling, the shining crockery, the girl's figure, knelt by the fire and warmed her hands, turning them from back to palm quickly and rubbing them one against another.

'The doctor was down by the brook, shooting,' she said. 'Did he come up?'

'He came in for a moment.'

Deborah rose from the fire and cut some slices of bread and began to make toast. She heard the girl's short sharp breathing. Her thin face was very white in the gloom. Suddenly she began:

'Would you mind if . . .' As suddenly she broke off, as though she lacked the courage or strength to go on.

Deborah looked up.

'Would you mind?' said the girl again. 'He wants me to marry him.'

Deborah felt her heart leap.

'But he must be fifty!' she cried.

'I know.'

'Do you like him?'

'Oh, yes, yes!'

Deborah turned the toast with an air of sudden resignation, her mouth set. She felt curiously shocked. The girl stood still, staring, and then spoke weakly.

'I'll do whatever you say,' she said.

'Do you want to marry him?'

'Yes.'

'Well, if you want to do it, there's no more to be said. You must do what you think best.'

She seemed with that to shake off her responsibility. Secretly she resigned herself to whatever might happen. She felt herself suddenly cut off from the girl.

Starling and the girl were married in the spring. She found it hard at first to grow used to the farm without the presence of another woman, but gradually the old stubbornness re-asserted itself. She flung herself into work again, hardening herself, labouring endlessly, trying to smother her solitude and the remembrance of death. But continually she felt old and broken up and she would ask herself why she should go on, why must she slave as she did, what did it all mean, what was the end?

The thought of Benjamin gave her strength again. Once a month he wrote from Palestine, cheering her with his garrulous letters and his old sardonic humour, and she smiled involuntarily at his jests, in spite of herself. 'When the blooming war is over,' he wrote, 'we'll have a tractor and I'll plough the big field twice over while you milk one cow.' Gradually she felt her thoughts shift from the dead to the living, her old common sense beginning to triumph over her pain. As the war drew to an end all her aspirations and hopes had become centred in Benjamin. She lived from day to day stretched with an agony of waiting and desperate hope for his safe return. When he returned she would give him the old Twelve-tree house. She would let him farm for himself. She would see him marry and prosper.

BOOK FOUR

Chapter 1

BENJAMIN did not come home until the March of 1919. He arrived by a train at six o'clock one evening and Deborah drove in the trap to fetch him from the station. His first words were loud and bantering. 'Still driving the old trap – same old cart-cushions, same old whip. Why don't you burn 'em?' She rapped him on the knuckles with the whip-handle in sharp humour. 'I'll burn you,' she said, looking him up and down. 'You'd keep going for a month or more, you great horse! What have they been feeding you on out there?' She ran her hand along his arms, pressing the thick, firm flesh, and she kept looking at his large, sun-tanned face with its cheeks taut and smooth with strength and health. She marvelled at him. He sat there beside her like a giant, filling more than half the cart-seat, the wood creaking beneath him. She stared at his hands resting on his knees, and she thought they were like great red hams; there was something almost terrifying about their largeness and strength. 'Well,' she said. 'It looks as if I shall be able to sack all the men now you're home. You'll do the work enough for fifty.'

'Ah,' he said, 'sack 'em and buy that tractor. That's what you want to do. Thought any more about that tractor?'

'Tractor?' she said. 'I've plenty else to think about. We've got horses, haven't we?'

'Tah! – horses. Who wants horses?' he said. 'I've rid enough horses this last four years to last me a lifetime. I want summat on wheels – wheels are the coming thing. Everything's going to be on wheels. We're all going to be on wheels. Mark my words.'

As they drove along the high road from the station the sun sank behind the dark line of woods in the west and the cold, still March twilight began to drop over the fields. The young wheat was showing in feathery lines of the brightest green and the sallows were half-gold, half-silver among the young hazel-trees, dusty-yellow with catkins, in the roadside copses. The earth was dried to a sand colour by wind and sunshine; the evening sky was clear, wind-blown, without a cloud. Benjamin looked at the wheat-green fields and the pastures and the catkined copses.

'Same old country,' he said.

'Glad to be back, aren't you?'

'Ah.'

She started. It was his father's voice, the same expression, the same dry, laconic intonation, making her think of Jess with the most vivid intimacy.

It was too dark to look at the farm that evening, but in the morning Benjamin wandered about the farm-yard in his shirt-sleeves, sizing up the place, prodding the pigs, smoothing the flanks of the horses. At eleven he came back to the house, calling her down from bed-making to cut him bread and cheese. She fluttered downstairs and cut the loaf and the cheese with an almost feverish joy, her whole being startled by the sound of his voice bellowing up the stairs like an echo of his father's. She cut herself some bread and cheese, not because she was hungry, but for the simple joy of eating with him.

'Same old farm,' he remarked.

'Same old farm, indeed!' she said, indignant. 'It's twice as big.'

'Ah, well! Same old farm only a bit bigger. Same old mullocking going-on, anyway.'

'You must remember we haven't had the men,' she said.

'Ah!'

It was so like his father's voice again that she started involuntarily. As he finished his bread and cheese she watched him incredulously, full of wonder. Soon he had swallowed his last mouthful and was looking for his jacket.

'Mind, man, it'll bite you,' she said. She spoke quickly, just as she might have spoken to Jess, and picked up his jacket from the back of the chair in which he had been sitting. 'You aren't going off anywhere?' she said.

'Ah, till dinner.' He struggled into his jacket, almost too small for his great, fleshy shoulders, and went towards the door.

'Aren't you going to put a collar on?' she said.

'Collar!' he snorted.

He strode off with his hands in his pockets. From the door she watched him go. He still walked with a faint rolling swagger which even his army erectness could not conceal. She went back to her beds, thinking of him, and afterwards she sat down and peeled many potatoes and stuffed the fowl she had killed for him the day before, happy in the thought of serving him.

At half-past twelve the kitchen was full of the rich odour of the baking fowl, the steam from the potatoes, and the crisp fragrance of browning pastry. As she stood over the fire, stirring the white sauce, she kept looking out of the window for a sign of Benjamin returning. The dinner, their first together for so long, was to be a great event. Now and then she opened the oven and looked at the fowl and basted it with spluttering brown gravy, sniffing the rich fragrance of baked flesh. The fowl was ready and the sauce had thickened to a white cream when a quarter to one struck, making her start for the door. The farm hands had knocked off for dinner and were sitting under a straw-stack in the sunshine, sheltered from the March wind, but there was no sign of Benjamin.

She went back and hovered about the oven and the table, waiting impatiently and anxiously, taking the fowl from the oven and putting it back again, prodding the softening potatoes continually, fretting over the spoiling dinner. She waited till half-past one and then miserably she carved a few slices of the fowl-breast and put the bird on the hearth and began to eat. Her stomach was empty, but her real hunger was dissipated in anxiety and disappointment. As she ate she made excuses for Benjamin. 'He's run across some old pals and he is staying there to dinner,' she thought, and it was a little consolation.

Nevertheless she kept the table set and the dinner warm after she had finished eating. There had been no pleasure in the meal. The sudden disappointment after a great expectation had left her tired and glum, and she sat by the fire staring and listening, too wretched to move.

At half-past two she heard his heavy steps on the wind-dried earth of the yard. She leapt up at once, full of relief and life, and took the fowl from the oven and carved off a leg and great portions of the breast, spooning a heap of spicy green stuffing beside the meat.

Outside, Benjamin hawked and spat and scraped his feet clumsily and then, pushing open the door, came into the kitchen. She looked up at once, smiling, but the smile vanished when she saw his face, unmistakably heavy with drink. Her heart seemed to beat in great irregular bounds. She tried to speak normally.

'Sit you down, while it's hot,' she said quickly.

He put his hands on the table and sat heavily down in his chair. She set the plate of fowl and potatoes before him, catching the odour of his breath as she leaned near him.

'You're a bit late,' she remarked.

'Ah.' He wiped his mouth with his hand, unsteadily. 'What's this?' he said heavily, peering at the food.

'Don't be a jabey. You can see what it is. Now don't act the goat, just because you've had a pint and a smell of the barmaid's breath.'

'Pint? Who's had a pint?' he flared up. 'Ain't touched a drop.'

'All right, all right. That's sufficient. If you're late you're late and that's all about it. Eat your dinner now. I've had bother enough to keep it hot.'

She stood by him and coaxed him to eat, and then humoured him while he ate. But his appetite had gone. He left his plate messy and unfinished, stumbling away from the table in disgust at last. She rattled the dirty crocks together, miserable and angry. He pushed his way out of the kitchen into fresh air. Later she heard him retching in the yard and her heart sickened as he was sick. He spent the afternoon on the sofa, his face hot in its stupor, sleeping heavily, and she let him sleep as he would.

For a week he slouched about the farm, doing nothing. He got drunk once or twice again. Every evening he dressed up and caught the new motor-bus to Staveston, going to the cinema or from pub to pub, showing off with a girl or two, always restless. At the farm he lazed about, smoking, shooting a little, working off the ill-effects of the night, his great body listless and sluggish.

She waited for him to begin some work, to lift a swill-bucket or harness a horse or milk a cow, to do some simple job on the land itself. She excused him instantly; he was not bored nor lazy but only resting himself, luxuriating quietly after the tension and strictness of war. She excused him patiently, her delight in him always so much greater than her disappointment.

'You might chop me some wood,' she said one afternoon. 'There's plenty in the spinney.'

Reluctantly he swaggered off with the axe and later she heard the ringing sound of the axe on the brittle oak boughs and the snap of wood. She listened with a deep satisfaction, but very soon the sounds ceased, and going to the kitchen door she saw Benjamin leaning on the spinney gate talking to a girl in a red hat. She heard the high, giggling voice of the girl and Benjamin's deep easy words flattering her and making her laugh afresh. The fence was between them and now and then Benjamin leaned over, trying to clasp the girl, but she wormed and dodged sinuously out of his reach, challenging him with laughter. Finally he vaulted the stile nimbly and caught her as she ran off, his great arms enveloping her as he tried to kiss her lowered face.

After watching them go laughing down the lane together, Deborah went into the spinney and found the axe and chopped the wood herself. As she chopped and then carried the wood into the house she felt a sharp jealousy rise up against the girl. 'Some giggling wench,' she thought bitterly. 'The fool.'

Unconsciously a tension grew up between them. It was in the air, on her part a reproachful silence, on his a sullen resentment that she should grudge him his pleasures. When he began to work at last there was no satisfaction in it for either of them; he worked on sufferance, giving every minute of time with reluctance. She was conscious of it to a point of pain. She tried always to understand his restlessness; it was the aftermath of war, she told herself, it was the convalescence after illness, enervating and fretful until the full strength had come back. She reasoned easily with her mind, but deep within her there was no conviction or rest. Since she had toiled and struggled until it was second nature to her she could not understand why work should not be as imperative as food and drink to him too. The way he downed tools early and swallowed his tea and swaggered off for the evening, not caring to spend a minute of ease with her, made her first dejected, then both lonely and embittered.

At haytime all her fears were suddenly destroyed. He became an unexpected slave to the mowing-machine; he drove it all day, tuning it up in the dinner-hour, his greasy fingers touching the screws and bolts lovingly, his whole being lost in the task of setting the knife or replacing it. He drove round and round the field tirelessly, like a child on a roundabout. The touch of the machine seemed to elevate him; he lost his old slouching listless air; his body tightened and quickened up as though it were a part of the machine itself.

'Best day's work you ever done,' he told her, 'the day you bought this. *Think* of the days when we had to mow every 'nation blade with a scythe. Licks me how we did it.'

'We worked,' she observed.

He became obsessed with a machine-madness, talking of nothing else. He spoke a machine-language which she did not understand. They must mechanize the farm, he told her; they must buy a tractor and a little petrol engine which would drive the chaff-cutter and the winnower; they must have a Ford in which to drive to market and take the milk to the station. He bought agricultural papers, showing her illustrations of the latest implements for saving labour.

She refused to be convinced, cautious as ever. He argued from the practical standpoint. 'A machine saves labour. You see that, don't you? A tractor does the work of three horses and a man and a boy. It saves labour – you save money.'

'And tractors are two for three ha'pence!' she said, satirically.

'Ah, they cost a bit at first, admitted, but look at the saving! Save their cost in a year.'

'So you say.'

In July they went together to the Agricultural Show. The trap had been painted a fresh yellow-and-black for the occasion. One side of the big show-field was lined with motor-cars. Seeing them, he was satirical about the trap. 'I wonder you don't want to come in a muck-cart,' he gibed. He armed her up and down the avenue of exhibits, dragging her from an electric milking-machine to see an electric water-pump and from that to an oil-engine and finally to a tractor working noisily in a cloud of petrol fumes. The implements were brilliantly painted in scarlet or green and their wheels and shafts flashed silver in the burning sunshine. She walked in a dazed fashion, marvelling. She looked a long time at a milk-cooler, fascinated in spite of herself, until Benjamin dragged her away to see a Ford, beautiful with shining enamel and new-smelling upholstery.

'Sit in it, go on,' he said, 'and see how you like it.'

'Don't be so silly, boy.'

'Go on, get up and sit aside o' me. They'll let you. Go on.'

'I'm sure I shan't. I should look well, with folks staring at me.'

Benjamin climbed into the car and sat in the driving-seat, fingering the polished driving-wheel and the gears. Deborah felt conspicuous and on edge, a little impatient with him.

'Were you thinking of buying?' said the salesman's voice.

'I'm sure I wasn't,' she said quickly, and walked off.

Benjamin stayed behind, talking easily with the salesman, discussing the points of the car, eyeing and caressing it as his father might have done a mare. Deborah waited a little distance off, fretting impatiently.

'How you dare, I don't know,' she said, when he joined her at last. 'I'm sure I daren't look at a thing when I'd no intention of buying.'

'That's what it's there for,' he argued. 'So's you can have a good look for nothing.'

'Licking the steam off!' she said in a huff. 'I went all hot and cold for you.'

'Well, that's what we want – a thing like that. Something to run about in quick – take the milk to the station in no time. Don't you *see* how we should save?'

'No, I don't!'

'You mean you won't see.'

'I don't see,' she insisted. 'When you have a farm of your own it'll be time enough to do as you like and have as many machines as you like, not until.'

They continued looking at the rows of implements, he like a child in his enthusiasm, she always cool and cautious, like an old dog, too sagacious to be led away.

'Know what we want?' he would say. 'A new drill – look at them horse-drills now – look at the rows you'd drill in one bout. All to save you work and you don't see it.'

'Your grandfather sowed his wheat broadcast, and he had ten quarter one year, I remember him saying. Ten quarter to an acre! There isn't a man in this show that's seen ten quarter.'

'Ah, his life was all work. Things have changed. You don't want to be sowing corn half the night, nor yet reaping it. We want a drill and a binder, that's what we want.'

By subtle manœuvres he took her to a place where many binders stood, like strange windmills, painted yellow and green, the paint shining like enamel in the sunshine. She stood fascinated, listening to the salesman tell how the corn was cut and swept up and tied in a sheaf and pitched out, all in a minute, in less time than it took to tell.

'Hear that?' said Benjamin. 'A kid could work it – reaps and ties and throws out in a jiffy. Come on, say we'll have one, come on. It'll save its cost in two harvests.'

All against herself she hesitated. He saw her hesitation, seizing upon it instantly.

'Come on, you know it's the thing. If you don't know when a thing's right nobody does.'

There was something flattering and persuasive about his words; they were so like an echo of his father's. And abruptly she succumbed and said 'All right.' A moment later she was in a panic.

'Ask the price,' she whispered. 'I'm not made of money. Ask the price first. Go on. . . .'

But Benjamin had edged away and she knew that she had committed herself.

The binder came in time for harvest. Benjamin handled it like a baby: it must not be touched or scratched, and only he

must drive it. Deborah, after the first shock of guilty extravagance had passed, watched it with pride as it rattled round
and round the golden square of wheat. She felt a pleasure in
the gay flicker of the sails, the soft swish of them on the dry
wheat-ears and the sight of Benjamin high on the seat, shouting above the din to the straining horses.

The last of her fears for him vanished; she felt secure again.
And then, one evening, Benjamin came home, hurled his cap
gaily into a chair and exclaimed:

'Well, you can get the flags out!'

'And what for?'

'For me!'

'And now what's the jape?'

'Going to be married,' he announced.

She stared at him in astonishment.

'Are you serious?' she said.

'Cut my throat if I tell a lie!' he declared.

She picked up her candle and struck a match, and lighting
the candle, prepared to go to bed, her lips set tight.

'You needn't be sniffy, need you?' he broke out, affronted.

'I don't think I am sniffy. But it's a bit sudden, surely?'

'What's that matter?' he asked, raising his voice. 'It's my
business. I'm marrying the girl.'

'And who is the girl?'

He was silent. She put her hands on the latch of the stairs'
door.

'All right! Her name's Ada. She's all right.'

'I hope she is. When did you meet her?'

'Last week. At a dance.'

'A dance?'

He was silent. Her stiff, cool attitude puzzled him.

She opened the stairs' door. 'Well, I'll say good night,' she
said.

'Can I bring her home?' he said suddenly.

'Well, I think I ought to see the sort of girl my son's going
to marry all in a hurry.'

The silent antagonism sprang up between them again. She
suffered a little, afraid of losing him so suddenly. The girl
arrived to tea on Sunday. Her name was Ada. All through
tea Deborah sat eyeing her secretly, trying to decide in her

own mind what character could lie behind the girl's powdered face, her bright, thin red lips, and her hollow voice with its forced, constant laugh. Sometimes, looking at her yellow, silk-smooth hair, close-cropped and full of lovely lights, she understood why Benjamin had fallen for her. But marriage was another matter. Finally she asked in her downright fashion:

'Why are you in such a hurry to get married, that's what I want to know.'

'Oh! we want to!' sang out the girl.

'I suppose so.'

'Well, what's the use of waiting? Once you start waiting you wait for ever. I know a woman who's been waiting for twenty years, if no more. You don't catch me waiting.'

'Where are you going to live?' said Deborah.

Benjamin and the girl looked quickly at each other.

'We thought you'd have us here,' Benjamin said.

'Tied to your mother's apron strings?' she flashed.

'You came here to live when you were married,' said the boy.

'Yes, and I learnt my lesson.'

'Well, where are we to live?'

'You're big enough to answer that yourself,' she said. 'You should think of these things beforehand.'

Benjamin argued, but she would not relent. If they couldn't marry and be independent they mustn't marry at all; she had no more to say. She was almost wilfully stubborn against them.

But afterwards, in secret, she felt troubled and she reproached herself. Wasn't she a little hard on them? Why was she like some old, ill-tempered dog?

Trying to reason things out, she thought at last of the Twelvetree house. She went about for some days ruminating, cautious as ever, exploring every point of the idea in her mind. She came to a decision at last and she spoke of it to Benjamin before the girl came to tea again on Sunday.

'If I put you in Twelvetree's old farm,' she said cautiously, 'could I trust you to look after things? Could Ada do the work? Don't say you could just for the sake of saying so. The farm was to have been David's – he was to farm that side and me this. Could you farm it?'

'On my own?'

'You'd come into it when I'm dead, in any case, so I'd better by half make it over to you while I am alive and I can see you reaping the benefit.'

'I'll farm it – I'll show you *how* to farm,' he said.

'It's a big thing,' she warned him.

'You'll see!' he said. 'When you see me across that hill ploughing a whole damn field while old Rook does a headland your eyes'll drop out. You'll see me. And harvest-time I'll cut my own wheat in the morning and yours in the afternoon. Farming! You don't know how to farm.'

'Well, we'll see,' she said.

Benjamin and Ada were married at Christmas. The girl lived in Staveston in a street of many box-like yellow brick houses, each like its neighbour; her father made boots in a back outhouse and there were six other children and an invalid brother living in the little, depressing, greasy-walled house. There were cars with fluttering white ribbons, however, to drive the guests to church; the church bells were rung; and after the wedding the bride and bridegroom went to London on honeymoon while the guests remained behind and ate and drank too much, merry-making till morning. Deborah watched the waste of money despondently.

Back at the farm she felt intolerably troubled and lonely. The trouble of one son bred also all the old, bitter, aching trouble of the other. She turned and tossed at night, without sleep, thinking of first one and then another, her mind diabolically sharp and awake. During the day she flung herself into the work of the farm, labouring desperately, never giving her mind time to develop a thought.

She was having the Twelvetree house papered and painted, and every day she went across to the farm to watch the workmen. The photographs of Benjamin and Ada, newly married, arrived one afternoon as she was setting out, and as she trudged up the rain-sodden hillside and slushed up to her boot-tops in the slime of the farm-yard she kept thinking of the slim, silk-dressed girl, with her powdered face and her narrow, small-breasted frame, and she could not help wondering how she would regard the farm-work, the swill-mixing, the cold root-cleaning of winter, the backache of planting and

217

hoeing, the eternal morning-to-night slaving in dirt and sweat.

It was a damp, windless December day. The empty house was full of the smell of fresh paint and size and the rank cigarette-smoke of the workmen. The tramp of feet on the bare floor-boards, the slapping of wet brushes and the voices of the men made hollow echoes about the place. Deborah wiped her boots carefully on an old sack at the kitchen door and then walked about the house, eyeing the workmen sharply.

'Here! are you cock-eyed, young man?' she called to a youth pasting up a frieze.

'Eh?'

'I'll give you eh! Look at the frieze, not at me. Do you call that straight?'

'Well, it *is* a bit out o' true, now you come to say.'

'I'll out o' true you!' she warned him. 'What do you think I'm paying for?'

As she walked away, the other workmen, who had ceased working to look at her, exchanged looks and winked at each other, amused by the sight of her short, black figure, her old-fashioned hat and her shaky umbrella.

She walked from room to room, upstairs and downstairs, criticizing the painting on a door, admiring the blue-flowered wall-paper on a wall. Now and then she stood at a window and looked out on the rain-dead land. She tried to defeat the sadness of the memories which kept rising up in her mind, but they persisted and at last she hurried downstairs and left the house, the thought of what might have been too sharp and cruel to bear.

It was still early when she returned to the farm. She stood in the kitchen and unpinned her hat and looked about her in bewilderment, her mind black with sudden despair and agony at her repeated memories. She felt not only intolerably lonely but utterly useless also, feeling that nothing in her life mattered or had ever mattered.

It was too early to get tea, and she stood looking out of the window across the farm-yard, at a loss for something to do. Idleness seemed to intensify her agony. She felt desperate, feeling suddenly that she must work until the last of her pain had been driven out by sheer fatigue.

She went upstairs and changed into her working boots and blouse and skirt. In the yard she found Rook and his son, recently demobilized, cleaning the pigsties. Taking a muck-fork she began to help them, working like a mad woman. Hardly knowing what she did, she strained at the wet pig-muck with all her strength, as though trying with every fork-ful to bury and suffocate the agony of her loss.

She worked silently and tirelessly. When the two men had knocked off she worked on into the twilight until the very pain of her fatigue began to drive out the pain of her mind. Every act was a blow flung at her own despair. She knew that it was her only salvation; she must work and go on working. Only work could bring her peace. She worked till darkness fell and went into the house at last reluctantly. She felt weary and chastened and she told herself that the worst had passed. But she felt uneasy and for the first time she began to be afraid of being alone with herself.

Chapter 2

As Deborah panted up the field-path to her son's house on a still November day, three years later, she felt that the hill seemed steeper every time she climbed it. She dug her umbrella hard into the soft turf in order to pull herself up, grunting to herself in disgust at her lack of breath and the stiffness of her limbs. All the way up the slope she heard the stuttering and moaning crescendo of a tractor, the noise magnified by the still air, and as she reached the breast of the hill she saw that Benjamin was ploughing a stubble field to the west of the farm-house. She paused to regain her breath and look at him. The tractor crawled along the strip of pale stubble like a big sleepy beetle, jerking and lurching and half-stopping at intervals, the engine missing fire or the wheels refusing to bite the wet land. A cloud of bluish smoke hung behind and above it. Deborah, pursing her lips tightly, watched the tractor travel the bout. At the end of the field Benjamin swung it round, half-turned it and reversed, bringing it round to the straight again. The engine revolved rapidly, roaring and belching clouds of smoke, and finally with a great jerk it stopped dead, half-pitching Benjamin from the driving-seat. It stood roaring fiercely as he accelerated, but there was no movement, and finally he shut off the engine and climbed down and bent over the bonnet. Deborah, hearing the tap of the spanner across the silent field, made a sound of impatience like a snort and then walked on to the house.

In the farm-yard a dozen dirty white hens were pecking about the cornstacks. She thought the stacks looked poorly built; they leaned and stooped at queer angles, as though a great storm had struck them. Plucking out an ear of corn as she passed she threshed it in her hands, blowing the chaff away gently. She munched a grain or two of the wheat, looked at the rest lying in her hand and then threw it away. 'Not fit for hen-food,' she thought. Crossing the rest of the yard she listened instinctively for the noise of pigs and cows, but it was too early for the cows to be up and the pigsties seemed empty. She believed that Benjamin had a sow about to farrow, and puzzled by the silence she went and looked into the sties. They were empty and the muck and straw in them were dry. She made a gesture of acute impatience. At the door of the house she knocked with the handle of her umbrella and then opened the door and called in her rather shrill voice:

'Anybody about?'

There was no answer except the crying of a baby.

'Anybody about?' she repeated. There was no answer still except the wailing of the child.

She wiped her boots on the sack at the door and went into the scullery. Her sharp eyes went at once to the floor, dirty with farm-muck and straw and hen-droppings, and she made a sound of disgust. The scullery led into the kitchen and she crossed the dirty floor and opened the door. In the room beyond Benjamin's wife was sitting before the fire, reading a novelette and warming her legs, absently rocking a perambulator with her free hand. The child in the perambulator was crying fretfully and another child, a boy of two, was creeping about under the table, guiding a toy train into reckless motions. The dirty dinner things were still on the table, and the floor, like the scullery floor, had not been swept or scrubbed for a long time. Deborah sniffed as she came in; the room smelt sour and stale.

Ada jumped up. 'Oh! you did give me a turn,' she said. 'I never heard you. It's this squawkin' kid. You can't hear yourself speak. Sit down. You'll find a chair somewhere if you're lucky.'

Deborah sat down in silence. The child in the perambulator, missing the rocking of his mother's hand, wailed out afresh as she hung her umbrella on the chair back.

'Oh! shut up!' snapped the girl. She rocked the perambulator angrily and said to Deborah: 'The damn kid makes me sick. Nothing but bawl, bawl, bawl, all day long.'

'Have you fed him?'

'Oh! I'm always feedin' him. He bawls when he wants to be fed and he bawls again when you've fed him. It's sickening.'

'Shall I nurse him a bit?' said Deborah.

'I don't care.'

Deborah took the child from the perambulator and held him in her arms, rocking herself and nursing him gradually to tranquillity. On the floor the elder child urged the train to a fury of noisy speed, crying lustily, filling the room with a great din.

'Oh! shut up!' cried the girl. 'If you want to make that row go and play in the stable. It's like Bedlam!'

'The child's all right,' said Deborah quietly. 'Let him be happy while he can.'

'They don't give you a minute's peace!' cried Ada. 'Will you shut up, Benny?'

The boy, bringing the train to a standstill by a table leg, made a sound of gently escaping steam. Infuriated, his mother suddenly bent and raised her hand to him threateningly. 'Shall I?' she whispered awfully. 'Shall I?' The boy cowered, turned white and instinctively retreated, staring with terrified eyes. 'I'll learn you!' said the girl. 'I'll fetch the devil to you! He'll have you!'

'No, no!' whimpered the boy.

'Well then, be quiet! Be quiet! You bawl again and see what you get.'

The boy retreated, silent and afraid. Deborah sat at first maddened and then with a pain in her heart at the sight of his white watching face stricken to silence by his mother's anger. The baby in her arms was dropping to sleep and she kept her voice to a whisper as she called the boy: 'Come and see what I've got for you.' As he came forward he half-watched his mother from the corner of his eyes, still afraid of her, and when Deborah found two pennies in her purse and gave them to him, one in each hand, he retreated in the same way, terrified even of her silence and stillness.

When the children were quiet at last Deborah sat looking at the girl. There was something frowsy and slovenly about her thin drab face, prematurely wrinkled, her uncombed hair and her dirty pink woollen jumper and short blue skirt.

'How are the hens?' said Deborah. 'Are they laying at all?'

'Laying! We don't get an egg apiece for breakfast.'

'What's the matter with them? What feed do you give them?'

'Feed! They take pot-luck most days. They find enough in the yard.'

'They want a bran-mash these cold mornings.'

'I dare say! But who's going to get a bran-mash here, with two kids to feed and dress? Not me, thank you.'

Deborah was silent. In her arms the baby was fast asleep, his head warm against her flat breast. After a time she spoke again:

'Has that sow pigged yet?' she asked the girl.

'Sow? Oh! we sold that.'

'Sold it? That sow was in pig! What the 'nation did he sell it for?'

'The tractor went wrong and wanted new parts or something and Ben thought the tractor was more important than the sow, so he sold her.'

'Well, he's sharp! He could have got credit for the parts, couldn't he?'

'He's finished gettin' credit.'

'But that sow was worth her weight in gold! She'd have had twelve or fourteen pigs, besides more litters.'

'Oh! well, it's done with now. I ain't sorry, either. I can't stand the rotten things.'

Deborah listened wretchedly; but suddenly she broke out sharply, unable to conceal her disgust:

'There's not much you can stand at all, is there?'

'No, there ain't! And I don't care who knows it! If I have another winter in this place I shall go scatty – muck, muck, muck, and nobody to talk to and kids bawling all day long. I'm sick of it.'

'You knew what you were coming to, didn't you?'

'Did I? Don't be funny.'

The bitterness of the voice made Deborah silent. She sat rocking the baby very gently, trying to reason out something to say.

'Why don't you get a woman in for the chickens and things?' she said at last.

'Very nice!' said the girl satirically. 'And who's going to pay?'

'You could get a girl for ten shillings a week.'

'I should like to see ten shillings a week for myself, let alone a servant. We're up to our necks in debt as it is.'

'In debt?' Deborah seemed to spit out the word as though it were foul to her taste.

'Yes, and too far in to get out in a hurry, either.'

'But what's he been *doing*?' Deborah demanded.

'Doing? What can you do with a place like this? We shouldn't make it pay if we lived here till Doomsday. Farming don't pay nowadays. It's finished.'

'You had a free start here,' Deborah reminded her. 'I was hoping you'd make a go of it, between you.'

'How? That's what I want to know.'

'Work!' she flashed. 'That's the only thing on the land. Work and patience and more work.' She got up suddenly and laid the baby in the perambulator again. 'I'll be going now. I want a word with Benjamin.' She kissed the baby quietly and then called the elder child to her and kissed him too. At the door she turned back and the sight of the unclean room, the dirty dinner things on the table and the frowsy girl made her feel quite sick.

'Work! That's the only thing!' she repeated. 'I never had time to read tales!'

'When I want your advice I'll ask fer it?' said the girl quickly, rising.

But Deborah had shut the door and was out of the house before the girl had finished speaking. Crossing the farm-yard hurriedly she tramped across the stubble field that Benjamin was ploughing. At the far end of the field the tractor still stood, silent now, with the figure of Benjamin bending over it absorbedly. A crowd of rooks pecking the new-turned land rose into straggling flight at her approach and flapped off and settled again on the farthest furrows. She did not look at them. She walked with bent head, observing the unlevel furrows and the hard broad imprint of the tractor-wheel on the rain-soft land. The stubble was choked with the dead and half-dead and still green weeds of summer and she knew what the harvest had been.

Standing by the tractor she looked on impassively. Benjamin drew his head away from the bonnet and wrenched the starting-handle and the engine began its chuttering, ticking unevenly, missing fire constantly. The boy climbed up into the driving-seat, grinning to his mother with his old sardonic look, calling to her in triumph above the din of the tractor:

'All right! We're off again!' A cloud of smoke filled the air with its stench, and Deborah retreated a pace or two, standing on the edge of the furrow, behind the plough. 'What d'yer think of her?' he called.

'Not much!' she flashed.

He did not hear. He had put the tractor into gear, and a moment later the engine quickened into deafening revolutions, starting into movement with a great bound.

As the tractor moved the plough seemed to leap suddenly from the furrow. Moving aside in alarm Deborah slipped on the greasy edge of the furrow. She lost her balance and fell heavily on her side; a bare flint on the furrow-edge caught her a sharp blow on the left side of her breast and she lay for a moment or two in an agony of pain, fighting desperately for breath. She tried to cry out, but no sound came, and Benjamin drove the tractor away up the land without seeing her.

When she dragged herself to her feet at last she had to stoop and catch her hand to her breast in pain. She felt sick and faint and every breath she took made a quick needle-stab at her breast. The field was swimming in a mist and the sound of the tractor turning at the bout-end was like far-off thunder. She staggered away to the gate in the hedge and leaned against it, gasping. The tractor roared into motion and began to return. As she heard it approaching she made a desperate effort and unhooked the gate. On the other side she rehooked it, biting her lips fiercely, and then waved her hand to Benjamin and turned and stumbled away down the field.

At the farm again she lay still on the couch. Presently she felt better, but getting up to give the hens their evening feed the pain stabbed her back to weakness again. She fell on her knees by the couch, biting her lips and fighting against the pain till she sank away into a cold faint of weakness.

She managed to drag herself to bed. She lay on the bed for a long time, too weak to take off her clothes. Every stab of pain seemed to age her. When she dragged herself downstairs at last to heat a poultice for her breast she felt like an old woman, cramped and feeble and half-dead. The poultice eased her and she undressed at last and lay in bed with the heat of the bran-bag pressing out the pain.

She fell asleep, but towards morning the pain woke her again. She lay on her back, fighting against it until the light began to filter through the dark blinds. Although her mind was alert and fresh after sleep the pain of her body seemed to arouse all the sleeping pains of her mind. Thinking first of David and then of Jess, she wondered as she had so often wondered what her life could have been if she had never lost them. Too exhausted to weep, she lay with a tormenting sense of hopelessness and emptiness that was worse to bear than her physical pain.

After a day or two the pain lessened. There were hours together when she felt nothing of it at all. But she was broken up, bodily and mentally crushed. If her spirit was vigorous her body was too exhausted to obey it, or if her body felt strong again her mind was absorbed in pain and the memory of former pain. When she tried to rest there was a fresh torment in inactivity. She had never been ill; she never had time to be idle. It was like a sin to lie there on the couch and hear the milk buckets clank in the cow-house or the pigs squealing to be fed, knowing she could do nothing. She reproached herself endlessly. Such a trivial thing! What was the matter with her? Could she do nothing against the repetition of pain? Sometimes she looked in the glass and was horrified by her sick, yellowish face and her grey hair. She condemned herself bitterly.

In December, Rook, coming for orders one morning, said to her in the kitchen:

'You don't look half-well, missus.'

'Who said so? I'm all right.'

'You look run down, like.'

Run down? Who's run down? I'm not so young as I was, that's all.' She spoke with all her old, flashing, downright spirit.

'I've been wondering about that field behind the spinney,' Rook said. 'It's about time we got it ploughed up and had summat in, ain't it?'

'It is,' she said. 'I'll come and look at it.'

She went across the paddock with him. They leaned together on the gate and looked at the field in silence. It was a
cloudy morning, and the unbroken land, beaten down by
rain, with the stones washed up white and stark among the
weeds, looked poor and dead.

'A bit o' beans might do all right, missus,' Rook said.

'When did we have beans on it last?' she said.

'Four years back.'

She did not speak. For the first time she felt that she did
not care if the land grew beans or charlock, wheat or coltsfoot.
She stared at the field blankly and then turned away.

'Let it lay another year,' she said. 'A rest won't hurt it.'

The winter tried her desperately. She forced herself to
work, but sometimes in the afternoons she went back indoors
on some pretext and rested secretly. The unutterable loneliness she had begun to feel at the end of the war began to
increase. She kept away from Benjamin, too tired or too
depressed by the last visit to go up to the farm again. If they
were in debt, she told herself, they were in, and they must
suffer. She had done enough. She tried to forget the dirty
house, Benjamin's lazy wife and the poverty-stricken look of
the place.

But in March she heard news that brought them all vividly
into her life again. Rook said one morning:

'Bad business up there.' He jerked his thumb towards the
farm on the hill.

'What? What is it? What is it?'

'The bums are in. Short notice of sale for Thursday.
They're clearing out.'

'Benjamin's clearing out? Benjamin?'

She rushed into the house without another word. She
snatched up her hat and coat and put them on. For one
moment she felt that she must act desperately: she must go up
at once and see Benjamin and talk with him and arrange
something. But suddenly it all vanished. She felt that she
could not go. If they were finished, they were finished. Let
the farm be sold and let them go their own way. She would
do nothing. Moreover, she felt bitterly that they did not need
her help.

227

Nevertheless she could not rest for thinking of them, and on Friday, not daring to go herself, she sent Rook to the sale. He was to buy the cows and the hens and the two corn-wagons, and he was to run up anything he saw going cheaply and buy that too.

She waited all day in agony for him to come back. He returned at tea-time. He had bought the cows and hens and the wagons and some oddments.

'Did you see Benjamin?' she said.

'No. They were saying he'd gone off about some partnership in a motor-bus. He's going to run from all the villages into market. That's what he's selling up for.'

'What next! My goodness gracious. What next will he do? Were Ada and the children about?'

'They say they're living with her mother.'

She tossed her head with all her old stoical resignation, trying to conceal her disgust and pain.

Chapter 3

THE little yellow motor-bus turned out of the village and hummed away down the hill like a quick, fussy wasp, the women who had climbed in at the church jolting and rocking from side to side with the speed, clasping their baskets tight on their laps. The engine shook and rattled and hummed like a threshing-drum, but at the top of the hill Benjamin shut off the engine and the bus coasted smoothly downhill, the cool air rushing in at the windows to drive away the stifling engine heat and the warmth of the July sun.

At the bottom of the hill a small figure in black was waving an umbrella, signalling him to stop, and he put on his brakes and brought the bus to a standstill. It was his mother. He opened the door for her to climb in and she pulled herself up by the door-handle, panting a little. He half-opened his leather cash-bag in readiness to give her change for her fare, but she said, 'Here, take for the return journey as well,' and he took the money without a word. She sat down heavily in the nearest seat, as though she were very tired, and he put in the clutch and let the bus glide away.

As the bus gathered speed she sat with her lips very tight, looking fixedly out of the window at the passing land. The potato fields were a dark green, the wheat fields a greenish yellow, the first oat crops ripening to whiteness under the July sun. The woods were sombre and still under the blaze of sunshine and in the distance the heat danced and quivered above the dark hedgerows. She stared meditatively, as though she did not see the land. Now and then she moved in her seat, restlessly. The jolting of the bus shook her mercilessly. At every swerve and lurch the pain came at her like a knife; it stabbed quickly and withdrew and then stabbed again and withdrew again, wounding her doubly in a single place, just beneath her heart.

For nearly eighteen months she had ridden in the bus to

market. Sometimes on days of stormy or bitter weather she would be the only passenger, and the empty bus would lurch and rattle more furiously, aggravating her pain. She told herself that she travelled by the bus because it was quick and convenient, that she had given up the trap because she dared not trust herself to drive. Nevertheless her eyes would constantly rest on the figure of Benjamin in the driving-seat, an expression of quiet pleasure and admiration coming over her face in spite of herself.

The bus swerved into the town and fussed through the streets and came to rest in the market-place. Benjamin flung open the door and the passengers began to alight. Deborah sat still, waiting for the bus to empty, and when the last passenger had alighted Benjamin turned and saw her sitting there, looking at him expectantly.

'I hope you're all right, my boy?' she said.

'Ah,' he said, 'can't grumble.'

They sat silent. He had grown even bigger, his face florid and a little coarse, his lips ripe and sullen and his eyes sombre and bloodshot, as though he were habitually drinking.

'How are the children?' she said.

'Benny's middlin'.'

He sat with his hand on the brake, anxious to start off again, speaking reluctantly.

'Shall I go and see him?' she said.

'Please yourself.'

'What time will you go home for tea?'

'Four.'

'I'll come down about then,' she said.

He did not speak. In silence she picked up her bag and her umbrella and climbed down to the pavement. He drove the bus away before she had time to collect herself and turn to look.

She walked about the town with some of her old briskness, doing her shopping, but by four o'clock she felt tired and beaten. She was shocked sometimes to see her reflection in the shop-windows, to see how bent her body was and how thin and drawn her face.

As she walked away from the market through the streets to where Benjamin lived she was glad of her umbrella to pull herself along. The sun poured down hot and stifling and the heat struck up again from the white pavements, making her eyes drawn and tired. The street was like a long gulley running from north to south and every house on either side was like its neighbour, a little brick box with a grey slate lid. Benjamin lived at the far end of the street. She remembered the house because of the yellow curtains, which had previously hung in the parlour at the farm.

She knocked at the door and waited. At the farm she would have knocked and opened and called in 'Anybody about?' but here she was never sure of her welcome. She waited uneasily. She heard a scuffle of feet and then children's voices, and a moment later Ada, holding a child in her arms, opened the door a fraction and peered out.

'Oh! it's you,' she said.

'Yes. I told Benjamin I should be coming down.'

'Oh! did you? Well, he ain't here yet.'

'He said Benny was bad. I thought I must come and see how he was. Is he better?'

'Oh! he ain't half so bad as he'd like to make out.'

'Can I come in?'

'Come in if you like.' Ada's voice was hard and reluctant. She pushed open the door another inch or two and retreated into the room, leaving Deborah to come in and shut the door.

The door opened straight from the street into the living-room and Deborah sat down heavily on a chair just inside the door. The room reminded her of the kitchen at the farm: it had the same sour smell, the same look of untidiness. Its varnished wall-paper was peeling and greasy and the floor-boards bare except for odd lengths of curling linoleum and carpet. But Deborah saw with relief that the table was laid for tea and that the kettle was boiling over a gas-ring on the hearth. She began to hope desperately that she would be asked to have a cup.

Ada stood jogging the baby on her hip. It was her third child, a girl of seven months; under the table the second child was crawling and in a chair in one corner sat Benny, looking at her with mute, timid eyes, his face sick and white with pain. Whenever she looked at him now she was reminded of David; he had the same pale, fretful, questioning look, as though he only half-understood what was going on about him.

231

She hung her umbrella on the chair and went to him and half-knelt by him.

'What's the matter with Benny?' she said.

He turned away from her, half-shaking his head.

'What's the matter?' He would not answer, and presently Ada said sharply:

'Don't be so daft, boy. Let her look at your ear. He's a damn' nuisance,' she went on. 'He won't let you touch him. He won't do anything. I've had enough, straight.'

'Let me look,' said Deborah gently. 'Let me look.'

She coaxed him softly and presently he turned his head slowly, cringing with fear and pain. A moment later she drew in her breath sharply. Suddenly she sprang to her feet with all her old briskness and strength of decision. On his ear there was a large abscess, oozing and ready to burst. The flesh of his neck was stiff and drawn with pain.

'I'm going for the doctor to that child at once. Why didn't you send for him before?'

'He wouldn't let me do anything! He wouldn't let me look at him.'

'He let me look! And he'll let a doctor look, I know!'

She picked up her umbrella, but she had not time to move again before the door opened. Benjamin walked in. His breath was rank with drink and his movements were heavy and stupefied.

'Hullo!' he greeted her. 'Off already?'

'Yes,' she said briskly. 'I'm off for the doctor.'

'Thought you looked middlin',' he said heavily.

'Middlin'! I'm all right! It's that child of yours. You ought to be ashamed of yourself.'

'What's that?' he muttered. 'I know what's wrong with him without asking you. You leave him to me.'

'Leave him to you!' she flashed. 'I should think he's been left to you long enough. Why, the child's not even clean.'

'What?'

'If he'd been clean this wouldn't have happened!'

She stood facing him, small, sharp, dynamic, regarding his big heavy face, flushed by drink and his rising temper, with all the contempt and fearlessness of her being.

'Tell her straight, I would,' said Ada.

232

'It's you he ought to tell straight!' flashed Deborah. 'Why don't you wash the child?'

'Who said I didn't wash it? Who said I didn't? You interfere too much by half. If you'd given us a lift up when we needed it we shouldn't have been here, but you never came near, did you? You took damn' good care to keep away. I know your sort! Telling me I don't wash the child! We don't want your help. We're as good as you, any day!'

'Ah!' Benjamin muttered.

'Don't you mutter at me, my boy!' Deborah whipped out. 'I've given you chances enough for a dozen men. You're big and lazy, though. Too big and lazy to wash your own children, that's what you are!'

'What's that?' he roared. 'Get out afore I do summat I s'll wish I hadn't! Go on!'

'I'm going,' she said calmly. 'Don't lose your temper.'

'Who's losing his temper? Who's losing his temper?'

'Tell her straight, I would,' said Ada. 'I've about had enough. Tell her straight.'

'Get out of this house and don't come back!' shouted Benjamin.

She stood firm, facing him calmly.

'I'll go when I'm ready.'

'Then you'd better be ready quick!' he shouted.

'I'd be ashamed of myself,' she said. 'Shouting about.'

'Go on! Get out,' said Ada. 'How many more times d'ye want telling?'

The words cut her bitterly, and suddenly she opened the door and went out proudly, neither speaking nor looking back.

The door of the house slammed shut with a noise that seemed to strike straight at her heart, waking the pain there. She hurried on with the consciousness of the pain deepening and sharpening to something more than a mere physical pain until she felt unhappy down to the very core of her being, all her hope and strength obliterated by a black wretchedness which she felt was too vast and deep ever to be washed away again.

She hurried mechanically to Starling's surgery and left a message for him to go to the child that evening.

233

From the surgery she walked straight out of the town, hardly knowing what she was doing. As she hastened along on the grass of the roadside in the hot sunshine she tried not to think of what had happened, but the bitterness of it crept into her most trivial thought. She walked with her old quick, almost scuffling walk, half-consciously hoping to obliterate the pain of her mind by exhausting herself. The sweat broke out heavily under her hot black clothes and she felt intolerably thirsty, but she knew that if she once paused, even for a second, she might never go on again. Half-way to the farm she heard the moan of a motor-bus behind her and presently Benjamin's little bus flew past her recklessly. She watched it race along the road, buzzing like an angry wasp, until it was lost behind a belt of trees.

At the farm Rook was knocking off and she met him crossing the paddock.

'Everything all right?' she said.

'Yes,' he said.

She saw him looking at her closely.

'What's the matter?' he asked. 'You look middlin'.'

'Me? I'm all right! What's the matter with me? I'm all right, man.'

She spoke quickly, with a sort of bluff assurance, but he stared at her again as he spoke:

'You want to be careful at your age. It's tidy hot, you know.'

'What if it is?' she snapped.

She walked on, as though impatient with him, and after watching her hurry into the house Rook walked on himself, meditating a little about her. He thought she looked sick and wild; he had noticed something wrong with her all summer. After opening the gate to go down the lane he stood thinking uneasily for a moment or two and then suddenly he hooked the gate shut again and walked back across the paddock to the farm-house.

In the yard he stood and listened, hearing sounds from the kitchen. The door stood wide open. Coming nearer he could see the figure of Deborah sitting at the table. Her head was bowed and half-hidden by her hands and she was crying bitterly. He did not know what to do, and after a moment of

234

embarrassed hesitation he walked away. He could hear the sound of her crying all the way across the paddock. She was crying as though she would never stop, as though she were weeping out her life.

Chapter 4

ON a late September morning Deborah was busy in the kitchen with her bread, waiting for the sponge to rise under the pink-and-white cloth covering the copper-coloured panchion on the hearth. Harvest was over and there had been a spell of warm, tranquil weather, and she felt rested and stronger already. She had fought against her bodily pain and the trouble of Benjamin with all her old stoicism and her old tendency to belittle all that went against her, so that whenever Benjamin's words rankled in her mind she made herself remember that they had been spoken in the heat of passion, and when the pain in her side came on she scorned herself for her weakness in not being able to bear such a trivial thing. She had not seen Benjamin since the quarrel. A week later, at the usual time, she had gone to catch the bus, determined not to alter her plans for him, but the bus had not come, and after waiting for more than half an hour she had come wearily back up the hill to the farm again. She did not know if Benjamin had changed his time-table or if he had gone bankrupt or what had happened. During harvest she heard that the bus was running again, but she was too busy to go and catch it, and when she finally travelled by it after harvest Benjamin was no longer driving. The bus had been painted over afresh and a red-haired young man in a clean white smock and peak-cap was driving. 'Where's the old driver?' she said to him. 'Ask me another,' he said. 'This is a new company.' In Staveston she went to the house, intending to inquire in spite of everything and to offer help if they needed it, but there were strange curtains at the window and the doorstep shone like a block of snow. She knew that they could no longer live there.

She gained a curious happiness from her ignorance. No news, she told herself, was good news; she had never been the one to fret for nothing. Sooner or later she would hear again.

If he were dead she would have cause to fret, but she would never fret for the living.

Nevertheless she found herself thinking of him uneasily as she stood quietly waiting for the sponge to rise. Suddenly, as though in answer to her thoughts, she fancied she heard his voice in the yard outside. She listened quietly; the voice broke off and began again and she felt sure it must be.

She knelt down by the fire and poked it quickly and then listened. Footsteps were coming across the yard and she heard them halt by the door.

'Come in,' she said.

Heavy feet scraped on the dry step. Looking up she saw a heavy, burly figure come across the threshold. She thought for one instant that it was Benjamin. But abruptly she leapt to her feet, staring.

'Ah, you may well stare,' said Jess.

They stood looking at each other, half-stupid, half-uneasy, for a second or two, she trembling a little, he not attempting to come a step farther in, until she spoke at last:

'Well, I suppose you'd better come in,' she said.

He came in. They stared at each other again, not knowing what to do or say. 'Bread day?' he said finally, trying to make his voice easy. She did not answer.

The sponge was rising in the panchion. She bent down and lifted the cloth and looked at it and then dropped the cloth again. With heavy eyes he stood and watched her; it was the same panchion she had always used; he recognized it by the red chip along the edge, as though he had seen it only yesterday.

In silence she busied herself with the bread. His eyes rested alternately upon her and upon familiar objects in the kitchen. When his eyes were no longer fixed on her, she in turn watched him. Though she would have known him anywhere he had changed greatly. He looked gaunt and old; the big powerful frame had not changed, but the flesh had hardened and dried, and the skin, which had been so fresh and tight, had withered and wrinkled. His face had a dead grey colour, his eyes were yellowish along the edges of the whites, and his hair showed a dirty grey colour from under his shapeless and colourless cap. She noticed something fresh about him each time she looked at him, but it was not until she had looked four or five times that she noticed his hands. All the time they were trembling violently. Soon she noticed that his lips were trembling also. Suddenly he saw that she noticed it and he clenched his hands together in an effort to keep them still, but every now and then they began to tremble involuntarily again. He sat like a man recovering from nervous illness. She could see him fighting to keep himself still, to keep up an appearance of his old strength before her.

When the dough was ready she began to pound it on the bare table, trying to conceal her inward trembling as desperately as he tried to conceal the quivering of his lips and hands. She gave up trying to collect her thoughts at last and only stared at him silently.

His jacket and trousers were crumpled and spattered with mud, and little specks of chaff and straw were clinging to the dirty cloth and to his cap and his neck-muffler.

'You've been sleeping rough,' she said suddenly.

He leaned forward as she spoke.

'Eh?' he said.

'Where did you sleep last night?' she said.

'Eh?' he said. She repeated what she had said the first time and he understood. 'Best I could find,' he said. His manner seemed strange and distant.

'Can't you hear?' she said.

'Eh?'

It was only a second or two later that his mind grasped the words. An expression of understanding passed over his face.

'Ah,' he said. 'I've been a bit deaf this two year.'

Having nothing to say she went on kneading the dough and cutting it into loaf-shapes for the tins. He looked round the kitchen again. The place was neat and bright, the dresser scrubbed white as a bleached bone, the plates like rows of blue-and-white mirrors; the woodwork had been painted and the hens no longer came in and dirtied the floor with their grey droppings; on the dresser stood a new lamp with a pink shade and a row of pendant beads along the edge of the shade. There was an air of comfort and prosperity about the place which impressed him powerfully. Outside he had noticed also the big wheat-ricks, the new white gates about the yard and the new-fashioned chicken-houses as he had come up through the spinney.

'Ain't done amiss,' he said tentatively.

She banged the dough almost impatiently. His words made clear to her the very essence of the situation. It maddened her suddenly that he should walk calmly in after so many years and comment on all her labour and sacrifice and suffering with words that were faintly grudging and envious, as though she had taken something that should have been his. She looked up sharply, with her bitter thoughts ready to shape into words, but suddenly she checked herself, feeling a curious pity for him beginning to assert itself in spite of her. He looked so old and tired and broken-up and she could not bear the everlasting trembling of his hands.

'Now you have come, are you going to stop?' she said.

'Eh?' He leaned forward sharply, but before she could repeat her words their meaning had penetrated to his mind.

'I come up to see if you'd got a bit of a jacket to give away.' He showed her his torn sleeves and a slit in one pocket. 'This ain't much good.'

She wanted to shout at him: 'Why didn't you come before? What makes you creep back after all this time?' but she could not do it. Something finer and softer kept asserting itself insistently within her, governing the tone of her voice and the things she said.

'Where were you going when you decided to come?' she said, speaking louder.

'Birmingham,' he said. 'I heard of a job there.'

She moved across to put her bread into the oven. Going back she saw his boots. They were breaking out at the toes and they had been laced with pieces of string.

'You wouldn't walk far,' she said.

They faced each other again, the strangeness between them lessening already and a hint of the old remote intimacy taking its place. As it increased she knew if he wanted to stay she would not turn him out. Yet she hesitated to say so.

She wiped the flour from the table with a damp cloth, scrubbing away every fleck of dough, scratching spots clean with her finger-nail. As the bread began to bake, sending out a hot fragrance, she glanced furtively at the clock on the mantelpiece. It was nearly twelve. Impulsively she took the white cloth from the table-drawer and spread it, smoothing it quickly with her flat hands. All the time he was watching her and breathing in the sweet smell of the bread, sitting there quite still except for the twitching of his hands and lips. Over the knives and forks she hesitated for a moment. Would he expect to stay? And suddenly she saw him sniff the bread, thinking she was not looking at him, a long eager breath of aching hunger. She laid two places immediately, at the ends of the table, so that they faced each other.

Seeing her set two places, and two only, he stared and looked puzzled. She knew a second later what was troubling him. Instantly she tried to divert his thoughts.

'You can stop and have a bite if you care,' she said. 'It's cold, but you're welcome.' She looked at his travel-dirty face and hands. 'You can go and wash while I dish up if you like.'

'Ah, I shan't bother,' he said. 'A bit o' muck more or less won't hurt me.'

'Just as you please,' she said stiffly.

The potatoes were boiling on the fire and she took off the saucepan lid and forked them gently. She wondered how often she had heard him say those words and how often she had made him wash the plough-muck or stable-muck from his hands before she would put the food before him. After looking at the bread in the oven she strained the potatoes and brought them to the table in their dish, following with the cold breast of mutton.

'Well, it's ready,' she said finally, 'if you are.'

'Ah.' He drew up his chair awkwardly, scraping it along the bare bricks as he had always done.

She cut the meat and gave him his plateful, pushing the potato-dish towards him. As he took it she saw him looking about him half-expectantly again. She cut her own meat desperately, bending her head.

'Help yourself to potatoes,' she said.

He spooned up the potatoes, the spoon shaking violently. There were moments when his hand hung stiff and paralysed above his plate, so that he looked like a clock-work figure which had run down in the middle of a simple act. It made him look half-pathetic, half-ludicrous.

He picked up his knife and fork at last. But before he could eat his thoughts came to his lips bluntly:

'Ain't the boys about?' he asked her.

She spoke in a hard voice, with difficulty:

'Benjamin's in business, in the motor business in Staveston. He was restless after the war. He felt he couldn't take to farming again.'

She turned away from the table to look at the bread again, opening and shutting the door of the oven quickly.

'Where's David?' she heard him say.

She found it impossible to lift her head in order to speak, and she remained bending and half-whispered:

'He was killed in the war.'

'Eh?' he said, not hearing.

'He's dead!' she said loudly.

He was watching her lips as she spoke the second time, and he understood and was silent. They went on eating together. Her appetite had gone and she ate mechanically, the food meaning nothing to her. He ate slowly, his trembling hands travelling backwards and forwards from his mouth to his plate laboriously.

'War?' he asked at last.

She nodded. He had finished the meat and potatoes. 'There's some pudding,' she said. 'You'll have some?'

'Ah, I don't mind if I do.'

It was a rice pudding, baked within a crust, with currants swollen fat among the steaming rice; his mother had baked it that way. She knew that he liked it and she filled up his plate, taking none for herself, and when he had finished the first plateful she pushed the dish towards him, saying:

'You'd better finish it up. I've had enough. Go on.'

He looked at her acutely as he took the dish.

'You don't look very lively,' he said.

'I'm all right!' she flashed at once. 'I'm a bit older than when you saw me last, that's all.'

The bitter flash of her words silenced him for a moment. He saw the old sharp pursing of her lips, expressing all the strength and uncompromising determination of her nature.

'I ain't such a chicken myself,' he said.

For a moment they gazed at each other openly, the old antagonism awake again, but the moment passed quickly. They had no longer the strength for quarrelling, nor the time, nor the inclination; the meaning and purpose, if ever there had been meaning and purpose in it, had long ago been lost. Looking at his quivering hands again and remembering his broken boots she was simply troubled instead.

'You're never going to walk to Birmingham?' she said, 'are you?'

'Thought about it.'

'What sort of a job do you think you'll get? There's young men can't get jobs.'

'I know. I see 'em – up and down the country, kids, never had no work.'

Looking at his trembling hands and dissipated eyes and his broken-up body, she wondered what chance he thought he could have. She marvelled at the depth of his fortitude and hope, pitying him again in spite of herself.

'You'd better stop here,' she said bluntly. 'You could do light work and I'd pay you and keep you.'

'Pay me?'

'That makes me independent.'

'Ah,' he said.

Soon afterwards she went upstairs and came down again with an old suit and a shirt and a pair of boots which had once been David's. She aired them briefly before the fire and then gave them to him.

'You better go up and put these on,' she said. 'I shall have my bread burning.'

When he came downstairs again she was washing up the dinner things. She turned and looked at him as he came into the room. She started involuntarily as she saw him. He looked to her for one moment like the embodiment of his own sons, wearing the clothes of one and having the big, careless body and the swaggering movements of the other. He had brought his boots downstairs in his hand and he came to the fire and sat down and pulled them on, exactly as he had always done.

'What d'ye want me to do?' he said, standing up.

'They're thatching the stacks. You'd better see Rook – he'll give you a job.'

'Rook? Rook Baxter?'

'Yes,' she said. She had been thinking. 'I'll pay you by the hour,' she said. 'Then if you don't like it you can leave off and draw your money.'

'All right,' he said. 'You're boss.'

When he had gone she sat down, telling herself repeatedly that she must think things out. But as she sat there she began to feel gradually that there was nothing to think out. If he had come back he had come, and that was all. There was something natural and inevitable about his drifting home. At moments she wanted to be angry about it all, about his colossal coolness in walking in after twenty years as though he had never gone away, but she felt always that anger was useless against the simple fact itself. For years she had thought dimly that he might return, cherishing the possibility of it secretly; there was no use in anger and pride now that he had returned.

He worked on the stacks all afternoon. From the dairy window she saw him going slowly to and fro with the straw, his movements like those of an old man; she saw him rest often, sticking his fork in the earth and shouldering all his weight upon it. The stacks were solid and sound as houses and she saw him sometimes lift his eyes to admire them. Once he pulled an ear from the wheat stack and threshed it slowly in his tottering hands, spilling the grains with the husks, and then threw his hand unsteadily to his mouth, munching the hard, sun-golden grain as he moved away to work again. She remembered his teaching her to thresh a wheat-ear in her hands in that way. As she watched him she felt uneasy with regret, half-dreading the time when he would come back to the house.

He came in again about four o'clock. He was finished. As he sat down heavily she thought his hands twitched more violently and that he looked sick and tired. His eyes were yellow and dead and as he wiped his hand across his brow she seemed to feel the cold clamminess of it in her bones.

'What's the matter, man?' she said.

He did not hear; his hands gave a sudden convulsive start; he could not control himself.

'Good gracious! What's the matter with you?' she said in a loud voice.

'Eh?' He quivered terribly. 'Give me a drink,' he said. 'I s'll be all right.'

She kept a bottle each of whisky and brandy in the kitchen cupboard, drinking a little of one or the other sometimes to ease the pain in her side. Taking down the brandy she poured out a wine-glassful and gave it to him quickly and he drank it off in a second, gasping. It did not stop his trembling. But after a moment the sick look went out of his face.

'What's the matter with you?' she asked, looking at him closely.

'That damned gas. I got it proper.'

'Then you went?'

He did not answer.

'I'll get some tea,' she said, corking up the brandy bottle and putting it back into the cupboard again.

Afterwards she was glad of the chance to slip away and feed the chickens and collect the eggs before darkness fell. Before she left the house she said to him:

'You can drive down with Rook's son to the station if you like. He takes the milk at five.'

'Ah, I might do that,' he said, getting up.

With relief she saw him drive in the float, half-wishing he had gone for ever again. She dreaded the evening; she had grown used to loneliness, and the thought of another presence about the house, and his presence more than all others, filled her with a fretting uneasiness. She lingered about among the chickens as long as she could in the twilight, shutting each trap-door with extreme care and counting every bird in every coop.

It was dark when she entered the house again. He was sitting huddled before the fire, hardly visible in its feeble glow. He had let the fire die down – an old trick with him. She piled it up again with wood and coal, flinging on the fuel impatiently, making him stir guiltily in his chair. Without a word she lit the lamp. He blinked in the bright, pinkish rays.

In the evenings she sat and read the newspaper and since she read slowly it lasted her till bedtime. She sat before the fire and looked at the front page; her eyes were still strong and she could read even the smallest print easily. For a moment she read in silence and then her conscience hurt her. She divided the paper and handed a part to Jess.

He shook his head. 'I can't see,' he said. 'I'm as blind as a bat. I can just make out the picture bits, that's all.'

With an unpleasant lump in her throat she gave the picture page. He took it and held it at arm's length, letting the lamp-light fall full upon it, and squinted his eyes.

She read on in a silence that seemed sometimes too intense and deep to bear; the flutter of the newspaper, the clock-tick and the fall of the fire were gigantic noises that made her start sometimes and look up in alarm. She had an illusion that she was waiting for some momentous happening. She stared with only a pretence of reading until the tension of silence and waiting exhausted her. She felt her heart leap with relief when he dropped his paper to his knee and spoke.

'Rum times,' he said.

'Yes.'

'What are we coming to?'

'I'm sure I don't know.'

'Won't ever be the same again, will it?'

She shook her head. The conversation faltered and the silence returned.

She had given up trying to read; she was merely holding up the paper before her, staring in thought, the shock of his return making itself felt painfully in the smallest things. She began to wonder more and more about him. Where had he been? What had he been doing? Why should he come back? Too proud to ask him she lost herself in a tangle of conjecture, giving it up wearily at last. With her common sense coming back to her, she wondered instead what he was going to do, how they were going to take up the threads of their life together again.

To her relief he spoke once more.

'Land's in a poor way,' he said.

'The land's all right,' she said quickly. 'It's the people on it. The land's still the same as ever.'

It silenced him. Almost at once she regretted it acutely. The silence was unbearable; she had to speak.

'Do you want some supper?' she said desperately.

'When you're ready,' he said.

It was still early, but she folded up the newspaper and tucked it under the chair-cushion and laid the supper-cloth, bringing cold meat and cheese and pickles to the table, with water to drink. As she saw him eye the water with a faint disappointment, she thought bitterly: 'If you're not satisfied you go elsewhere, Mister Particular. You won't get me to kill any fatted calf for you.'

They ate in silence. He did not touch the water. After supper she said:

'You can sleep in Benjamin's old room.'

'Ah.'

She sat infuriated: no thanks, not a word, not even a gesture of gratitude! From the mantelpiece she took down her candle and straightened the wick. As she did so she saw that his hands were quivering violently again. Her pity rushed up at once and she said:

'Can't do anything for that everlasting trembling?'

'Give me another drop o' brandy.'

While he drank another wine-glassful of brandy she lit her candle, and when he had drained his glass she walked to the door and said: 'Well, I'll say "Good night." I get up betimes.'

'Ah, shan't be long myself. Good night.'

She gripped the banisters in anger as she went upstairs. As she lay in bed, with no desire to sleep, she called herself a fool over and over again for the placid way she had accepted him back again. Why had she done it? Why had she suffered his ingratitude so meekly? What had come over her? She catechized herself unmercifully. Nevertheless, at the back of her mind, she knew with absolute certainty that it was because somewhere and at some time, even though remotely, they had possessed each other. They had touched the core of one another. She had borne his sons and she could not escape that. It was as though she were chained to him. Nothing could change or alter that, and at last some of her old fatalistic resignation came back to her. 'If he's back, he's back, and you'd better make the best of it.'

Next day he worked on the stack and they met only for meals. In the evening he begged for brandy again and she gave it him and afterwards they divided the paper, he looking at the pictures with squinting, tired yellow eyes and she reading the news with the same dread of silence. They talked briefly of the land also. Once more she had the illusion of waiting for something to happen, though she did not know what. Sometimes she was seized with a kind of mild panic because of it. How long must it go on? How long must they go on sitting there, night after night, in that awful, silent toleration of each other? The next day was Sunday and she dreaded its coming, with little work and hours of leisure. How could they bear it?

On Sunday afternoon they walked round the farm together. It was a bright, windy afternoon, with an eternal rustling of dropping and dying leaves in the spinney. The shadows of the trees were long and soft on the bare land. The wind, bearing autumn odours and flying thistle-seed and leaves and straws, was warm and tiring as it gusted from the south-west. After skirting the big hawthorn hedge to the north they returned up the cart-track under the willows, where the leaves were dropping thickly, filling the cart-ruts and drifting up against the big earth clods of the fallow field. As they came up the track a hare leapt out of the ditch, under their very feet, and Jess made a movement as though to drop on it, but the hare was bounding away over the fallow before he had bent his body.

He laughed and she smiled faintly. 'I'm past my time for dropping on hares, I think,' he said.

When he had watched the hare out of sight he looked at the field itself and observed to her:

'Don't you cultivate it nowadays?'

'Of course I cultivate it!' she said. 'And I've had some tidy crops off it, too. It's been artificially manured I don't know how many times. And it's been worked – and worked properly. It's a different field from what it used to be, by a long way.'

He looked at the stretch of big, weathered clods, weed-bound and sun-hardened, with the long drift of yellowish soil, strewn thick with a belt of white stones, running along the brow above the dip.

'Looks like the same old field to me,' he said. 'Bad as ever.'

'What do *you* know about it?' she snapped.

He was silenced. They did not speak to each other again until tea-time.

After tea she fed the pigs their swill; it was tedious, dirty work to mix the pollard with the kitchen scraps and water from the big swill-tub, beating it to a fine brown froth, and then hitch the buckets to the hooks of the sway-tree and carry them to the sties and fill the nose-worn trough, beating back the screaming pigs as they fought to bury their snouts in the swill. The six sties of pigs meant six buckets and three journeys to and fro. The sway-tree itself was heavy and the weight of the buckets grew greater at every journey, the swill spilling over her boots and stockings as she staggered over the rough yard, half-running in order to relieve the weight a little. At the second journey she felt the pain in her side shoot up, half-crippling her for a moment. She set down the buckets and leaned against the pigsty door, panting and biting her lips as the pain shot up through her breast. She did the last journey by stages, half-kneeling on the ground to rest at intervals. The pain spread, the centre of it like a hot wound. Finally, she made a great effort and brought the buckets to the sties, spilling the swill as she staggered. After resting a little she opened the sty door and filled the trough with swill; the young stores, lusty and ravenous, charged her madly. In a moment she was knocked off her balance and thrown to the ground, the pigs leaping about her in their frantic pig-hunger, squealing and snorting until they could bury their sucking snouts in the troughs. She struggled upright and held on to the sty rails, gripping them to fight back the pain in her breast and the trembling of her limbs after the shock of falling. Hardly knowing what she did she lifted the last bucket into the adjoining sty, kicking back the lumbering blue sow with her foot, and spilled half her feed on the straw. The pain was worse than ever she remembered it; it was so alive and powerful and insistent that she could almost grip the centre of the agony with her hands. Involuntarily her hands leapt to her breast, trying to tear out the pain. The farm swam sickeningly before her eyes and she felt the cold sweat of a swoon break out on her forehead and she began to go hot and cold by turns. She saved herself from falling by gripping objects in her path across the yard, an old harrow, a cart, the swill-tub, the door of the kitchen itself. She walked into the kitchen in intolerable pain and sat down in a chair, vaguely conscious of Jess sitting in the twilight on the other side of the dying fire.

Little by little the pain seemed to melt away, leaving her

strengthless and sick. She kept her eyes shut. Jess noticed nothing, but she had no strength to speak or reproach him. She had not even the strength to open her clenched hands.

By and by she dropped into a kind of half-doze brought on by sheer weakness and exhaustion, and when she aroused herself the room was dark and cold and there was no sign of Jess. She got out of her chair to poke the fire and dropped back instantly with a cry of pain. It was as though she were being kept back at the point of a knife. She tried to move again and the pain returned. It was futile. She felt like a child. Tears of weakness sprang from her eyes and began to run hotly down her cheeks and she had no power to stop them or wipe them away. She had never before felt so old and weak. It was as though all the tears that her strength had kept back had broken loose at last. She felt them falling on her dress and her hands and she tried to wipe them away in the darkness, but very soon her hands were wet with them and she gave it up at last, letting the tears come as they would, silently and bitterly, blinding and choking her.

Later, having a sudden insane notion that she might sit there and cry for ever, she pulled herself up with a tremendous effort. Still crying, she went to the cupboard and got down the brandy bottle and a glass. The room was quite dark and she tilted the bottle to the glass by instinct. She heard the brief trickle of the brandy and then it ceased. She tilted it still more until finally she was holding it upside down. It was empty. She cried more helplessly as she realized what had happened, and her whole body trembled with her sobbing so that she could not hold the glass. She groped up to the cupboard again for the whisky bottle; it seemed light in her wet hands, and in a moment it had slipped and fallen, breaking on the bare bricks. The sound of the breaking bottle was light and hollow, so that she knew that too must have been empty.

She managed to drag herself to bed, crying all the time, feeling at last like an old, weak woman, worn-out and useless. Lying down, she felt easier, and presently the flow of her tears broke. She dried her eyes on the sheet and lay silent. In the silence and with her tears no longer troubling her, she began to think vividly, her mind filling with clamouring thoughts, not of herself, but of Benjamin and David, and then of Jess. She put the thought of David away from her quickly, not trusting herself. She thought of Jess clearly, seeing him with a kind of second sight. From the first she had seen through him easily and she had forgiven him easily because of it; now though she saw through him just as easily she felt that it no longer mattered whether she forgave him or not, just as it no longer mattered that she had slaved and built up the farm. I'm finished, she thought wearily. She looked out of the window, wondering where he had gone. It was like him to come back, so like him that she was amazed she had neither been ready for it nor had made provision against it. She saw now the meaning of his trembling hands. His eyes were sick with drink. Why hadn't she foreseen it?

She began to cry weakly again and as the tears flowed the pain aroused itself in her side. As she put her hand against her bare flesh to stop it she felt a lump there. She started terribly and drew her hand away. It's nothing, she thought, but she remembered Mrs. Mortimer taking her hand and making her touch the lump on her side. I'm a fool if I don't send for Starling, she thought.

Hoping suddenly that Jess might have returned she called 'Jess! Jess!' several times, but there was no answer. In the following silence the clock downstairs struck ten. She waited, lying on her side to ease the pain, crying a little and biting her tear-salt lips.

A little later she heard him return. She heard the click of the broken whisky bottle as he stumbled about. Looking for matches, she thought, and finally she heard him shake the box.

'Jess! Jess!' she called.

He did not answer; she heard him kick against the broken glass, muttering.

'Jess! Jess! Come here a minute!'

She wondered why he did not reply and then suddenly she remembered that she might call all night and he would never hear.

Lying silent again, she thought: 'Perhaps I shall be all right. I'll lay till morning. I'll lay quiet and see what morning brings.'

Chapter 5

THE yellow October sunlight kept brightening and dying over the walls of the bedroom, the light appearing and vanishing as the clouds rolled over the sun on the quick west wind. Leaves blown up from the spinney and the garden kept striking the open window, finding their way sometimes through the aperture, creeping along the floor, fluttering on the white counterpane. Deborah lay still, watching them and waiting also for the breaking and vanishing of the sunlight. She felt warm and at rest. The pain which had wracked her for three weeks, hardly existed. Every now and then a cloud came over the sun and she shut her eyes briefly. When she felt the yellow sunlight filter through her drawn lids again she opened her eyes with a start almost of joy to find the room flooded with light.

'The sun changes everything so,' she remarked.

Anthea was sitting in the sunlight under the window, reading a book.

'You mustn't talk,' she said.

'What difference does it make?' she said in a low, sharp voice.

The girl did not answer, and Deborah shut her eyes, making a little sound of disgust with her thin lips. Coming to the end of a chapter the girl shut the book and turned to look at her, starting violently. Had it happened? She held her breath and looked hard at the absolutely still, yellow face, with its placid, almost transparent lids and its reposeful mouth. The face did not move, but the breast was rising and falling faintly and the girl drew back. Deborah had lain there for three weeks and Starling had come to see her twice a day, giving her morphia to ease the pain, and alternately Anthea and Rook's wife had sat with her. Her body had become as thin and frail as a shell, looking as if another touch of pain would break it. But somewhere, in the heart of it, there was a

251

tenacious, almost wilful toughness which would not surrender. She clung with the old determination and defiance; she would not die. She had even become skilful at concealing the pain, only sudden involuntary cries giving away her agony.

She opened her eyes and stared at the girl. The sun was shining again.

'How many eggs to-day?' she said.

The girl made a wild guess. 'Nearly forty,' she said. 'You mustn't talk.'

'Forty! Good gracious, what's he doing with them? Not an egg to three hens!'

'You mustn't talk.'

'What's he up to? He ought to be doing that ploughing

She lay and thought a moment, panting quickly. 'He ought to be doing that ploughing.'

'Not to-day. It's Sunday. You mustn't talk.'

'I don't care. Where is he? Fetch him up. I want to talk to him.'

'You mustn't talk!' It was useless.

'I'll get up if you don't fetch him!' said Deborah. The voice was wonderfully sharp and defiant.

'Promise to close your eyes while I fetch him.'

'All right.' She lay exhausted.

A long time seemed to pass without a sound, and she lay with her eyes shut, not out of obedience, but because she had not the strength to open them. Now and then she felt herself sink away, in a curious dark swoon, as though to sleep. Finally she heard the girl's footsteps, followed by heavier feet, returning upstairs, and she pulled herself back to consciousness with a supreme effort as the door opened.

Someone came into the room, and as the door was shut quietly she opened her eyes. Jess was standing by the bedside. His eyes had a curious sombre look of drowsiness.

'Were you having a nap?' she asked.

'Ah. How d'ye feel, my gal?'

'As right as they'll let me.' She looked at him sharply. 'Have you done that ploughing?'

'Eh? The fallow? Ah, we made a start.'

'A start!' she croaked. 'You ought to be finished. I want that wheat in.'

'It'll be in time enough.'

'It ought to have been ploughed a month back – directly after harvest.'

He stood silent, his great body loose and awkward, his long arms hanging heavily by his side, as though he did not know what to do with them. The sombreness of his eyes gave a heavy, thoughtless, pathetic look to his face; some strength was still left in his great bones, but he had no longer the will to use it. As he stood waiting, trying to keep his hands from trembling, his eyes were only half on her face, as though it hurt him or made him ashamed to look at her. A moment or two of immobility seemed to bring on a strange, stupid, fuddled look, so that she startled him when she spoke again.

'If you don't plough that field we shall lose it again. You know what it used to be. Why don't you do it?' She was growing excited, and suddenly she tried to raise herself up in bed, but as suddenly she sank back again.

'Now, you've talked enough,' said Anthea firmly. 'Lie still now.'

She turned to Jess, who was staring uneasily.

'You must go.'

'Eh?' he said.

'It's time you went.'

'Ah, I'll go!'

He went out heavily.

In the stillness of the room Deborah fought to regain her breath, and the girl stood over her until she was breathing again. 'Try to sleep,' she said. There was no answer. She went back to the window and took up her book.

No sooner had she begun to read than the voice, perverse and restless as a child's, broke out once more:

'He's been drinking again, hasn't he?'

'You really mustn't talk.'

'I want you to have the farm,' said Deborah. 'You would have had it. He'll drink it away. I know he will. You see how his hands keep twitching and trembling? That's drink. He told me it was gas, but it's drink. I know.'

'When the doctor comes I shall make him give you a sleeping-draught. You must stop talking.'

253

'All right, all right.' She hated the draughts like poison. She closed her eyes.

Presently the sunlight on her eyes aroused her again.

'How many eggs was it you said?'

The girl kept silent until the voice defied her twice. 'How many eggs did you say? How many was it?'

'About forty.'

'It's not enough. It's not half enough.'

'Never mind.'

'Go down and make sure, will you? Count them yourself. *He* won't know.'

'Will you be quiet if I go?'

'Yes.'

Going downstairs the girl met her husband in the kitchen. The eggs had not been collected for the day and she decided to say she had found another basinful, making seventy all told. She waited with Starling a moment or two and then they went upstairs together. Jess she had not seen.

Back in the bedroom they found her lying with an immobility that seemed for a moment like death itself. Starling bent over her and instantly she started, as though he had aroused her from a dream.

He drew away quietly. She opened her eyes, fully conscious.

'How many eggs?' she said, seeing the girl.

'Over seventy. I found another basinful.'

'That's more like it.' The doctor moved and she saw him also. 'Oh, you're here, are you? I don't want your old sleeping-draught, I'll tell you! Many birds this year?'

He smiled. 'Not many. The spring was too wet.'

He walked away to the window and her eyes followed him, contrasting his grey-haired figure with the slight, timid body of the girl. She opened her lips to speak again, but her tongue stiffened and no sound came. She felt strong and quiet, strangely serene to the depths of her being. She made a great effort to speak and the words broke from her throat in a sudden dry rattle.

'I want you to have the farm,' she said. 'You two. I want you to have the farm.'

Her voice was desperate. Starling and Anthea looked at

each other. How could she give them something that was not hers to give? She rambled on:

'It'll be nice for you. The land's all right. It's only the people on it. It wants working, that's all.' Her voice was like the rattle of a dry leaf, drifting farther and farther away. 'Is he ploughing that field? He never would plough it. I want wheat on it. If it isn't ploughed we shall lose it – we shall – lift me up. Lift me up. I want to see if he's ploughing it. Lift me.'

Her voice died away abruptly. A strange serene look, an expression of happy elation, came suddenly over her face, as though she were really being lifted up and were looking at that old field with the new brown furrows lying sweet and straight in the late sunlight.

Starling crossed her thin hands on her nightgown. The girl, after waiting a moment, moved quietly across the room as though afraid of startling her back to life again, and drew the blind, filling the room with a strange yellow twilight.

The sun had set when they were ready to leave the house. Rook's wife had come in for the evening and was upstairs, laying out the body. Jess they had not seen, but going out into the paddock they saw him leaning on the gate by the spinney, gazing over the fallow field.

'Go and sit in the car while I tell him,' said Starling.

Starling walked across the paddock, rustling the dry apple leaves with his feet. Jess was staring at the field with a lost, sombre look on his heavy face. As Starling came up behind him and touched his shoulder, he straightened his body with a great effort.

'How is she?' he said.

'She's gone.'

'Eh?' A second later he understood.

They stood for a moment staring at the field; the twilight was deepening rapidly and a flock of starlings, flying eastward, went over the field with a great murmur of wings. The evening chill was creeping up from the brook. Starling could feel the colder air on his face and hands.

'She was asking about the field,' he said. 'She asked me to tell you to plough it up and have wheat on it.'

'The field's no good.'

'I've seen some good crops on it.'

'I dare say. But what good's wheat? They won't buy it. No good at all.' His voice was stubborn and short. He had gripped the gate with his hands in order to hide their everlasting trembling. 'The land's no good,' he muttered.

'If you sell the place I'll buy it,' said Starling.

'Eh?' His hands gave a great convulsive quiver in spite of himself. 'The land's no good, I tell you.' He looked old and broken-up and he turned away stubbornly again, as though he wanted to have done with it all.

A moment later Starling walked away, leaving him in the same dejected, meditative attitude as he had found him.

As he stared over the field Jess dimly heard the paddock gate click shut and then the starting-up of the car and finally the sound of the engine dropping farther and farther away. He stared at the fading outlines of the woods and the hedges and the field itself as though he did not see them. The sky was empty except for an occasional flock of starlings that appeared and vanished quickly. The field lay rough and fallow, without a furrow turned. It looked to him just as it had looked in his father's time, as though it had never been touched, the same old field difficult to plough and worse to reap, never worth the trouble of seed or harvest.

He stared a little longer, lost in thought, shrinking from going into the house. The air was cold and full of the damp odours of dying leaves from the spinney. He could feel the coldness coming up from the brook, chilling his trembling hands. As he turned away from the gate at last another flock of starlings flew over the farm and the spinney, but he could not see them in the darkness. A pheasant cried in the spinney and was silent. The first star had come out behind the trees, hanging like a lantern. The cold wrapped about him damply, making him shiver.

He put his quivering hands in his pockets and turned towards the house.

It was time to go.

Recent titles from Robinson Publishing

If you cannot find these titles in your bookshop, they can be obtained directly from the publisher. Please indicate the copies required and fill in the form overleaf in block letters.

Please fill in the form below in block letters:

NAME_____

ADDRESS_____

_____

_____

_____

Send to Robinson Publishing Cash Sales,
P.O. Box 11, Falmouth, Cornwall TR10 9EN

Please enclose cheque or postal order to the value of the cover
price plus:

In UK only – 55p for the first book, 22p for the second book,
and 14p for each additional book to a maximum £1.75.

BFPO – 55p for the first book, 22p for the second book, and
14p for the next seven books and 8p for each book thereafter.

Overseas – £1.25 for the first book, 31p per copy for each
additional book.

Whilst every effort is made to keep prices low, it is sometimes
necessary to increase prices at short notice. Robinson
Publishing reserve the right to show on covers, and charge,
new retail prices which may differ from those advertised in text
or elsewhere.